THE TALE OF THE SHAGGING MONKEYS

Trippin'

Anthony Bunko

Copyright @ 2009 Anthony Bunko

The right of Anthony Bunko to be identified as the Author of the work has been asserted by him in accordance with the Copyright, Designs and Patent Act 1988

All the characters in this book are fictitious (except for the mad woman in the rolled up carpet and the sexually active goat on page 543), and any resemblance to actual persons, living or dead, is purely coincidental.

All rights reserved. No part of this publication may be reproduced, stored in a retrieval system, or transmitted, in any form or by any means without the prior written permission of the publisher, nor be otherwise circulated in any form of binding or cover other than that in which it is published and without similar conditions being imposed on the subsequent purchaser.

anthonybunko@hotmail.com

ISBN - 9798647920003

DEDICATED TO: -

STEVE 'JAC' FEALEY

"STEP LIGHTLY……..STAY FREE……."

Chapter 1

'Would you like a saucer of milk with that, Sir?'

The mini-bus found itself at the wrong end of town at precisely the wrong time of night. The driver hastily pulled it around the sharp bend and into the relative safety of the well-lit high street. Its windscreen wipers, like some punch-drunk street fighter, sparred with the more nimble, faster drops of rain. The persistent onslaught of drizzle was making it a very one-sided contest, until a sand-brick from the adjacent block of flats ended the bout by shattering the windscreen and frightening the fucking life out of the bus driver.

The sound of smashing glass also startled Jac, who stood alone in the doorway to the kebab shop waiting for his lift to arrive. He had decided at the last minute to treat himself to a proper meal before his seven-day excursion in the sun with his best mates.

There had been no need to scan the brightly coloured menu board taking centre stage in the compact takeaway; he knew exactly what his last supper would be. It was the same choice every time he entered his favourite den of gastric delights; a large, old fashioned, English style, doner kebab with extra garlic and   chilli sauce…light on the salad.

'You know what these foreigners are like with their food. It's all this pasta shit, or snails, or things that glow in the fuckin' dark,' he told the newly arrived Greek waiter who nodded politely only because he could not speak a word of English.

Jac had grown up in a town that had discovered iron production, but had then left it on the doorstep for entrepreneurs dressed up as friendly milkmen to pilfer. This in turn led to this once prosperous upstart of a boomtown slowly grinding to a shuddering and spectacular halt.

From the doorway, he observed how the hand of misfortune had squeezed the breath out of the place. It had been replaced by boarded up shop windows, which were desperately searching for someone to give them the kiss of life, or at least, a lick of paint.

Ever since he could remember, the town had been cold and grey. But these days the cold really chilled to the bones and the grey embedded itself onto the faces of its occupants. Disillusioned individuals wandered aimlessly about like dead, flesh-eating zombies.

For that reason, Jac loved the nights before a tour of duty; if only for the excuse to travel far away from the smell of despair and wash the grime of desperation out of his skin, for a short while at least.

In his mind, there could be nothing better in the world than escaping for a few days. OK, that may have been a slight exaggeration; there were lots of things in Jac's life that could be better.

He could be a successful footballer for Manchester United, earning about one hundred and twenty grand a week or a 21-year-old underwear model waking up in Ibiza with a beautiful, hairy arm-pitted, French girl with eyes like Marine Boy and a tongue that young

American punk kids wearing stupidly baggy jeans could skateboard on.

He paid the waiter and bit into the pita bread sandwich. A rebellious section of the red-hot chilli sauce squirted onto his overalls, nearly burning a hole right through to his skin.

As he licked his fingers, he wondered if he had really put his mind to it, if he could become a famous footballer who modelled underwear in his spare time, earning one hundred and twenty grand a week and waking up with two beautiful, hairy arm-pitted French girls. Maybe it was time to buckle down and get serious about his life.

A car passed by and spat jets of rainwater in the direction of the doorway. It instantly snapped him out of his dream world and back to the reality of life as a lonely 33 year old carpenter.

'Bastard,' he muttered to himself. 'Where the fuck is Kinsey?' He turned his jacket collar up to shield the food from the cold breath of the wind.

He cursed himself for getting banned from driving. This meant he now had to rely on unreliable people like Kinsey to give him a lift.

Before the driving incident, which had sentenced him to years of hanging about on street corners, his life had appeared to be pleasantly warm with a fine, light wind blowing in from the south. It all started to go grey and cloudy the day that Father Time, and his mate Johnny Law, finally caught up with him while he was minding his own business and studying hard from the book 'Hints and Tips to Fuck about With Life'.

'For Christ sake, forgive and forget why don't you, it was only a joke!' he shouted at a passing police car that just happened to be sneaking through the streets disguised as a Royal Mail delivery van.

He recalled the trial and how his solicitor tried to justify his actions. He shared with the jury how Jac had always been a big time practical joker and how a child psychologist had once told his mother that Jac used humour as a safety net for his lack of self-confidence and that if he was not allowed to indulge, he would surely commit suicide. The lawyer purposely forget to mention Jac's mother's response that she didn't know what the fuck the shrink was on about, all she knew was she was sick to death of finding dead slugs in her beef and leek broth.

The incident with the bus had backfired and Jac now realized that it was a stupid thing to do. But what was done was done. Time could not repair what happened on that cold Saturday night in Merthyr Tydfil town centre.

What angered him most was that most murderers received less of a sentence than was handed down on him. Bloody Psycho Hendrix, who killed two security guards in the middle of Tesco with a can of beans and a jar of Value beetroot, had gotten off with a meagre ten year sentence. He was last seen planting flowers and vegetables in a local comprehensive school like some bloody reformed Alan Titchmarsh. He even had his own column in the local paper: -

'The Supermarket Killer – Turning over a new leaf....

Top Gardening Tips.'

'Fucking top gardening tips!' he yelled out. The only thing Psycho Hendrix knew how to plant were the part remains of his poor victims. Now, Psycho was telling thousands of readers how to spruce up their allotments while poor Jac Innocent Morgan waited for a lift in the pissing down rain and got treated like Lenny the Leper with a particular nasty bout of chicken pox.

'Justice...what bastard justice?' he whispered to himself. He threw his empty kebab box at a mangy black and white cat which had strolled past the doorway.

He still couldn't understand why he had been the only one singled out. There were lots of people on the bus that night. It was full to the brim. The seats, the aisles and all the baggage racks were occupied. So why did he take the entire rap?

OK, so it was his idea to break into the bus depot on that fateful night. And he had suggested drawing the moustaches on each other so they would look older and yes, he had come up with the idea of sitting on the beanbag for extra height. After all, everybody knew that the pigs were always on the look out to nick short drivers with pencil thin moustaches. He rightfully pleaded guilty to those charges.

But it was not he who insisted that the bus stop outside the Labour club and the entire establishment be invited to a free magical mystery tour to the Big Shitty; that was entirely Alex's doing.

And, it was not *his* idea to have everyone take their clothes off and dance around in the buff; again, all Alex. Although, it was a bloody good call; Jac wished it had been his idea.

He had driven the bus that night and may have sampled a drop or two of alcohol, but not eight times over the limit that the police reported. And the gorgeous blonde sitting on his lap as the bus careered around the corner of the shopping centre was not giving him a blowjob as the local paper had stated in its biased story of the event; although he wished she had been. After the crash he couldn't have a wank for three months.

He had lost control and skidded through the hot-dog stand across the park and ploughed into the brass band, who had just finished their first, and last, open-air night concert. But he strongly disagreed with the prosecution's accusations that he was trying to drive the vehicle while standing on his head and drinking a yard of ale at the same time. He simply couldn't remember that bit.

By the time the police arrived at the scene, everyone except for Jac, had done a runner and the bus was deserted. For his sins, he was trapped in the driver's seat with his trousers down, covered in lipstick and blobs of white stuff; two arms and one leg, broken.

The story he gave the arresting officer was that he was merrily watching his favourite brass band when a crazy bus crashed into the crowd and he landed in the position which they had found him.

Because of the conflicting evidence, an identity parade was set-up. Because Jac was incapable of standing, the line up was carried out at the local hospital. The police roped in seven innocent suspects plus Jac. They were all decked out in identical wheelchairs with plaster-of-Paris covering most of their bodies.

Three in the line up were schoolboys with false moustaches attached to their top lips. The other four were travelling midgets, who were each a quarter of the newly formed tribute band....

'The Mini Feet Preachers.'

One eyewitness, who had lost an eye in a laughable fishing accident, mistakenly identified one of the midgets as the driver of the bus. Jac was sure it was the Titchy James character that had been fingered. There was absolute chaos as the on-duty policemen fought a running battle with the remaining three-quarters of the famous miniature band. It all came to an abrupt end when the other sixty witnesses confirmed Jac as the perpetrator and driver of the runaway motor vehicle.

'What a set-up!' he exclaimed to his solicitor as they dragged him down into the cells.

'He was framed!' his mates in the gallery shouted at the top of their voices, but to no avail.

Now, years later, he had just about finished his community service and was still unable to drive a car. Trevor, the owner of the half-inched bus, had banned him and his family for life from travelling on his luxury coaches. And he was still getting annual death threats from the Brass Band Society of Great Britain.

He was getting more and more irritated thinking back to the sheer injustice of the whole situation. He finished the last of the kebab and wondered if his digestive system could handle another one.

Back in the high street as the minibus with the smashed windscreen came to a halt outside the kebab shop and the driver got out chasing the offenders, Jac couldn't help but smile. After all this time, he had become an expert when it came to throwing away all of yesterday's disturbing memories and an even greater expert on switching his thoughts to tomorrow's exciting adventures.

He was looking forward to spending the next couple of days relaxing with his best mates and playing fuck with everyone that crossed his path. He went back into the takeaway and joined the queue.

****

Billy 2 amp Kinsey sat angrily behind the wheel of his car. A face like thunder, shoulders carrying hailstones and a body surrounded with bolts of lightening.

He was extremely incensed with the old guy in front of him in the Morris Minor who had no business stopping suddenly when the traffic lights had just, for that split second, turned to amber.

'Wanker! You complete and utter wanker!' he screamed out loud. The words echoed around the car and finally settled down just above the dashboard. He beeped his horn violently and flashed his main beam murderously at the thoughtlessness of the vehicle that blocked his way.

At the next set of traffic lights, Kinsey filtered into the other lane. He pulled up along side the old man and lowered the passenger side window.

'Oy! You! Yes…you! Sterling fuckin Moss!'

The old guy was oblivious to the abuse that was being directed towards him. Kinsey layed on his horn again. The old man turned to face Billy. He nodded politely and smiled.

'Yes…you…it's you I'm talking to Mister Magoo!' Kinsey shouted.

The old man couldn't hear a word. Firstly, he had not unwound the window and secondly, he was as deaf as an earless doorpost.

Kinsey gave the bloke one of his long hard stares. 'Yes, I thought so.' He gestured, menacingly. 'Now I know what a cunt looks like! Alright you cunt?'

He then shot off into the town centre happy in the knowledge that he had made another stand against the evil old cunts that were making a habit of slowing up the flow of traffic on the roads of the Welsh Valleys.

Billy 2 amp Kinsey had probably one of the shortest fuses that had ever been slotted into a human brain. No one knew if it had been a design fault or just a freak of nature.

He had been officially stamped with the nickname after throwing a steam pie at the owner of Queen's Café, after it burnt the inside of his mouth. Unfortunately, he didn't consider the consequences of his missile throwing actions or the hours of painful plastic surgery that Mr. Rossi, the owner, had to endure because of it.

But the name, 2 Amp, suited him to a tee. He had almost won a competition set up by some local students during rag week to find the person with the nickname that most describes its owner.

He was voted in the top three of all time and only lost out to Alan Rat Boy Price, who finished second. Rat boy not only had an unfortunately long face similar to a rodent's, but he also had black, shark-like eyes. For some strange reason, Alan was excused from ever going to biology lessons in case the sight of a manic second year carving up the body of a dead rodent was too much for him to handle.

The favourite and eventual winner of the prestigious title was Roberto Monster Cock Thomas, for reasons that shouldn't need any explanation. It was worth pointing out that when Roberto was thirteen, he had a cage welded around his torso with the words 'Beware, do not feed the beast' carved in large letters on a wooden sign that hung from the door.

Even today he was banned from wearing spandex unless under close supervision of a paramedic. A quick flash of the giant marrow was enough to convince the judges of his star quality.

After winning his award, Monster Cock took his trophy, unlocked the cage and headed for Hollywood. All the males in the town wished him luck and hoped he would never come back. To this day, he is still one of the few male porno stars who can give himself a blow job, though this did require some expensive and ground breaking dental work.

From an early age, Kinsey always had a big problem controlling his temper. His sports teacher, Mr. Brown, once wrote that Billy could have a big future in sports if he could just learn to count to ten now and again. A week after the report, he was suspended from school for strangling Mr Brown, who had unforgivably given Kinsey an offside penalty in the last minute of a school football game.

The night air was painted blue once again as Billy's car crawled behind a suspicious looking post office van which was taking photographs of everything that moved.

In the distance he saw a bus driver with half a brick in his hand chasing a gang of twelve year olds toward the no-go area.

Hope his wife has got him well insured, he thought, but drove on deciding to mind his own business. He made it his motto to never get involved with domestics, strange religious cults or pathetic heroes chasing street urchins.

During his journey he tried to avoid eye contact with the line of ladies of the night who applied their seedy trade from the alleyways of the dark streets. In the old days, girls selling their wares were called Pin Money. Nowadays, it was known as hypodermic needle cash.

The disguised post office van ignored them; it was looking for bigger fish to fry.

Kinsey suddenly had to brake hard to avoid Christine. The one time winner of the Rose of Tralee competition, was now sadly, a fully paying member of the Heroin Club. She walked out in front of his car while holding the hand of an overweight businessman who was in town for a plastic cutlery convention.

Her vacant eyes, which stared at Kinsey for a split second, indicated the emptiness that flowed through her veins. The warmth and life that had at one time filled her up had been taken away for dirty cash.

The odd-couple disappeared into the privacy of the old bakery.

In a mood that was spiralling toward resentment, he continued on his way. This was not a new state of mind for Billy. In fact Kinsey had been born anxious, quickly developed into high-strung and after years of refinement had mastered the art of anger.

He was an explosive character. A ticking time bomb full to the brim with six inch nails. Perhaps the only man-made thing that could come close to matching his aggression was a bottle of extra fizzy and extremely disconcerted Dandelion and Burdock pop; Dandelion and burp-a-lot pop as it is known by all teenagers throughout the world. Both the liquid substance and the boy looked quite placid but could get very agitated when shaken.

Unpredictability summed up Billy 2 amp Kinsey perfectly, and the fact that he worked as an electrician for his father's business was even more profound.

He had recently married Julie after a long engagement period and they had just had a little baby boy. Kinsey wanted to name him Billy Tyson Gladiator Kinsey the second, but Julie christened him Josh Kinsey instead. Billy was not pleased and out of spite, told people the sprog's name was Hercules.

After several years of therapy and a thousand bottles of Valium, his doctor had instructed him to take a long rest. He hoped that the trip with his mates would help him relieve some stress.

Kinsey spotted Jac standing in the doorway chit-chatting with the mangy black and white cat. He pulled up along side.

'Hey, make sure there's no cat shit on your shoes before you get in,' warned Kinsey.

Jac checked. He threw the remainder of his second kebab to the furry animal and slid into the warm car.

The starving stray, which hadn't eaten a thing for four days, sniffed at the food, licked the chilli sauce and wailed before pissing on the kebab and strutting away.

'Don't say a word, just have a puff of this.' Kinsey passed Jac a half-smoked joint. 'Listen to this new CD I just got.'

He turned up the volume, *'You get what you give'* by the New Radicals blasted out of the radio.

The car shot off into the night. It nearly hit two old women fresh out of the Castle Bingo hall. Kinsey grinned, aimed and then fired his special steering wheel gun which he had purchased from Gun Lovers monthly at the two old hags.

Of course, the gun wasn't real. The more the pity he had thought on the day it had arrived. It was a fake Charles Bronson vigilante special Magnum gadget which he attached to the dashboard of the car and fired red laser beams at unsuspecting victims.

'Take that you losers!' he screamed while blasting the two old ladies in the back.

He pulled the sun visor flap down and filled in the column labelled, Pedestrians Annihilated.

'Another two hundred points to me,' he said triumphantly.

Jac shook his head and let the music and the weed drift into his soul.

Chapter 2

'The jigsaw pieces are back in town'

There was a lot of activity in the lounge of Dowlais Rugby Club that night. The room looked the same as most rugby club lounges. It was a cross between a very poor workingmen's club in downtown Beirut and a deserted Indian restaurant in Blackwood. Even the cast of Changing Rooms would have struggled to alter the very core of this male orientated flocked wallpapered palace.

The club at Dowlais was positioned high on a hill looking down upon the rest of the town. It was an eerie place. It made the house in Psycho look like a showroom for Barrett Homes.

It had been erected on the site of an old Edwardian refuge tip, which many claimed was still causing serious health issues for the residents of the community. There were rumours of two-headed babies and deformed grandmothers attributed to the old cesspit. Although the stories were without substance, it added to the ominous reputation that surrounded the place in a big murky cloud.

Old Nessy Howard, who was seventy-two years old, did actually have two heads. Well, not actually two heads. She had a normal one and a stubby thing on her left shoulder which had no facial features but a mop of curly brown hair. She also had a wickedly deformed spine due to a major cock-up during birth. Despite this well known medical fact, many of the residents insisted that Nessy had once been a beautiful woman until the fumes leaking up from the Edwardian sewage system had caused her sudden and savage appearance.

It was during the annual protest marches, organised to complain about the horrendous smell seeping through the drains, that old Nessy would be pulled from the attic, tied to a flagpole and lofted up as a token symbol of the cause.

This went on for years until the tragic day she passed away after the residents got drunk and accidentally left her tied upside down on the pole in the car park of the club. She suffocated on the stench of her own under garments. During the panic that pursued, the organisers decided not to bury her. Instead, they had her stuffed with sawdust and straw so they could use her every year to lead the march until their fight against pollution was won. The only compromise to her dignity, and their sense of smell, was a fresh set of clothes. She became an instant martyr.

There were definitely many visual signs that things weren't quite right in this small part of the world. It was a place most people only dreamt of leaving; no one ever actually succeeded in achieving that goal.

Back in the club, a quiet buzz had been building up over the last couple of weeks. Not the same buzz that the flies the size of baby seals make on those rare summer days when they descend on the area to feast on the bare flesh of their victims. It was a friendly buzz mixed with excitement and possibility made even louder with this years piss-up that was neatly disguised as the end of the season rugby tour.

Tonight was just another typical night in loon-town with the familiar cast of characters running through a very typical script.

At the far end of the room sat old Harry and his best mate, Fred the Taxis, playing dominoes. The two had been friends for nearly sixty years; a friendship that had taken them through many revolving doors. Since Mavis and Elaine, their respective wives, had passed away several years earlier within four months of each other, the widowers had spent most of their grieving in fierce domino competitions in the intense arena of the four walls of the club.

The games were deadly serious with forfeits given out to the loser each week. This week's prize for the winner was a week of piggy back rides to and from the club.

The week before, Fred's penance was to make Harry two crumpets and a mug of tea each morning and to empty out his nightly bedpan. That was the wrong week to lose the game. Old Harry purposely didn't go to the toilet all day. It was pay back time for the week he had to wash Fred's underpants. He couldn't get his fingernails clean since.

Sitting by the door was Father John, the Catholic Priest for the community. On the outside he was a very intense serious looking man of God, but for the people who bothered to look more closely at his face, he was a suspicious church opponent that asked lots of questions concerning the whole Catholic Church thing; especially the need to eat fish on Fridays. Father John hated fish with a passion.

He found himself, most Fridays, travelling to a small transport café outside of Cardiff disguised as a builder. He put in a great deal of effort when he dressed up and always wore a check shirt with a pillow stuck down the front and crack-arsed jeans for the authentic look.

On his arrival, he would sit by the free-standing gas heater, order and consume the big mega, gut busting, all day breakfast. When he finished dipping his last piece of toast into his giant mug of tea, he would take out his rosary and quietly pray through the beads three times. The nightly church services that followed were conducted with bean sauce cemented onto the side of his lips and skin that reeked of bacon.

He had gained an enormous influence on the diocese since he had been posted from Kilkenny.

His first act was to change the choir. The old was comprised of the blue rinse brigade, who couldn't actually sing a note, and a one-armed organ player called Rory who could play but was terrible at solos. He replaced them with a younger generation folk group made up of local school kids and an ageing ex-Clash roadie called Mickey Flea.

Father John insisted the band played a new brand of God music on the altar. It became the main centrepiece of the whole communal mass, mixed with a backdrop of railway station graffiti and a life-size plastic, singing Virgin Mary, which would belt out a funky version of 'Like a Virgin' when a candle was lit.

This made him extremely popular with the modernists, but equally unpopular with the powerful and set in their ways, traditionalists.

'Cruel…the folk group are bloody cruel,' the spiteful Mrs. Griffiths had put in her letter to the Pope concerning the revolution that was taking place in her church since the long-haired, devil worshipping priest had taken over.

The Pope put the letter in a pile marked up for the Church police to investigate. The complaints in the letter tray concerning Father John grew bigger each day.

Father John's radical approach was tested to the limit when he commissioned a local artist to paint a mural in the entrance of the church. The painting depicted the Last Supper. But that was not the problem. The problem was that he had asked the artist to make all the apostles resemble pop stars of the recent decades.

To many of the congregation, this was the most serious act of treason he had committed so far. Mrs. Griffiths had gone on a hunger strike because of it and protested outside the church doors, screaming out for his head to be served on a plate and his bollocks to be fed to the pigs.

The painting was hung to the right of the alter. Obviously, Beatles' greats Paul and John were represented on the work of art along with Cliff, Rod and an extra jolly Noddy Holder. Most people didn't mind their presence in this modern day pop star-religious hall of fame canvas. It was the introduction of Gary Glitter as Matthew, Alice Cooper as Judas, and a slightly off colour James Brown as God's son, which really tugged on the heartstrings of the faithful.

But whatever people thought of Father John's unusual methods and practices, financially the church had never been better off. He was always one step ahead of the competition when getting hard cash to support the church.

When the collection box income started to decline, he decided to open up the church and its function for sponsorship deals in the area. This proved extremely popular and profitable.

For a sum of £200 per year one could display the company's logo on the back of an alter boy's cassock and hold up placards during the mass sponsoring local funerals or the midnight Christmas church service.

The money was rolling in, thick and fast. One famous UK frozen food company sponsored the funeral of the town's hard man and convicted poet, Malcolm Knuckles McCormick, for the godly price of five thousand big ones.

For their money, the company had full advertising control of the day. Malcolm was buried not in a coffin, but in a giant two-for-one beef burger box and during the funeral march thousands of leaflets dropped from the sky announcing the big summer give-away sale.

Sadly, success also brought with it jealousy and greed. Bank statements started to come up missing and rumours were rife of lavish Confirmation and first Communion parties. Although greatly exaggerated, they started to undermine everything that Father John wanted to bring to this slightly backward part of the world.

In the club that night, he sat alone on the beer stained table clutching a photograph while making best friends with a pint of cider and a little tot of whiskey.

By the jukebox sat Alex quietly sipping his lager while waiting for his best mates, Jac and Kinsey, to arrive and hopefully brighten the gloomy cloud that hung over the building.

Jac and 2 amp walked into the lounge discussing last night's Oasis concert on MTV.

'He's a cool fucker though,' admitted Jac, looking around the room for Alex. He saw his mate and waved.

'He's a big headed twat,' returned Kinsey.

'Who are you talking about boys?' interrupted Father John. 'That Barry John fellow is it?'

'No…no…sorry Father,' Jac replied, going red with embarrassment. 'Liam Gallagher from Oasis.'

Now to most Catholic priests the words Liam Gallagher would be locked away in the same drawer as things like vagina or transvestite, but Father John was different. He not only knew what the most forbidden expressions in that lost drawer meant, but at some point in his life he had emptied the contents out on the floor and looked through them eagerly. Now every week along with the mandatory Station of the Cross newsletter update from Rome, the postman delivered the new edition of the NME and The Face magazine in a plain brown bag.

What most people also didn't know was that he had actually gone to see Oasis live at Reading the previous year disguised as a bangle seller.

'Oh him…he is a big headed twat, and his brother Neil…he looks half werewolf with them eyebrows. He's hairier than the inside of Sister Elizabeth's thighs, and she's like a Bargoed pit pony!' Father John replied. 'That bastard Barry John's no better mind.'

Jac, glowing red, tried to change the subject quickly. 'Didn't see you in church on Sunday, Father.'

'Sorry boys, I had some business to sort out. I just couldn't make it back in time.'

The two boys glanced at each other, confusion written all over their innocent faces.

'Fancy coming to Portugal with us, Father?' Kinsey asked. 'It should be a great laugh.'

'I would love to boys.' The priest took a sip of his cider and quietly added, 'but they took me passport off me.'

'Who did?' both boys said in unison.

'It's a church thing boys. It's a stupid church thing. Don't ask!' He picked up the whiskey chaser and emptied the glass in one. He looked up towards the ceiling, shaking his head.

The boys noticed the words 'Fresh Fruit and Fish at Sam's Market Stall' engraved into his white collar.

Kinsey wondered how much it would be to advertise his father's business with mini-neon lights for maximum effect.

To overcome the silence, which was about to take root in the conversation, Jac said, 'Do you wanna drink, Father?'

'No…I'm alright. Thanks boy. I'm seeing someone tonight about hiring the Church out on weeknights for line dancing.' He winked at the pair and continued, 'Don't forget when you are away…don't do anything that I *would* do!'

He handed them two cards advertising the new home communion delivery service which was starting next week. The card highlighted the free small bottle of wine and crackers to every household. It stated that portable confessional boxes were available to hire at discount prices.

The boys walked off trying to analyse what this would mean in the scheme of life but failed in their assessment.

Father John went back to looking at the photo and whispering either the words to the Lord's Prayer or the lyrics to Lust for Life by Iggy Pop. It sounded strangely the same.

The boys headed to the bar. Jac shouted across the room to Alex to see if he required a top up. Kinsey ordered the drinks and turned to enquire about the reason Father John had missed Mass.

'It's not the first time either,' explained Jac

'What did you all do?' asked an intrigued Kinsey, who glanced in disgust back towards the priest.

'It was great,' Jac exclaimed. 'Rory, who luckily had his false organ hand with him started to belt out Christmas songs; Slade, Wizard, Shaky, and all that stuff. You should have seen it. Even old Mrs. Griffiths, who was being drip fed tomato soup intravenously, started singing and dancing to "Do they know it's Christmas time at all", and this was in bloody May.'

Barry the Bar handed over three pints of lager.

Jac continued with the story. 'Then someone shouted out for us to have a game of Bingo. So someone went next door to the club and got the bingo machine and all the congregation started with the eyes down, legs eleven and all that bollocks.'

Kinsey stopped him a second to count his change. People always counted their change when Barry was working. Barry was renowned for not giving customers the right change.

'Sorry my mistake,' he would always say. 'Should get me one of those calculator thingies.'

What the bartender didn't know was that everyone knew that in a previous life, Barry had served time for embezzling funds from an ex-employer. What they didn't bother to ask was why. If they had asked, he would have told them he had done it to pay for his mother's cancer operation. They wouldn't have known that Barry's mother died when he was born and the real reason he had embezzled those funds was because he thought that he would get away with it and he needed a new car.

Barry was not only an embezzler, but because of his stint behind bars, was also a very convincing liar to boot.

'No way!' Kinsey replied, having satisfied himself that his change was correct.

He turned the conversation back to the church story, 'What did they use for prizes?'

Jac went on to explain that anything not nailed down had been raffled off. Walking home was like a scene from the riots in Brixton; full scale looting everywhere you looked.

The best thing about that day, he added, was that one old biddy by the side of him suddenly tapped him on the shoulder and said that she'd had a sweat on for number six. When the bingo caller shouted number six, she screamed out, 'House!' and ran up to the altar to collect her prize. It was a crucifix on a six-foot pole. When she returned to her seat she looked Jac in the eye and excitedly told him that it was just the thing she had always wanted.

Everybody went home with something; Bishop's hats, statues or ceremonial dresses. He informed Kinsey that he had won one of those big purple robes they use in funerals.

'What are you going to do with it?' Kinsey enquired, sipping a drop of lager.

'I gave it to my Nan for her birthday. I went up to see her last night, and there she was doing the ironing in it while my Granddad was fast asleep by the fire. She cut a life-size cardboard mask of the Pope out of some magazine and had it around her head. She said she wanted to frighten the fucking life out of him when he woke up.'

Pints in hand, the two laughing boys headed towards Alex.

In the top corner of the room, the dinosaurs were gathering in their usual resting-place, decked out in cheap blazers, uncoordinated ties and army-issue white socks with grey slip-ons.

This was the land of the committee-men and the top relic was Big Ken, the chairman of this prehistoric outfit.

Everything about Big Ken was big. When he was a smallish baby, his mother entered him in a 'who has the head most like a whale' competition held at Minehead Butlins. He not only won it hands down, or head down, but so impressed the organisers that they asked his mother to be a guest speaker at the annual 'Bonny Baby Big Bonce' convention, staged in Bournemouth each year.

Big Ken had been chairman of the rugby club for the previous five years. In that time, the club had rolled a couple of sixes, and climbed several ladders in the snakes and ladders game of life. Unfortunately it had also landed on some mean-looking hombre reptiles and found itself travelling downwards towards the start of the board.

No one could criticise Big Ken for his effort or his heart, which was in the right place. The problem was his thought processes were sometimes still stuck on the platform at the 'where to go next' station, instead of sitting in business class, eating expensive egg mayonnaise sandwiches and gulping down boiling hot tea in a wafer thin porcelain cup.

'OK!' Big Ken brought the meeting to order by tapping his pint on the table. 'Committee meeting starting!'

Peter, who would make an ugly, buck-tooth ferret Dean Martin look-a-like, interrupted Big Ken and piped up 'We haven't done the roll-call Ken.'

Big Ken felt a sudden bout of coldness invade him. He looked at Peter and asked, 'What the fucking hell's bells are you on about, you twat?'

'It was agreed two meetings ago that all further committee meetings linked to the tour should start with a roll call, Ken. You must remember we put it in the red book.'

Now, Peter 'O' Neil crawled through life as an estate agent. He made a decent living from lying and swindling newly weds out of their hopes, dreams and happiness for the next ten years of their lives. He was a very slimy person. In fact his nickname at school had been 'Frog Spawn.'

Over the years, some people had questioned if Peter was actually human. Fuel was poured onto the fire when a small boy, named Derek, thought he had discovered a cold and disturbing secret at the 'O' Neil's household. One day the youngster entered Peter's garden to retrieve his ball. No one answered his knocks at the door, so he went around the back. When poor Derek glanced through the window he allegedly observed something so frightening that even today, ten years on, it still makes him wake up screaming in sheer terror and piss his pyjamas. Derek swore on the Holy Bible he saw something in Peter's kitchen slithering on the floor like a giant slug with no arms or legs. By the side of the creature were the remains of what Derek thought were the carcass of a small dog, perhaps a poodle or a stubby Jack Russell. He ran home and told his parents.

The police were called. After a thorough search of the premises, the police apologised to Mr 'O' Neil and left, but not empty-handed. Peter had talked them into putting a deposit down on a nice three-bedroom property which had just come on the market. Derek was sent to see a shrink. From that day on, he wore the sad label of the 'strange boy with the twitchy eye who snooped around people's back gardens'.

What everyone had missed during the commotion, was the disappearance of Ollie the news agent's pet poodle.

Back in the lounge, Big Ken shook his head. 'But I can see that everyone is here,' Big Ken protested. 'Is everyone here?' his voice raised several decibels.

Most of the committee members, who to be honest had only come to the club that night for the two free pints and to get out of the house for an hour, all nodded their approval.

'OK, let's start.' Big Ken turned to face his audience.

Before he said another word, Keith, who was nervously fiddling with his glasses, pronounced, 'We did say Ken that we would do a roll call and rules are rules and if we break this one it could mean that we start to drop various other important rules and where would we be then?' The words rolled out of his mouth with not a full stop or comma in sight. He looked down at the orange floor tiles and moved his glasses up his nose towards his eyes.

Now Keith was the type of person whose life revolved around the rugby club and expected the rugby club to revolve around committee meetings. He also expected the meetings to be held together with rules and regulations. These were rules and regulations that he made up, or someone else had made up, and he had of course seconded.

Big Ken was becoming impatient. Big Ken was not known for his patience. He was known for his big head and lack of brain cells. In fact, when patience was actually being given out, Big Ken was not even at the back of the queue. He completely missed it, slept so late that he had to have a note off his mother excusing him from ever using any patience again.

Due to this twist of fate, Big Ken would normally deal with different situations by either smashing his large fists on to the table or into the side of someone's poor eardrum. One was worse than the other, but it was all according to whether one was a table or an eardrum.

'OK,' interrupted Big Ken, 'Have the fucking roll call, but make it quick.'

Peter fumbled for his brief case and unlocked the clasps.

'Hey…you made that look so easy, especially with your fake plastic arms,' Small Jeff piped up sarcastically.

'Fuck off,' Peter snapped back and opened up the big red book. He found the right page, pulled his pen out and clicked the top of it. Big Ken's eyes burnt right through him. Everyone shuffled about nervously.

'Ken Jones,' Peter finally called out triumphantly.

There was a particularly nervous long pause. Big Ken drank his pint. All eyes fixed on the brown liquid that disappeared down his large throat.

'What?' Big Ken said, suddenly feeling all the eyes on him.

'Are you present?' Peter continued.

'Are you taking the piss?' Big Ken screamed. 'Of course I'm fucking present you dozy, snake-skinned, alien creature twat. Now if you don't hurry up I'll stick that book and briefcase and him, pointing violently at Keith, up your ring-piece.'

Peter sprinted through the rest of the roll call faster than Linford Christie and his oversized lunch box, had ever sprinted out of his blocks.

With an angry glare which was directed at no one but intended for everyone, Big Ken growled before continuing with the speech he had started a million years ago. 'So can I start this bloody meeting?'

The silence that greeted the question and the absence of any substantial eye contact politely invited him to finish his story.

'Boys, I'm excited about this tour.' His tone softened.

While he talked to the old, boring familiar faces in the room, he imagined in his overactive mind that he has just walked out to a standing ovation in the Albert hall. His support act of the rat pack had already been on to warm up the crowd. Even Frank, Dean and Sammy pulled up chairs at the side of the stage to watch this great man in full flow. A spotlight lit up Ken's face and a Welsh choir began to softly hum a fine tune behind him.

'I haven't slept for weeks boys. We are going to win this bloody tournament; I can feel it in my water.' He looked around and left time for a dramatic pause. 'We are going to put Dowlais Rugby Football Club on the bloody world map.' He banged his hand down onto the table. All the eardrums in the room breathed a heavy sigh of relief.

There were nods of approval from the committee-men. In his minds eye, a lovesick groupie, with a tiny skirt on and a 'Big Ken for King' tee shirt ran up the aisle. She dodged the security guards to plant a kiss onto his lips and stuff her red panties and phone number into his pocket. There was a roar of appreciation from the packed crowd.

'We are going to put Welsh rugby back to where it belongs on top of the tree. I am sick of these bloody stuck up, fancy-Nancy, big-minded English bastards and their professional approach to our national game.'

'Well said, Ken....well said.' Keith was showing signs of solidarity towards his leader. Only thing was, he had orange spots floating in front of his eyes after finally looking up from those terrible floor tiles.

Back on 'ego-trip' mountain in Ken's cranium, the audience was cheering and clapping wildly to every word that flowed out of his mouth.

Another beautiful girl, this time of Chinese origin, pronounced her undying love for the almighty Ken and jumped from the balcony to her instant death.

Big Ken thought, 'what a waste, she could have taken off her top before she jumped.'

She was swept under the carpet by a 'seen it all before' council worker. There she slept, not with the fishes, but with the remains of a skinned poodle and the ashes of a fat three-stone cat.

'It's about time we shoved that bloody chariot right back into the Bristol bloody channel.'

There was a standing ovation and thousand of flowers littered the stage. Ken closed his eyes and sucked in the adulation.

Keith, who now felt that he was on a roll, shamelessly nose-dived straight into arse lick territory by starting to sing, 'You can stick your bloody chariot up your arse.'

All the committee members began to sing along. They painfully got through three verses, arms linked and swaying to the beat.

At that stage, Ken had not only left the building, but had been out on the tiles until dawn with Frank, Dean and Sammy and was now getting into a hot tub with two bunny girls from the Misty Moves Gentleman's Club.

He didn't feel the large moth crawling over his forehead.

'What a bunch of tossers.' Jac said to Kinsey on hearing the pathetic noise coming from the corner of the room. 'The future's bright. The future's full of tossers like them lot.' He got up and headed for the quiet of the toilets.

In the background, the domino game had started to get ugly. Fred knocked one of Harry's dominoes onto the floor, and then started to rifle through the unturned dominoes on the table. Harry looked up with suspicion at Fred. They stared at each other like two boxers sizing each other up before a World Championship fight.

'I saw you cheating,' accused Harry.

'I never cheat,' stated Fred defensively.

'You do too you rat lilley bastard.'

The two contenders jumped to their feet and took the fighting stance; shoulders back, fists clenches at their sides, leaning into each other so their noses were almost touching. Shouts from the imaginary fans in the packed arena cheered them on.

Ding…ding…ding. Before the first punch was thrown, the invisible ghost referee shouldered his way in between the two old blokes and directed them to their respective corners. Fred and Harry touched gloves and went back to their seats, the game recommenced.

Back in the land where time was revolving backward at a rapid pace of knots, Justin had taken control of the floor.

Justin was the youngest member of the committee. He was the one person that all the players, players' wives, girlfriends and fans loathed with a vengeance. Not because had never played a game of rugby in his twenty-eight years of life. Not because he was only on the committee because his father was a Mason, but because he was a middle class, over-weight, Hammy Hamster-faced knob of a boy with a smug and arrogant expression that never left his chubby face.

To be fair to Justin, it wasn't his fault. He was an only child and had been spoiled rotten by his parents. And, his pure white skin and the sissy lunches of Belgian chocolate, crust-less cucumber sandwiches and 'have a good day' notes that his mom packed him everyday, caused the other kids to bully him relentlessly his entire school career. As much as he scrunched up his face or went days without sleeping in an attempt to make his face look weather beaten and rough like the tough boys in class, they would still beat him up and shove his face in a toilet bowl of smelly yellow piss water every morning.

He relished his place on the committee because it gave him the feeling of respect and authority he had longed for his entire life.

'The itinerary for the week is extremely busy,' Justin announced. As he spoke he made quotation mark gestures with his fingers.

Small Jeff butted in loudly. 'What do you mean the It..ali.an is busy?'

'Itinerary, not Italian…you idiot,' Peter interrupted. 'It means the things we are going to do each day.'

Half the group chuckled at the stupidity, the other half remained dumbfounded with vacant faces just like Jeff's; also caused by the Edwardian shit tip some argued.

Small Jeff was Big Ken's older brother. Unfortunately, ever since his sibling had been christened Big Ken, apparently making him Small Jeff to the rest of the world, he had a chip on his shoulder the size of a Mt. Everest. He blamed his father for the cruel and unusual nickname, so deep in fact that when his Father died, he refused to go to the funeral. He went mackerel fishing instead.

'Why didn't he just say that then?' Small Jeff said not even trying to hide his irritation. 'Just because his father got him a job with the council…all of a sudden it's ITINERARY this and ITINERARY that…it used to be 'things we have to do today' when he worked at Pizza Time.'

'Hey, Justin, I didn't know you worked for the council,' said Peter, who looked genuinely interested.

'Yes, I do…and my father did *not* get me the job. I went through the same interview process as everyone else.' Again, he made quotation marks with his fingers reminding everyone of why they despised him.

'What department do you work in?' Peter enquired.

'In the "my father got me the job because he's big in the fucking Masons" fucking department,' Small Jeff shouted proudly for the crowd.

Everyone laughed except Big Ken, who was starting to lose his temper. His knuckles were white with rage.

'In the Leisure and Services Department act…ua….lly. And I am responsible for arranging the burials at the cemetery,' Justin fired back.

'That should come in handy looking at the age of you lot,' Jac quipped walking back from the toilet, broad satisfied grin on his face.

'Fuck-off, Shorty…this is a committee meeting.' Small Jeff turned his aggression onto new prey.

Big Ken slammed his pint down onto the table. The tone of his voice was strangely calm. 'Can we get on with this bloody meeting please? I want no more talk of graves or Masons or fuckin' Italians.'

Everyone's eyes burnt large holes into the floor, as Big Ken asked Peter the one question that everyone was dying to know. 'Right Peter, how much dosh is in the kitty?'

All greedy eyes fell on Peter. This was what they had all joined the committee for. Fuck watching thirty grown men chasing a ball around in the pissing rain, they could watch it on TV if they really wanted to. It was all about free meal tickets and using their power to get more free meal tickets.

Most of the men around the table craved power and money. In one of their pre-season team-building sessions, an unhealthy obsession with Nazis, Jack-Boots and Margaret Thatcher was uncovered. One of the committee-men even admitted that he often dreamt of walking straight into an off-license, dressed in full SS officer gear, handing over a large sum of cash and then driving off with all the booze and fags in a Chieftain tank with furry dice on the dashboard.

As they waited to hear how much was in the kitty, they closed their eyes and imagined an unlimited free buffet of warm beer, pork scratchings and ham rolls. Unfortunately, the dream was shattered by the sound of the domino table being kicked over.

Fred and old Harry both rolled about on the floor like two tortoises trying to get up off their backs.

'Go and sort those two out, Pete,' Big Ken sighed in an 'it's not those two fucking idiots again' kind of depressed tone.

Peter coughed. 'It's Keith's turn to sort out any unusual disturbances in the clubhouse when there's a meeting taking place,' he quietly added, while conveniently staring somewhere else.

'What the bastard hell are you talking about?' barked Big Ken.

'It was stated in the committee meeting dated the 12th of October that…'

Big Ken stopped him in his stride with one finger and slowly grunted, 'Right I will go and sort out Ali and fucking Frazier over there and when I return I am going to sort out that little red fucking book of yours for fucking good.' He gave Peter a stare that would have frozen the fires of Hell.

Big Ken stormed over to Fred and Harry and bent over to pick them up. He muttered, 'Boys. I am in a very bad mood. That prick over there,' He pointed to Peter who was nervously smiling back, 'is getting on my tits. So you two oldies had better stop this fighting every night or you will be banned for life, which looking at the both of you isn't probably that long anyway…so fuckin' behave.'

'He's always cheating at dominoes,' Harry shouted.

'I am not.'

'Yes he is.'

'Well you asked my Mavis out in 1947 and you call yourself a friend?'

Everyone in the room sighed openly.

'That's not the real reason is it? It's because you should have been watching that equipment that night,' Harry slammed his reply back towards his friend.

'Harry, you bastard, it was your turn. You were the one that was blind drunk.' Fred swung his fist at his mate.

'Ha…I always knew there was a reason behind this,' snarled Harry, ducking and diving behind Big Ken.

Everyone in the room knew the script by heart and the story of the great 'butterball' explosion at Yardley's Butter factory in 1953. It happened because a drunk Fred and Harry had neglected the giant vats of hot cooking butter. The blast covered a three-mile radius and took an army six weeks to clean up. Of course they both got sacked not only for the explosion, but for wasting hundreds of gallons of the prized Yardley's butter, which was the butter by appointment to the Queen.

Not surprisingly bread and crumpet sales rocketed in the area. But stranger than that, bright yellow sewer rats started to emerge from the drain holes. A special documentary was produced and narrated by

David Attenborough, called 'The Fat Yellow Coated Rats of Irontown'. It was shown late on Wednesday 26th April 1964 on BBC2.

Fred and Old Harry never worked in the food industry again.

Dangling from Big Ken's arms, the gruesome twosome tried desperately to kick and spit at each other.

All of a sudden, *'Anarchy in the UK'* by the Sex Pistols blasted out of the jukebox. Everyone turned to look at the offending piece of equipment that was causing the noise. Jac walked away from it, pretending to play air guitar as he headed back to his seat.

Big Ken immediately dropped poor Fred and Harry, who fell unceremoniously onto the floor. Johnny Rotten's snarling voice pumped out of the speakers.

'I am an Antichrist,
I am an Anarchist
Don't know what I want
But I know how to get it
I wanna destroy passers-by'

With uncontrollable amounts of steam coming out of his ears, Big Ken marched over to the jukebox and pulled out the plug. He turned to face the table in one movement and yelled: 'WE ARE TRYING TO HAVE A COMMITTEE MEETING YOU PRICKS!'

Big Ken forgot to compensate for the sudden loss of the loud anti-social music. The word 'pricks' rebounded around the clubhouse. It knocked a photograph of the 1974 rugby team, sporting Showaddywaddy sideburns, off the wall. The team members in the

1975 photograph next to it, who all looked the spitting image of Dave Hill from Slade, smiled. The Boy George look-a-likes in the 1988 team photo stubbornly sucked in their cheeks and refused to look in either of their directions.

'Sorry Ken, we thought that you were all just counting out your twelve pieces of silver,' Alex smirked.

Meanwhile, Peter and Keith had flapped over to Ken to offer support. They conveniently perched on either side of Big Ken's shoulders.

'Stop being a smart arse or I'll wipe that smirk off your face,' he indicated to Alex. 'And I'm warning you three now, I don't want any of the nonsense we had on the last tour.'

'Who... us?' said Jac, a mocking grin balancing on his lips.

'I don't wanna smell any of that WACKY BACKY,' the big man said in a very crisp voice that would have snapped a twig if it was walking through a jungle. 'Or find any of those C's that you junkies keep popping every night.'

'E's, Ken,' corrected Peter.

'What...?' said Big Ken, flicking the large moth off his larger head.

'It's E's, not C's, Ken. I thought you would like to know.'

'Right that's it... outside. You've been trying to pick a fight with me all fuckin' night.'

Big Ken turned to face Peter. He started to roll up the sleeves of his shirt. 'We haven't done the roll call, Ken. It's not in the Red book, Ken.' Big Ken sarcastically replied. His features bright red; spittle dribbling down his bottom lip.

This was in opposite contrast to Peter, who had just turned ten shades of white. His ears dived for cover, waiting the onslaught of Big Ken's fists.

'But…but,' Pete started to stutter like a back firing motorcycle.

The boys knew that Ken was now balancing on the edge of his limit. One wrong word and it would be a Blitzkrieg Bop all over again in the lounge.

They had seen Big Ken perform several times in the past. It was not a pretty sight. The worst, and still the most talked about, was the day of Benny Mackintosh's wedding.

On that fateful afternoon, Trashy and his three brothers were ushering people to their seats in the church. Trashy, just happened to say to one of the guests that he thought the wrestling on ITV with Dickey Davies was a big set up. Unfortunately for Trashy, Big Ken overheard this statement. What Trashy didn't realise was Big Ken was the number two fan of 'Queeny tight pants,' the blonde-haired darling of the wrestling circuit.

At first Big Ken quietly asked Trashy to apologise to all the fine men in the wrestling fraternity who risked their lives and limbs for other people's enjoyment, week in and week out. Trashy's X-rated reply to Big Ken should never have set foot in the house of God. In fact, if God had been listening and not fast asleep in front of a roaring fire, after drinking too much sherry and Iron-Bru at a 'New Angel wing' designer party, he would have sent a lightening strike so powerful that Trashy's ashes would have fitted into a matchbox. So it was left to Big Ken to take the mantle of the 'Avenger' on his own set of shoulders. After staring at the floor for several minutes, he unleashed the 'Whale

Head'. It was a scary place to be. Bodies lay beneath the pews and the altar; blood splattered over the statues of the Mary and Joseph. Someone's front teeth were found in the holy water.

The outcome of the day was quite simple. Firstly, the wedding did go ahead, but there were no wedding photographs for obvious reasons. Secondly, Queeny had a lovely letter and a bunch of flowers from someone he thought was called Tishy.

In the club house, the boys tried hard not to smile. They had decided to visit Orange Tile City; their bottom lip biting hard to stop their shoulders from shaking.

Just at that moment, Steve 'Lusty' James strolled in carrying his kit bag. Ken saw Lusty and his attitude immediately changed.

Big Ken loved Lusty. Not in a 'man plays with another man's flute in the toilets by the Crown Court' sort of way, but in 'Lusty is the best Player in the Town' sort of way.

'Hello Steve,' bellowed Big Ken proudly.

'Hello Big Ken,' replied the handsome newcomer

'You scored two great tries on the weekend Steve. I was telling my wife in bed on Saturday night how you reminded me of a young Phil Bennett.' Big Ken pretended to swivel his hips and dummied with an imaginary ball.

Peter and Keith feigned to play along. Behind the big man's back the rest of the boys made wanking gestures. Peter saw them and considered informing Big Ken for all about two seconds until he realised it may backfire like his last comment.

Ken spotted the kit bag resting on Lusty's back. 'Been training have you, Steve?'

Lusty, with a stone-faced expression, nodded confidently. He placed the kit bag under the table out of harms way.

'That's my boy.' Big Ken turned to the other boys, 'If only you lot had the dedication and attitude of this boy.' He put his arm around Lusty and muttered to himself, 'My secret weapon.'

Lusty's face broke out into a smile. It was more of 'if only you knew what was really happening' type of smirk than an 'oh thank you for appreciating all my good work' sort of grin.

He thanked Big Ken and winked at his mates.

Big Ken turned to face the boys who sat around the table. 'Now keep that bloody racket off until I go home.'

He turned to Peter, raised one finger like a giant hammer and muttered: 'Come on shit face and don't you say another word until I go home.' He snatched the red book out of Peter's hand and put it under his arm.

Peter, who had finally returned back to a colour that resembled human skin, headed slowly towards the toilet. His ears popped out from undercover of his shirt collars and removed the small protective crash helmets that they had put on.

When the smoke had cleared, the dust settled and the dinosaurs had retired back into their box, the four life long friends sat alone at the table.

Jac was the first to address Lusty, by mimicking Big Ken. 'I was telling my wife in bed on Saturday that you were exactly like a young Phil Bennett, blah, blah, blah. Fucking Tony Bennett, more like.'

'More like Tony the shagging fucking tiger,' snorted Kinsey.

They all laughed.

'Should've heard what she was telling me in bed,' Lusty cut in, while he took a seat next to Alex.

'You haven't?' Kinsey said; a look of disgust on his face.

'Let's just say that not every old piano plays a fine tune,' he said quietly in a voice huskier than normal.

This was too much for Kinsey to take in. 'What the fuck are you on about? Who do you think you are...? Eric 'Lusty' Cantona...piano...seagulls..!! You should be locked up.'

'Castrated more like,' advised Alex. 'Not Big Ken's wife?'

Lusty stood up laughing and offered to get the drinks in. He strolled to the bar.

Steve 'Lusty' James' life had never really deviated far from the path of women. He already had two failed marriages and five official children against his name. There were many rumours of many more little unofficial sprogs running about trying to cling onto his Levi jeans.

In the local newspaper section on young babies it was quite interesting, and frightening for all the supposed dads in the town, to see how many of the kids on the pages actually looked like dead ringers for this Warren Beatty look alike.

Women had always been attracted to Lusty. They were like iron filings swimming towards a horny magnet. He was so attractive he really should have carried a health warning printed on his body somewhere.

Even when he was in the scouts, girls, and their mothers, and often their grandmothers, used to flock to see the young handsome kid in his little tight shorts. Lusty was quite oblivious to the fact until one night while the scout troops were out camping. Akela, the scout leader, sneaked into his tent. She had told the other little ugly scouts to go and pick fire wood and take as long as they liked. She took Lusty by the hand and told her scout lover to pick whatever he fancied. That night, underneath the full moon, he was introduced to the joys of older women with big, swinging tits. That night he qualified for his 'erecting a tent' badge. That night, call it fate or not, the legend of Steve 'Lusty' James was born.

Now from that day on, a night out with Lusty normally ended up with some lovely looking girl shimmying up to Steve, taking his hand and walking him off into the night.

There was a phrase coined in the English dictionary that described Lusty's journey through this sea of fishy fingers. It simply read ... 'Jammy twat.'

Alex called order to the proceedings by opening up the conversation just as Lusty placed the fresh pints of lager onto the table. 'OK let's get down to business. Lusty, have you got the presents?'

'Of course, captain,' he responded promptly.

'What do you mean the presents?' Kinsey enquired, looking to the rest of the group for some clarification.

'Well, it's quite simple. On the last tour to America, Wigsy worked out that we spent at least 15% of our time shopping for presents,' replied Alex.

'And cock books,' Jac quickly butted in.

There were general nods of approval for the cock book remark.

Alex continued with the explanation. 'So, to a normal person that's acceptable, and it's nice to have time off the pop, but to Wigsy it's a massive waste of precious drinking time. So he suggested that all the shopping is a non-value activity and should stop. So this time we decided to get all the presents before we go.'

Wigsy was the club drinking champion. If there had been an Oscar for drinking, it would have been no contest. Wigsy would easily have lifted the 'Best Film', 'Best Actor', 'Most Interesting Musical Score' and probably the 'Best Foreign Short Film with Sub-titles' award.

He was the undisputed king of the drinking ring. All comers welcome. All new comers destroyed. Macho Lager, a local brewing company, sent him a year supply of their product just for wearing their merchandise. He drank the years supply in two weeks and gave the tee-shirts away to a charity shop where his Gran worked.

'Voila.' Lusty tipped all the wears from his kit bag onto the table. Out fell perfume and toys and lots of other goodies.

'You told Ken that you had been training,' said Kinsey.

'Training to become a shoplifter,' was Lusty's smiling reply.

'Lusty…you *are* Liam Gallagher,' Jac interrupted, with an added look of admiration.

Wigsy walked into the room and ordered his fifth drink of the night. Lusty threw him some perfume and two toy trucks.

'Top man, Lust …how much do I owe you?'

'You can buy me a pint in the sun, Wigs.'

Wigsy strolled off clutching his pint and his presents like little trophies to be taken back to his strange world. He was now happy in the knowledge that there would be no searching around poxy, knick knack shops on this tour. To make the trip complete, he would be explaining to the barman on his arrival that he would like his beer cold and plentiful. A drunken man lost in lager paradise.

The boys started to divvy up the contents of Lusty's treasure cove.

'What about the C's...no sorry... the E's?' Alex jokingly announced.

Lusty produced a big bag of white tablets from the inside pocket of his Levi jacket. Eyes lit up at the magnificent sight.

'Lusty. Will you marry me?' asked Jac.

'I'll have to fuck you first, Jac!'

'I have the WACKY BACKY.' Alex again mimicked Ken. 'What about the Speed, Jac?'

Jac stared at the table. The boys could sense that there was something wrong.

'Sorry, boys, I couldn't get any.' His voice trailed off in disappointment.

'You're fucking joking!' Kinsey yelled out in complete horror.

'I tried everywhere, honest. I even went to see Danny 'Cut it to fuck and mix it with baking powder' Harris, but he was out of flour and chalk and wouldn't give me any of his personal stash.'

Kinsey, whose short fuse had ignited, quickly barked back, 'Tell me you are messing about... tell me Jac... tell me!'

'I've got some liquid Viagra.' Jac sheepishly looked away.

'Liquid Viagra? Liquid Viagra?' Kinsey protested in a high pitched voice. 'Who are you...Jac and the fucking beanstalk? Look Mam, I haven't got any money, but I have these lovely, useless, fucking beans instead. You fucking useless, fucking Coco the clown, fucking moron,' he snapped.

'Cool down, Kins, I'll see what I can do,' muttered Lusty.

'Well I'm not going,' said Kinsey, who folded his arms and looked in the other direction. He stared straight at Old Harry who was trying to force a double blank domino block up Fred the Taxis nose.

'Don't be so soft,' Alex grinned as he got up to get another round in.

'There's no way I can spend seven days in the sun, drinking like a lunatic without any whizz,' Kinsey said desperately. 'I'll end up like that tramp Maxy. I'll be rolling in the gutter with sick all over me like last year, and you lot standing over me pissing yourselves laughing.'

A long silence, held in a half-nelson death grip, amongst the boys was deafening.

Lusty talked into his mobile phone like a professional drug dealer, 'Whizz…yeah…great…amount, wait a minute.' Unfazed, he motioned to Kinsey, who immediately held up ten fingers.

'About ten grams…a speed ball…yeah…tonight. Great… thanks, Lippy.' Lusty held up a lit match to Kinsey's face, blew it out and said, 'Explosion denied. Now get the drinks in, you short fused idiot.'

Someone shouted for Barry the Bar to turn the sound up on the TV. Barry dropped a bag of change from the fruit machine onto the floor in surprise.

'That's Merthyr, ain't it?' proclaimed Small Jeff.

The sound went up. There was quiet in the lounge.

The newscaster was introducing the story. 'And now we can go live to the scene of the hideous crime and our reporter Lisa Bari.'

Lisa Bari was standing outside Dowlais Catholic Church. The rain was driving down hard. There were camera crews dotted around the perimeter wall of the church building.

'Hello Ladies and Gentlemen. Today this small community has witnessed one of the most shocking and disturbing crimes in a town that has a long history of shocking and disturbing crimes. Last Sunday all the possessions belonging to this church were stolen. The Police suspect it was the work of a European cartel which specialised in exporting religious artefacts. A spokesman for the police added that they had no leads to go on, since there had been some sort of veil of silence amongst this tight-knit community.'

At that moment, in the background, a small child rode past on a chopper bike with an Archbishop's hat on.

The camera crew, who had been starved of a big, juicy story for the last three months, shouted for him to get out of the way, they had criminals to catch. They were also praying deep down that this assignment would bring with it lots of overtime. The last big pay-day they had was the hi-jacking of farmer Boris's Pig lorry by the splinter group of the animal liberation front, 'The Veggie's are for life, not just for decoration society', on the M4.

Thirty long days and nights the siege lasted. Then the SAS went in. The result changed meat transportation forever. The Tele-printer in the newsroom on that cold November morning highlighted the extent of the gruesome result:

- *SAS - 6 killed*
- *Veggie is for life society - 12 killed and 1 maimed*
- *Boris's prized Pigs – 56 burned alive.*
- *Boris and wife perished in the blaze*

- *Japanese News team travelling to scene in minibus 220 killed*

Of course, out of every disaster emerges a nugget with a silver lining. The overtime was great and the pork wraps were the best anyone had every tasted.

Back at the Catholic Church at Dowlais, Lisa continued. 'Father John, the local Priest, has not been seen since the incident and was unavailable for comment today.'

All the eyes in the rugby club slowly left the TV set and headed in the direction of Father John, but all they found were the remains of a pint of cider, an empty whiskey glass and a signed photograph of Iggy Pop.

Chapter 3

'Ethel Candy fined 20 shillings'

The morning rain sounded like a series of jazzed-up soft drumbeats on the snared windowpane of the Davies' household.

In the warm bed, Alex and his wife Claire were trying their best to keep their motion to the same beat as the rhythm of the elements outside. Their lovemaking was passionate. It was always passionate. Well, as passionate as a couple who have been married for at least a million years, could be.

'That feels great,' Alex whispered. He slipped into his wife for the first time that morning. He had just finished the compulsory oral sex examination between her legs and although he knew he wouldn't be getting an A+ grade, too much drink last night, he would have been disappointed with anything less than a B star and a pat on the back.

'Slower…slower…faster….faster,' enthused Claire. Her eyes closed and fingers clenched tightly. Her breath warmed the side of his neck. She had thanked her lucky stars that he had finally stopped trying his pathetic attempt of arousing her with his index finger. It was actually making her feel more sore and drowsy than erotic.

'Move your leg over a bit, darling…bit more…more ohhh…that's nice…ohhh yessss,' Alex felt the tension of last night moving inch by inch out of his body. It's a great way to cure a hangover, he thought to himself.

'*I wish he'd brush his teeth before he climbed all over me. His breath smells like stale cheese,*' Claire confided with the little old cleaning lady, who occupied a flat inside her mind.

'How does that feel babe?' Alex asked hopefully.

'It feels…great…ohhh,' Claire exaggerated just a little. In fact, her exaggeration levels had shot straight off the meter, something that she wished her husband would be doing quite soon. She had lots to do this morning and all this pointless messing about 'down by the river' just because he was going away for a few days was not helping in the slightest.

'*Go on my son, she's loving it,*' Alex convinced himself. '*Stick the tongue in there; that always gets her going.*'

Alex tracked down her lips and sent in the tongue without a warrant, for a quick mouth to mouth strip search and tickle.

'*Oh no…not the fucking tongue. I think I am going to be sick.*' Claire could feel herself heaving.

'*Just think of something else.*' The little old lady, whose name was Ethel, grinned back, while polishing the large stately mirror with a rag.

'*Like what?*' Claire asked, hoping for a bloody good suggestion as his breath smelling of stinking bishop cheese had sent her imagination AWOL.

'*What about that lovely new dress you just bought. Or that chocolate orange you have hidden away from the kids in the kitchen drawer?*'

'*I've eaten it, Ethel,*' she answered sheepishly.

'*You didn't give me a piece, you selfish tart,*' Ethel replied obviously upset. She stopped rubbing the glass.

'*Don't get a strop on now Ethel...don't forget I'm the one with this lager tasting badger tickling my tonsils.*'

'*Well you married him,*" Ethel shrugged her shoulders, and started to Hoover Claire's secret room that was situated just behind her open mind.

'*You told me he was the best out of the bunch,*' Claire snapped back, remembering the night that the two of them had sat down to study all the options that were open to her at the time. It had been a tough time. There had been much soul-searching that had required a bottle of gin and a large box of Milk Tray to help ease the pain. She had told Ethel about all the ex-loves of her life; their strengths, which didn't take long, and their many weaknesses, which lasted most of the night. It had come down to a straight choice between Alex and a Spanish guy she had met when she was sixteen. Alex had won only because he spoke slightly better English and had a car. The Spaniard had had a much better tongue but his breath smelt of garlic.

'What did you say babe?' Alex unknowingly interrupted the silent conversation between the two women.

'Nothing love...keep going...faster...faster,' She pulled him in tighter and stormed back to confront Ethel.

'*Ethel, you just listen here. You are in my mind and you don't pay any rent and your food is free. So in the future, if I ask for your advice, I expect you to understand the situation and be more constructive. If you keep getting all uppity every time I need someone to comfort me,*

I'll go back to talking to Shirley. You wouldn't like that now, would you?"

There was a look of horror on the older woman's face. Although Ethel had never met Shirley in person, her reputation had preceded her.

Shirley had occupied the flat in Claire's mind before Ethel. She was younger than her and apparently enjoyed the odd smoke and drink. In the end, Claire had summoned her with an eviction notice, shortly after she had woken up one night and found the imaginary woman using Claire's body to satisfy her sexual cravings with a loofer.

'I am sorry Claire. Look, why don't you finish him off and we'll have a nice cup of tea and a Viscount biscuit, 'round about eleven.'

'OK, that sounds good,' Claire closed the door, leaving Ethel to get things ready for their daily morning chat.

Claire took a deep breath and re-entered 'husband-ville', without the aid of a safety net.

Alex was also trying hard to concentrate on the job at hand. Should he go for the quick finale? Should he stick it out for extra time? Should he go back to giving her oral pleasure? Time was getting on and Kinsey would be here soon and he still had lots of things to do. He made a snap decision.

'It must be at least twenty minutes,' he told himself. *'I think it's time I walked "doggy style" alley.'*

He knew what walking "doggy style" alley normally led to and led to quickly. *'And she loves it too,'* he vainly reminded himself. His face broke into a wide grin as he positioned her on all fours facing away from him.

'*She's still got a lovely arse mind,*' he nodded as he admired his wife's derrière.

'*Thank God for that,*' Claire thought to herself. '*He'll be finished in about five jerks of a rat's tail.*' She was glad Shirley was gone; she used to love this position and would often moan loudly in her brain during their love making.

'Oh yes… yes… that's good, big boy.' She knew that this would send his guns blazing. She reached under and tickled his balls for good measure.

She giggled to herself while Ethel relaxed upstairs on the settee reading this month's edition of Cosmopolitan.

Alex could feel his train about to arrive at the station called 'Cum-Town,' when all of a sudden, the bedroom door burst open and in ran Rachael, the two-year-old from Hell.

'Daddies going to Pert…ugall….Daddies going to Pert …ugall.' The two-year old happily announced the fact to her favourite doll.

Alex shot off Claire like his penis was on fire. Claire rolled the opposite way and fell off the side of the bed causing Ethel in turn to topple off the settee.

'Go see your brother, Rach,' Claire said nervously, while desperately climbing back under the covers.

Alex, who was trying to cover his modesty, sneaked under the blankets.

Rachel ignored her mother's pleas and clambered onto the bed. Alex's dog-on-heat manhood was oblivious to the young intruder that had stopped his morning performance. His angry buzzing bee could still smell the nectar deep inside the flower begging to be extracted. It headed back towards the garden of Claire's Eden, dragging his master with him. It huffed and puffed and tried to barge his way in.

'Stop it Alex! Not in front of the children,' she moaned, feeling his manhood standing proud against her leg.

'But…I won't see you for a week," he pleaded, still being led by his one-eyed dog. It was jerking away with a mind of its own.

Meanwhile, Rachel who had climbed high up onto the headboard was pretending that she was balancing on the top diving board at 'Dirty Pants' swimming baths. She saw her landing target and dive-bombed. Her foot landed straight between Alex's legs.

'Ohhh...Fuck...Ohhh….' Alex recoiled in shock. In the distance a wounded dog whimpered and looked for solitude back in his kennel, tail firmly between his legs.

'Stop swearing, Alex,' shouted Claire

'Ohhh…Fuck it…I'm going for a shower.' A doubled up Alex got up and slowly and carefully turned towards the en-suite door, slamming it shut.

Claire winked at Rachel. 'Good girl, Rach.' She'd really had enough of the morning session with Alex and was already thinking of the special offers at Asda.

Alex looked long and hard into the mirror above the sink. He stared at the face of someone he thought he knew quite well. There were signs of age popping up all over his face. In his prime, he could side-step and jinks his way from the unwelcome grasp of Father Time, but the introduction of two devil kids had slowed him down considerably.

A few grey hairs and crow's feet were starting to take root on his relatively handsome, but rugged face.

'*Still looking reasonably good,*' he told his reasonably good looking reflection. '*OK, not in the same class as Lusty,*' he continued, '*but not too many people are.*' If Lusty was the male version of a Roll-Royce, he thought that he, Alex Davies, was perhaps the equivalent of say, a two-litre Mondeo Titanium, with all the toys; CD interchanger, sunroof, air conditioning…the full works.

He thought at one time he fit nicely into the three series BMW category. But after seeing all the beautiful people strolling on the beach a recent family holiday to the Italian resort of Rimini, he downgraded himself a couple of models.

He had always got by as far as girls were concerned. There had been plenty of girls before Claire appeared on the scene. There had even been a couple of girls since he met Claire. He breathed in and checked his side profile in the full-length mirror.

But girls had never been that high on Alex's list of 'must-do' lifetime achievements. Dragging himself out of the gutter of a poor working class existence was his number one priority.

He worked hard at it. In some cases he worked twenty-five hours a day. He liked the hard work and long hours. He drove himself non-stop until he could truly say that he could see the light at the end of the tunnel that was glowing brightly. It was now starting to pay off. A nice four bedroom house with big a mortgage but with payments he could afford. A wife, who although was starting to talk to herself a little bit too much lately was lovely and two demanding but beautiful kids.

And, there was still some money left over to spend on the luxuries of life.

It used to be so different. He remembered sadly what it was like to have nothing. He had felt the pain and still had the battle scars to prove it. His parents were good parents. Perhaps even, great, but they were always poor parents.

'Not a ha'penny to rub together', could have been the less than fancy nameplate that could have easily hung above the door. Times were tough on that council estate and no matter how sunny it was outside, it always felt cold inside.

'Even the black rats wore overcoats,' his dad used to say as all seven of them snuggled under the blankets.

He recalled the Christmas Day mornings that were the worst times he could remember. Seeing all his mates out in the street playing with the latest fashionable toy or calling for him in brand new yellow football boots was very hard to take, especially for his parents. He prayed every night for God to send one of his angels into Rancy's flat on the fourth floor and pinch one of his train sets.

'Come on God, he will understand if you take one. He's got bloody three anyway.'

Although he prayed hard every night, he never did get that train set until several years later. Too little too late, by that time his prayers were focused on copping a feel of Maria Martin's tits, or tit, right or left, he wasn't fussed. Just like some of the older boys had told him. And fair play to his Holiness, he did actually listen to him this time and granted him his wish one bonfire night in the playground by the school field. He went home and prayed that next time he could also put his hand on her honey pot. This must have upset God because not only did Maria move to a different area, but he came down with a bout of acne, which stopped girls going near him again for nine months.

From an early age, he made a promise to himself that he would get out of the life of nothing and try on someone else's shoes for a change; a real leather pair with no holes in the sole, a pair that actually fit.

He had his first paper round at the age of thirteen. This was not your average 'a couple of Sunday mirrors and colour supplements' and then be home to watch 'Wait until Your Father Gets Home.' No, this was the biggest and toughest paper round in the history of paper rounds. 1024 houses on a Sunday morning with nothing more than the aid of an old shopping trolley, fur-lined gloves and a flask of Bovril.

While all of his mates were tucked up in bed, he was earning the grand sum of £6.20 for his efforts from Glen 'the robbing bastard' Snape, the local shopkeeper. He also got about £2 in tips and an extra £1.75 from old Mr Mansfield for helping him to apply cream to his enflamed piles.

'Can't reach due to the arthritis, my boy,' Mr Mansfield would explain to Alex, while bending over and pulling his PJ's down.

It had been a very unpleasant job. Alex would blank the task out of his mind as he dipped his digit into that cold gunk, and without looking, spread it over Mansfield's bright purple hanging baskets.

'You are a saviour, my boy.' Mansfield sighed as he pulled back up his black, silky pyjamas.

He would always give the boy one chocolate finger biscuit, which Alex thought was very bizarre. He never ate that strange snack.

Then one day, earlier than normal, Alex let himself into Mr Mansfield's house. He placed the week's newspaper on the bedside cabinet and put the money into his bag. He was dreading the pile covering operation. The drawer of the cabinet was slightly ajar and what he saw on further investigation made him physically sick and very angry. There in the drawer was a packet of fake stick-on 'lifelike' piles, which had been imported from Hamburg. By its side was a saucy novel entitled 'Little French Au-Pair Boys Get Smacked in the Monastery'

Alex went ballistic. He confronted Mr Mansfield, and after he inspected his pile-free chocolate starfish, he decided that he would have his revenge. Mr Mansfield begged Alex not to tell anyone. From that Sunday on, for the next two years, Mansfield, or Mr Pervyfield as he was now called, would have a large cooked breakfast ready and a bowl of hot water for Alex to soak his feet in during his round. Alex also took a £2 tip and half a pack of chocolate finger biscuits. Mr Mansfield eventually moved away.

Alex's next job was as a tea boy in a local button-making factory. Within a week, he was planning his move up to manager of the photocopying room. Within a week of getting that job, he was devising an action plan on becoming the office supervisor. He was quickly promoted after the previous supervisor fell down the stairs.

This job progression continued up to the present day, where he now had the grand title of 'Sales and Marketing Manager'. He had already written the blueprint for his next move into the world of directorship.

His strive for perfection was relentless and he still gave himself yearly, weekly and even daily objectives. Some of these tasks were simple to achieve, while others were stretching. He had begun to taste the good life and he was never going back to eating poor pie again.

If he did have a major regret, it was that because he always planned everything to the smallest detail, he lost all spontaneity from his life. His diary and movements were often planned weeks in advance and he rarely, if ever, strayed off course.

On this tour 'to-do' list, he had written only two words, 'Be Spontaneous.' This had taken him four hours to process.

He met Claire while completing a degree in 'Environmentally Safe Social Ladder Climbing' at the local technical college. It was love at first sight.

She's the one that will help me on this journey, he had told himself. They married six months later.

He finished shaving. He checked his love handles and decided that he would make losing half a stone a must on next month's 'to-do' list, along with his stretched target of 'learning to swim with dolphins'.

He got the baby oil out of the drawer and made sure the bathroom door was securely locked.

After the shower and showing his dog the bone, Alex went downstairs to see the kids. Claire was in the kitchen making some toast and bringing Ethel up to speed with last nights gripping episode of Eastenders.

Alex observed his children. They seemed content watching some hi-tech cartoon on the box. He couldn't help wondering why kids were like light switches; either on or off. And when the siblings were turned to off, they were like two sweet angels singing in the choir of loveliness. When they were switched to on, they turned into Viking devils, whose sole aim was to rape and pillage through his life.

He remembered reading an article by Russell Grant in Hello magazine. Russell was going through his famous Chinese astrology and meat ball diet phase at the time. He had written that when Capricorn was revolving around Pluto: -

- Never try to enter the mind of a child.

- Never try to change the mood of women.

- Never try to think that you can get a decent cup of tea in Greece.

These words had an everlasting effect on Alex and he was extremely pleased that Russell had been given his own TV show and he wished that 'Cooking for the Stars' would be a great success.

'Are you going to buy us lots of presents, Daddy?' Rachel asked during an advert.

'Only if you and James are good and look after your Mummy when Daddy's away,' Alex's mind pictured all of the gifts already wrapped and stashed away in the garage.

'I wanna football,' James shouted as he momentarily disengaged from the TV.

'No problem, James, my boy!'

'Why can't we all go on tour with you, Daddy?' Rachel asked, pleading with him through giant puppy eyes.

Alex never believed in lying to his children, but situations like this always caused for a little white one. It wouldn't cause any harm.

'It's because of the Queen. She made a rule that all special daddies had to go away and enjoy themselves or go to prison. Now you wouldn't like your daddy to be locked away in a dirty prison cell, would you?'

'*Listen to all that crap,*' Ethel, who had overheard the sexist explanation, hissed, '*Yes you should be locked up and the key thrown away.*'

'Why can't Mummy go and enjoy herself as well, Daddy?' Rachel asked innocently.

'Mummy enjoys being here with you fab kids,' he answered, not so innocently.

'*Cheeky bugger,*' Ethel said, '*a chance for the both of us to go away and enjoy ourselves would be a fine thing.*'

Claire decided not to go there and carried on making the breakfast.

Alex was starting to get restless. He dived onto the floor and changed into the dragon of the lake. He chased the kids around the room for a while using up some of his nervous energy.

Kinsey pulled up outside in his car and honked the horn excitedly. He had already blown away two old twats in a Rover, a mini-bus packed with nuns and destroyed a jogger in a shell suit with matching headband. This was turning out to be a great day.

Alex, with a big broad smile on his features, hugged and kissed his children goodbye. He walked into the kitchen, replacing his 'Thank fuck its Friday' smile with an 'I don't think I will go' look of despair.

'Is that Kinsey beeping?' Claire asked.

'Think so, love, but I'm not really sure.' He lied, unconvincingly.

'Does he want some breakfast?'

'No time love, we are late already. You know what he's like if he's kept waiting.' He caught around her, kissed her and looked deep into her eyes.

'If you don't want me to go, I'll make up some excuse that the kids are not well or something.' It was Oscar time in the Davies household. Alex was concentrating hard so that he would not fluff the well-rehearsed 'I'm going away to mess about like a young kid' yearly speech.

'*Tell him that it's a good idea and you think he is better off staying home with his wife and kids. Go on...He'll pooh himself,*' Ethel yelled out angrily.

'Don't be so soft, go and enjoy yourself. You work hard enough all year,' Claire replied. She was looking forward to a bit of peace.

'Are you sure?' Alex tried hard to hold back the smile.

'Of course...But watch yourself, no getting into trouble like last year.' Her face changed into serious mode as she thought back to the sight of him hobbling up the path on crutches after apparently falling over drunk.

'Thanks love.' He kissed her again and snatched a piece of toast and picked up his bag. 'And you look after yourself, any problems, go see my Mother.' He then added, 'and don't forget...behave yourself.'

Any love that was floating about in that kitchen was quickly extinguished with these last two words. He knew he shouldn't have said it, but they just slipped out.

The silence choked him tightly around his throat.

'*Don't stand for that girl, smack him in the mouth,*' Ethel shouted, as she threw down her magazine. She picked up her sweeping brush and started to beat the top of Claire's head. But Claire didn't need any inside help to sort this one out.

'Butt out Ethel, I can handle this!'

She turned and shouted, 'Oy!…you are the one fucking off to Portugal. I'm staying here as usual with fucking Hansel and Gretel in there. Now piss off before I change my mind.'

Alex tried to reach over to kiss her but she pulled away. When the silence had quit strangling him, it was quickly followed by her coldness, which felt like a kick in the balls. He was losing this one badly so he decided to take his bag and head for the hills. She followed him towards the front door, eyes burning into the back of his exposed neck.

Ethel was bouncing up and down and screaming, *'Hit him with something…go on …hit him.'*

'Shut up Ethel.'

He made a last attempt to go for broke and turned and got hold of her by the door and after a token struggle, lips finally found lips. Deep down they knew that they were made for each other.

As soon as the door closed Alex cried out, 'YES' but not too loud. In his imagination he had just putted the winning ball in the Open. He pictured himself running over to the gallery and high-fiving all his adoring onlookers.

Meanwhile, on the inside of the door, Claire whispered quietly, 'YES'. In her mind she told Ethel to put the kids in a dog pound for children as she climbed into a Jacuzzi full of bare-chested twenty something men.

Alex threw his stuff in the back of Kinsey's car.

'Yessssss…come on…here we go,' Kinsey banged the steering wheel.

'Did you give Julie one before you left?' Alex enquired.

'Of course I did,' he lied. 'I gave her all of my best moves. I even went down for some Bin Laden beaver… tongue like an Anteater me. I left her clutching on to the ceiling. Her mother will have to pry her down with a crowbar.'

They both laughed. The noise somehow convinced the driver and his passenger that their morning dip in the lake of romance had gone a long way to satisfying the desires of wives being left behind.

'It's got to be done…keep the cats from roaming,' Alex added.

Kinsey turned up the CD and *'Rockaway Beach'* by the Ramones pierced the morning air. He shot his make-believe gun at the sky, before firing it at a postman getting hounded by a three-legged dog.

Chapter 4

'All aboard the Skylark, All abroad the Skylark'

Lusty walked bare-footed across the floor of his freezing cold flat. He opened up the fridge and took out a bottle of a substance that in its former lifetime had been milk. He smelt the congealed blob. It made his head recoil in horror.

'*Fuck it…it won't kill me,*' he said to himself, as he poured the so-called milk en masse into his mug.

He picked up the mail and sat on his threadbare settee to read what the postman had delivered. There was a postcard from Tracey in Bolton, who he had met at a rave last month. She was on holiday in Crete with her fiancé, Brian.

'Wish you were lying next to me!' Her suggestive message had ended, followed by several kisses.

'Dirty, sly old bitch.' He placed the card carefully in the bin.

'Bills, bills, and more fuckin' bills.' He grimaced as he took a sip of tea. The unopened brown envelopes also found an early burial in the overfilled swing bin.

He opened a letter from the DSS. It read:-

'Dear Mr James,

According to our records, you have been claiming invalidity benefits for over eight years now. We would appreciate it if you could contact the office immediately, so that we can arrange an interview. The outcome of the interview will hopefully be your re-introduction back into the working population.

Yours sincerely

Mrs W.P. Butterworth''

'And you lot can fuck right off,' he yelled at the letter as if it was a public address tannoy system straight to the DSS office, and, in particular, Mrs W.P. Butterworth herself.

He just couldn't see the point in getting a proper job when all they ever did was take all his money off him in the name of the CSA. Well they could go and fuck themselves, he thought as he ripped the letter up and buried it deep at the bottom of the bin.

Subconsciously, he was afraid that the letter would some how come back to life and follow him around like a vampire that Peter Cushin couldn't quite kill off. So he picked every piece carefully back out of the bin and flushed them down the toilet.

Although Lusty had done a thousand and one jobs in his life, only two had actually been a job, in the formal sense of the word.

The first proper job he had was a holiday rep on the sunshine island of Ibiza. The location, the booze, the music and the birds were great;

out of this world. What he couldn't understand were the mundane tasks in-between the partying like taking overweight Brits to the airport or sorting out issues with people's hotel rooms and shit like that. They did not tell him about all that poxy messing around during the training sessions.

He lasted in the role for a total of three months, but stayed in Ibiza for two years, mainly living in a commune which travelled around with the famous flea market. He met a boy from Stoke, who played bongos, and they made a living from busking and selling small quantities of the best Moroccan hash. He survived on nuts, sunshine and the kindness of middle-class rich girls, who instantly fell in love with his dark handsome features and his firm tanned body.

But even paradise can get boring and after waking up one morning underneath a palm tree, he decided that it was time to go back home and see what his mates were up to in the land of rain.

The second attempt at settling down into a normal job life came during his second marriage to a half-gypsy contortionist called Cathy.

Alex got him a job on the assembly line of a massive television-making organisation he had named 'Phoney Electronics'. From the start it was a disaster waiting to happen. The only thing Lusty had ever assembled was a coconut bong before a Christmas dance when he was fifteen years old. So the thought of wearing a dreadful white boiler suit, calling everyone 'Sir' and sitting like a robot on a production line, switching 36" TV's on and off, proved too much for a free spirit like Lusty.

On his second day, and after his tenth unofficial fag break, the tension between Lusty and his supervisor, who happened to look like Karl Malden from the Streets of San Francisco, finally snapped.

After a public dressing down in front of the other associates on the line, he quit.

During the short time he had worked there he couldn't help but see the funny side of how big organisations treated most of their employees like brainless robots. Then they thought that giving them names and calling them Associates or Cast Members would somehow change that fact and make everything rosy. He found it even funnier to think that the people who make up these 'groundbreaking' names were not and would never be Associates or Cast Members.

Lusty told Mr Malden exactly where to stick his television sets, and it was not up his rather large nose. He then proceeded to strip out of the shackles of the white prison uniform and march through the cheering assembly lines and into the locker room.

Girls fainted and the older women physically shook at the site of this Greek god in his boxers, rebelling against the giants of the Electronic world. The toilet cleaner, on the afternoon shift, thought a giant 'slug-rollerblade' convention had taken place in the women's toilets on that day. She wore out two new mop-heads trying to get the sticky substance off the tiled floor.

That was thankfully the end of Lusty's clocking in and out days.

He got on very nicely without the need for conformity. His most recent scam was to raid the nightly bins of the local Health and Beauty parlours. He dug out all the previous day's bikini waxes on muslin wax strips, and sold them on the Internet for a healthy profit, to pubic hair perverts.

The car carrying Kinsey and Alex pulled up to the shops in the Gurnos housing estate.

Kinsey took his plastic gun off the steering wheel and put it into the glove compartment. This was not the place to mess around with firearms, even if it was a fake one. This was a hard place.

Only last week, during a family feud over pigeons and fishing weights, Denny Ridley shot and killed his older brother, Johnny with a sawn-off shotgun. Lisa Bari and her action team were quickly on the scene to get the rundown. What they didn't expect was the hostile reception that was awaiting them. The TV crew's equipment was stolen, their van burnt out and Lisa was mugged and stripped of all her clothes, including her bra and expensive M&S panties.

This place was a no-go area. Outsiders were not welcome. This was a sprawling concrete wasteland of hopelessness. It had its own sinister heartbeat, its own language, its own diseases and its own rules. It prided itself on looking after its own kind, except on a Friday night when a western style free-for-all occurred outside Jim's chippy. In the morning, soiled condoms, cheap gold chains and broken teeth littered the bloodstained kerb side.

It was 10.30 am on a Friday morning and the square, which contained a couple of run down shops, a betting office and strangely, an un-vandalised telephone box, was full of zombies walking aimlessly around in search of life and their latest fix.

'Don't these people work?' Alex enquired, but made sure that his voice could not be heard outside the protection of the bodywork of the car.

'You must be joking! The only person that works around here is Sam the Bookie, and he's only on a three-day week,' Kinsey replied rather seriously.

Alex looked up and spotted Maxy the Tramp 'Isn't that you Kins without your speed fix?' he joked.

Maxy the tramp was staggering around the corner carrying a three-litre bottle of cheap, strong cider. It was his first little gift of the day, compliments of the people who issued him with his weekly giro.

Maxy was the unfortunate estate drunk who also doubled up as the town's homeless tramp throughout the week. Everyone in the town felt sorry for him, especially when they passed his forlorn figure sleeping in a shop doorway on a Saturday afternoon. Yet no one was willing to hold out a friendly hand to help him climb back on the rails. Everyone felt it better to help from afar.

'What a mess!' grunted Alex glumly.

Maxy used to be in Kinsey's class at school and was a real bright kid. He was especially good at drawing horses and shit like that. Then one day his father ran off with a younger woman, his mother died suddenly and his RE teacher took an interest in his loneliness, and it was all down hill from there. It was then he stumbled into a giant vat of memory-loss cider and piss stained clothes.

'Hi Maxy, go and have something to eat.' Alex threw the down-and-out a £2 coin.

There was silence while Maxy scrambled on the floor for it. They all knew that food was way down on Maxy's list of things to do. He held the coin and his cider tightly, smiled back in their direction with mud coloured teeth and headed off towards a condemned block of flats.

The occupants of the car suddenly felt that they were being watched. Then from across the street the Pozzoni brothers slowly came strutting up to the window.

The Pozzoni boys were two local gangsters, still only fourteen and fifteen years old, but quite infamous for spreading terror around the estate. Rumours of drug trafficking and an estate-wide protection racket were just two of the nicer things linked to these two small, big-time villains. They had convictions as long as their arms and police surveillance helicopters tracked and recorded their every movement.

Dorian Pozzoni, the younger of the two, was dressed in an over-sized fur coat and sunglasses. He strolled up to the car and tapped on the window with a hockey stick.

'What do you want?' Kinsey snapped, unwinding the glass.

'It will cost you a fiver to park here, mate!' Dorian spoke with a slight lisp. His eyes were cold and calculating, mainly from years of physical abuse and mental torture from a drunken father and an uncle with a heroin addiction.

'Firstly I am not your mate, mate! ... And secondly unlike your father, whoever the fuck that is, I pay road tax, so fuck off and go and pick some conkers.' Adrenaline rushed through Kinsey's veins.

'Do you know who we are?' said Dorian, accompanied by a James Cagney curl of the lip.

'Yes…some fucker who should be in kindergarten. Now just piss off before I phone for the child catcher off Chitty Chitty Bang Bang.'

Wayne Pozzoni, the silent but nastier one put down the BBC boom mike he had been holding and started to undo his fur-lined parker. Wayne was the brains and also the muscle behind this two-boy crime wave organisation. He had a reputation for finishing off the many scraps that his younger brother started. He feared no one. He was a home-grown psychopath with a baby face in a grown up body.

Lusty finished the last drop of tea, picked up his travel bag, checked the room and closed the door. He jumped down the steps from his third floor flat above the shops. He passed the ghetto graffiti which informed the underworld of the local gossip.

'Terry Shelley is a police informing pig and will be hung, drawn and quartered.'

'Jason shagged Lisa – twice'

'£5 for a blow-job plus swallow - phone Greg on 354767'

'Kerry has a small dick – Lisa and her mother and her gran.'

'Jason is a thieving bastard who'll lose both his hands.

He emerged from this dark corridor of urban information into the morning air and the ugly looking stand off between his best mates and the evil afterbirth of the lollipop gang.

'Hi boys,' Lusty chirped up. He looked at the two mini-gangsters. 'These are my best mates….give them a break.'

'Yeah, we'll give them a break, starting with their fucking fingers,' Wayne mocked.

'Yeah and then their heads,' Dorian added.

Lusty knew that this was deadly serious because Wayne rarely spoke unless it was to demand money from his victims.

The whole square stopped to observe the situation, except for Maxy who continued to rifle through a bin for his dinner. He picked out a bag of three-day-old chips and a half eaten pie and started to eat them.

The noise of the overhead helicopter broke the silence and the eye contact.

'OK Lusty, but you owe us big time. You hear…Big time,' Dorian said with a menace far beyond his youthful years, as he spied the metal bird overhead.

The two criminals put their coats back on, turned up the collars and marched into the nearby cake shop. They went straight to the front of the queue. Wayne, whose veins in his neck were sticking out, slammed his fist down. He either didn't notice or didn't really care about the freshly made sponge cake on the counter. Cream and jam shot all over the customers and staff.

'Give us two diet cokes with two of them bendy straws,' Wayne screamed at the terrified assistant.

Alex and the rest jumped back into the car and drove off.

'Thanks boys. Great start to the day,' Lusty said, already remembering the words 'Big Time,' that he knew would come back to haunt him in the shape of two permanent nut cases seeking revenge.

'They're only little kids,' protested Alex.

'Nasty little kids with an arsenal of weapons. You don't want to mess with them.'

'I can't understand it. Why do you live around here anyway, Lust?' asked Alex.

'The reason I live around here is the fucking CSA are crippling me, it's all I can afford…but I have a plan… a master plan,' he replied while watching a gang of eight year olds using a brand new car as a home-made trampoline.

'It's your fault anyway for being so bloody late,' Kinsey retorted, turning the tables back on Lusty. 'If you had been on time we wouldn't have seen the little lords of the ringworm.' He chuckled at his own humour.

'I had to go back to find the tour tape,' Lusty explained.

'Great…you can't go on tour without the fucking tour tape,' Alex piped up. 'It would be against the God of all tours.'

Kinsey pulled the car out of the estate and put the gun back on the steering wheel. The final couple of bars of Rockaway Beach transported them out of the Twilight zone that they called home.

****

The tour bus bound for Heathrow airport was already revving impatiently outside the rugby club when Kinsey's car pulled up.

Their proposed means of transport looked like it just returned from rescuing hard-line Palestinians from a minefield in the Gazza strip. It was decorated dark green, had no air conditioning and its toilet facilities consisted of a plastic bucket surrounded by a shower curtain and a can of air fresher. One of the side windows near the front was missing, probably pierced by a sniper bullet. A Golden Wonder crisp packet box with duct tape ensured that the wind, flies and smell from the tip were kept firmly outside.

'Watch where you step,' said the green-toothed bus driver, 'There's a little bit of rust here and there… nothing to worry about.'

Alex and Jac carefully threaded their way towards the middle of the coach. Wigsy followed, cracking open another can of Stella.

Keith and Peter were perched in the front two seats. Keith asked everyone who got on the same question. 'Have you got your passport, boys? Have a check, just in case. It would be a shame to be left on the runway. OK?'

He repeated it like a warped record to all the new faces that climbed onto the steps.

After questioning another four boys, Peter pulled Keith to one side and said, 'Look Keith, stop asking everyone about their passports. We have been organising this tour for the past two years, so if they are stupid enough to have forgotten it now they don't deserve to go.'

Deep down Peter hoped some of these idiots did actually leave their passports behind. He knew they called him terrible names behind his back. They didn't appreciate anything he did for 'his' club.

'But Pete, you know what these boys are like…forget their own heads if they weren't screwed on.'

'They are old enough to sort their own fuckin' lives out,' he answered back sharply. 'Now shut the fuck up.'

Without Keith noticing, Peter felt inside his jacket just to make sure his passport was there. He smirked when he touched the cover. At that moment, if he'd had a thin moustache he would surely have rolled the edges of it and laughed while, at the same time encircling himself within a big, black cloak. He didn't have either, so he went back to reading his book, 'The Slithering Aliens Are Coming to Porth.'

Kinsey and the gang headed for the seats with the card table. Two youth boys were occupying it.

'This table is reserved, boys.' Kinsey informed them.

'For whom?' they questioned bravely.

'Us...the old folks. There's a pecking order on this bus, so fuck off up the back with the rest of the young mongoloids. Come back in five years when your balls have dropped.' They didn't argue, they got up and headed for the back seats, muttering to each other. Dave, who was seated behind, turned and asked Jac if he had he heard about Matthew and his wife.

Now, Matthew's wife was well known for throwing a tantrum fit at the last minute and trying everything in her power to prevent her husband from going on every trip. Last year she tried to slit her wrists with a Bic safety razor and the year before he mysteriously came down with food poisoning which kept him in bed for two weeks.

Apparently she had a dream that he met a black girl and never came back. She wouldn't listen to reason and through spite she cut up all of Matt's clothes and threw them away. He phoned Dave to explain he was really sorry but he wouldn't be coming yet again, but added it was time that he either had her committed or seriously killed.

What no one could understand was she told everyone how much she hated his guts and that he was the worst husband in the world and she wished she could leave him tomorrow.

'Least she didn't poison him again,' Alex snorted.

Finally, the bus stuttered, coughed and slowly pulled off to a massive cheer from all the boys. Jac looked down the long, unimpressive valley and shouted out, 'Goodbye smelly grey town….I hope I never see you aga….' He was stopped in full cry, as the bus came to a sudden halt. It sent everyone shooting forward. The air reverberated with the sounds of moaning and shouting.

'Ay…driver, you fucking green toothed idiot!' screamed Wigsy, who had tipped half of his can of Stella over the table. There was a tear in his eye as he bent down and tried to lick up the escaping liquid, only to stop, repulsed at the taste of 25 years worth of filth.

The coach door opened slowly and up the bus steps appeared Matthew with only his pyjamas and a pair of pit boots on. There was another massive cheer.

'Quick, I told her I was putting out the wheelie bin, so hurry up and let's fly,' Matt proudly announced.

With a face full of white teeth, he grinned and headed for the back of the bus. His foot crashed through the rusty floor and he was saved from a quick tarmac water slide exit by the string of his pyjamas and the hand of Big Ken hoisting him back to the insanity of the inside of the coach.

'I wonder if he has his passport.' Keith said to Peter.

'Fuck off Keith!!!!!' and he hit him with his book.

Twenty minutes into the journey, Alex wandered up to the front of the bus and started talking to Nick the driver.

First thing the boy noticed were his white socks, green teeth and egg stained tie. On the dashboard was a photograph of the Queen Mother and a comb covered in loose hair.

'Hello Drive, everything going well?'

'Yes, had a bit of trouble with the engine, but I fixed it. I'm a fully trained mechanic, see. Plus I used to be a…'

Alex stopped him in full flow and looking at his watch. 'Hey mate we'll have to move it a bit to catch the plane. You'll be pulling up on the runway to meet it at this rate.'

'No problem, sonny. It wouldn't be the first. I've done it before many times.' Nick boasted.

Alex wasn't sure if he meant getting the bus there on time or driving it up on the runway. But whatever he meant Alex knew that he was in the company of a master liar. Perhaps he misunderstood the driver's name. Maybe it was really 'Prick' not Nick.

He changed the conversation by asking Nick the Prick, 'Who's that old hag?' pointing to the photo of the Queen mum.

'That's the Right Honourable Queen Mother. I am her favourite fan. We had tea together last week. I am booked to drive her and her mates to Brighton next Sunday.' The porkies were escaping thick and fast from his mouth.

Alex needed to get out before the floodgates opened and swallowed him up. 'Any good sounds, Drive?' he asked checking the box of old cassettes.

'Yes, I've got The Eagles Greatest Hits,' he said with pride, 'and a great Doctor Hook album.'

Alex looked disgusted and dropped the tapes into the bin.

'Sorry Drive, we can't go all the way to London listening to that crap.' He turned to face the boys and shouted, 'Lusty, bring down the tour tape.'

There was a cheer from the boys and a definite moan from the committee.

'Not that puke rock stuff,' Peter mentioned to Keith.

Lusty went into his bag and took out the famous tour tape. The transportation of the cassette resembled a scene from 'Raiders of the Lost Ark', with gold light shining out of the surrounding case. The tape was uncovered and inserted into the tape machine.

'Let the tour begin,' Alex bellowed and walked back to his seat. There was a fifteen-second pause and then the opening bars to 'Police and Thieves' by The Clash blasted out of the buses inadequate sound system.

The gang of four just sat smiling at each other. They all turned and looked at Matt in his night-clothes and they smiled some more. Without saying a word, Lusty removed two of the biggest joints that had ever been made, from out of his jacket. He followed it by pulling a jumbo size pack of Ritz biscuits from his bag.

'For when the munchies kick in.' Lusty said in a deep Jamaican voice.

Jac lit up one of the joints, took a deep pull and muttered, 'This is the life.' He cracked open a can and started singing:-

'Police and thieves in the street.'

The rest of the bus joined in,

'Oh Yeah...Fighting the nation with their guns and ammunition.'

In the front of the bus, Big Ken sniffed the air. He noticed the strange smell coming from the middle rows. 'Wacky Backy?' He was just about to jump up when he thought to himself, 'Fuck it, we're on tour.'

He went back to looking at page three of the Sun, and swallowed another two 'quiet life' tranquilizers.

They arrived at Heathrow airport and they all piled into the checking-in queue. The Committee-men pulled rank and marched straight to the front of the line in imaginary jack-boots and Nazi SS uniforms, knocking over everything and everyone in their path.

'Ay....You fuckin' cheats,' shouted Wigsy. He was really pissed off with them, especially because their actions caused him to spill his can for the second time that day. He made a note to purchase one of those hats with the plastic bottles attached to the sides and the long plastic straw just to protect his precious liquid from any further catastrophe.

Big Ken and Peter strolled up to book in first.

'I would like a seat by the window please my love,' Big Ken asked the rather attractive young lady.

'I'll see what I can do, Sir.'

Big Ken winked at the girl and whispered to her, 'Don't sit me next to him,' pointing to Peter, who was bent down getting his passport out of his jacket.

The lady giggled and winked back at him. Big Ken smiled and wished he was ten years younger. He gave her his best 'Elvis' impression, and pulled his dandruff filled comb through his dandruff filled hair. *'It's great to be in charge!'* he told himself.

The two men gave their passports to the attendant. Big Ken's was checked and handed back. The lady checked Peter's passport, then looked in a confused fashion at the man before her. She did this several times. Peter shuffled awkwardly.

'He's a world famous drug smuggling alien, love,' Jac shouted out from the back of the impatient queue.

The woman called over her colleague, who also went through the same routine. Then a security guard was summoned over. His gun was already cocked. They showed the copper the photo. He grinned and indicated to leave it to him.

The airport security policeman tried extremely hard to hide his sheer delight at this situation. He'd been waiting for this opportunity to display his skills ever since he had passed his basic training. Now Rhian, the pretty passport control operator whom he had been bashing his love stump over for the last three months, would finally see what he was made of.

'This punk needs his oversized wings clipped down to size,' he said excitedly to himself as he pulled up his black leather gloves and eyeballed Peter. He knew exactly what to do. He had been practising the drill in his basement for a lifetime. He had even persuaded his

mother to buy him an uncooked chicken out of his allowance so that he could perfect the drill.

'Handcuffs…legs apart…slap on the gloves…apply the KY jelly, if they were lucky. This one, he had already decided, would be having the dry bobsleigh run. Bend them over….insert the two fingers and recover the drugs. Easy. Like fuckin' clockwork.'

During his training he'd gotten his mother to insert a small bag of talc into the fowl's anal passage to make it more realistic. His record for arresting the bird and retrieving the contraband was around thirty seconds on a good day. 'A world record surely', he had put in his letter to Norris McWhirter, he of the Guinness Book of Records Fame.

The only real setback he had experienced was the time it took him over one hour to find the shipment of pretend drugs from the new Asda free-range BBQ chicken. He finally found it by smashing the chicken to bits with a lump hammer. How could he have known that his mother had inserted the stuff in the wrong bloody end by mistake? That was not in the airport security police manual. He never asked her to help him again in his quest for perfection.

'Excuse me sir, can you collect up your belongings and follow me,' he demanded of the committee-man.

'But why officer, there must be some mistake,' Peter answered nervously.

'I was only joking about him smuggling drugs.' Jac said quietly. 'But he is a bastard alien though.'

The officer clicked his knuckles loudly. 'No mistake Sir. Please don't be awkward.'

'What's wrong officer?' Peter was nearly in tears.

The policeman showed Peter the passport. There, staring back at Peter where his photo should have been was a photo of Kathleen 'O' Neil…Peter's wife.

He looked confused and started to shake. The policeman grabbed tightly around his arm.

'Please Sir, don't make this any worse than it already is!' grinned the security guard, who was even contemplating unleashing the 'terrorist tool' that he had designed and made out of an old broom stick, some masking tape and the top of a sardine tin.

'It's a mistake. I must get on that flight,' shrieked Peter, as his whole body began to spasm.

'Sorry Sir, unless you can prove to me that you have had a sex change recently, Sir, or should I say Kathleen, after checking the name. You will not be going on the flight.' *'That was it,'* the officer noted to himself, *'this punk's having the full works'*. He would be dishing out the legal and illegal bits they had taught him at the training camp.

Chinese whispers had already started through the line of waiting people. A huge cheer went up from the boys when they realised what was going on. Even Keith smiled a little 'told you to check your passport, didn't I, you bastard' sort of smile. Peter looked around for someone to say something in his defence, but no one did.

Suddenly, Big Ken came running up behind Peter and the police officer, who was now marching the prisoner away through the crowded terminal building.

'Hey, hang on a minute,' said Big Ken trying to catch his breath.

'Thank God, Ken….tell them…tell them.' Desperation was oozing from Peter's every word.

'Peter, where's the Kitty Money?'

Peter felt the floor of his world open up. His shoulders dipped, he handed over the cash to Big Ken from his money belt, and fell headfirst into the volcanic pit of utter despair.

Big Ken started to count out the notes and headed for the duty free shop. He shouted back at Peter, 'You'd better shave that beard off, Kathy, before you get in trouble.'

'You're only as good as your last game,' Alex said to Kinsey on witnessing Peter's sudden fall from grace. 'You're only as good as your last game,' he repeated. The whole crowd nodded in agreement.

Peter chased after him and threw himself at Big Ken and held onto his leg. He pleaded, he cried, he even screamed out loud.

'I need to get on that plane.'

'Get off you nutter,' Big Ken warned him. He kicked out at Peter, who seemed to be starting to metamorphose into a woman.

Finally, the copper dragged Peter off Big Ken's leg by his curlers and tights. He bungled him into a room and slammed the door closed. The sign on the door said:-

"Do not disturb… (Even if you can not stand the screaming)"

In brackets underneath were the chilling words

"We are watching you!!!"

****

They all boarded the 727 and as each prepared in their own little way for take-off, an announcement from over the tannoy system caught their attention.

'Ladies and Gentlemen, this is your captain speaking. My name is Glen Miller and your co-pilot for today's flight will be Mr Buddy Holly.'

Everyone looked at each other in frightened amazement. One elderly couple from Chepstow stood up and tried to get off.

The air stewardess violently snatched the intercom off Jac and told him in no uncertain terms to return to his seat straight away and stop being so childish. She gave him another cold stare as she walked past him leading the elderly couple in the direction of the cockpit. They had demanded to see that the pilots were actually real people and not two dead 1950's big band and rock 'n' roll stars.

During the flight Justin looked out of the window at the big fluffy clouds and turned to Small Jeff and said, 'This is the only way to fly!'

Small Jeff thought about the statement for a few minutes and then harped back. 'Of course it's the only way to fly. How else could we do it, on the wings of a fucking giant butterfly? Now, shut up and give us one of those strawberry sherbet lemons you are hiding in your pocket.'

Another air stewardess came over to Lusty. The good-looking girl whispered something in his ear and led him away in to the first class section of the plane. They strolled passed Wigsy who was sitting alone cracking open another cold can of Stella. He thought he smelled the odour of expectant sex wafting past him as the couple walked past.

Chapter 5

'Johnny's fingers caught in the pie'

Alex awoke with a startled jump. He had dreamt the tour was already over and he'd somehow slept through it all. Worse still, he was being asked by Witchy-Pooh, the receptionist, to settle Wigsy's bar bill which ran into millions of pounds.

His near hysteria turned to a pleasant grin when he looked across and saw Kinsey flat out in the next bed. His mate was in the nude and had a pair of flashing devil's horns on his head. The batteries must have been running out because only one of the horns was still glowing.

Relieved, Alex made his way out of the bed, painfully. He rolled his furry caterpillar tongue back inside its rightful cave and headed for the balcony. The sunlight hurt his eyes.

After coming to terms with the shock of the morning light, he refocused his eyeballs. He had to admit this was one hell of a good hotel. The swimming pool below had been designed in the shape of a big double bass with palm trees and blue sun loungers making up the frets. A tennis court, mini golf area, an outside bar and a small sports complex helped to decorate the surrounding scenery.

He wished he had put 'use the gym everyday' on his tour 'to-do' list. He had so far failed to do the 'be spontaneous' item, but this was only the second day and there would be lots of opportunities to do something off the cuff.

The only real blot on this copybook paradise landscape was the building work being carried out to the partial erected shell of a proposed 3-star apartment block opposite. Two giant mechano set cranes slowly moved empty pallets to a space where nothing ever seemed to get done and no one seemed to care. There never seemed to be any workers actually working on its construction.

Alex scanned the poolside to see if he recognised any familiar faces at this ungodly hour. Wigsy was already there, sitting on his very own stool by the bar. The waiter had just given him a pint of lager with a lit sparkler spitting flashes towards his face. Alex laughed to himself as he saw a confused Wigsy throwing the sparkler, unceremoniously over his shoulder, to the obvious disappointment of the waiter. He sank the drink in one long swig and slammed the mug back on the bar demanding a refill immediately, but without all the bells and sparklers. Wigsy was an uncomplicated creature.

Everyone else enjoying the 10.30am sunshine was unfamiliar to him.

'The vampires must all be locked away safely in their coffins,' he thought to himself.

On further inspection, it dawned on him that all the people playing volley ball and shouting at each other as if they were separated by different continents were actually German.

'Trust the noisy krauts to be the first to everything.'

He recalled the war story his Grandfather used to tell him. It was during the Second World War. All the British fighter pilots had woken up early for the dawn raid over Berlin only to find on arriving at the runway, the Luftwaffe had gotten there first and placed all of their towels on top of the planes. The raid was cancelled. They had to wait for the evening when the sun went down and the Germans had retired to the bar to sample spicy sausages and strong lager before they proceeded to blow the shit out of them.

His Granddad had a million stories like that.

His reminiscing was interrupted when a waiter came sprinting out of the breakfast room with Big Ken in hot pursuit. The waiter dropped the tray he had been carrying by the pool side. Without hesitation, he dove into the water and swam to the other side like Mark Spitz with four pairs of arms and pumped up on performance enhancing drugs. He leaped out and scrambled over the fifteen-foot hotel boundary fence without once looking back. Big Ken had given up the chase at the edge of the pool. He threw what appeared to be a red mouse in the direction of the fleeing waiter and stormed back into the restaurant.

'What was all that about?' Kinsey joined Alex on the balcony, his devil's horns now not flashing at all.

'Beats me,' Alex answered, while scratching his nuts.

Moment's later, Jac burst into their room. He was unable to contain the laughter which was in danger of engulfing him.

'You won't believe it…fuck me that was the funniest thing that I've ever seen.' Tears the size of golf balls rolled down his face.

After a few minutes, he gathered his senses and started to tell the boys what had happened in the breakfast room.

He explained how the previous night he had found an unused tampon in the toilet of a night-club they had gone to. That morning he had gone down to the breakfast bar to get a cold drink. All the committee-men were there dressed like Hitler's youth in a 'coming out' rally

Anyway, he remembered the contraption in his pocket and decided to have a bit of a craic. So he unwrapped it and dipped it in tomato sauce and dropped it in one of the mugs of tea that the waiter was taking to the table.

After about five minutes and several gulps of tea later, Keith noticed this string hanging out of Big Ken's mug and informed him that they must have left the tea-bag in there. So Big Ken nonchalantly picked the fully formed tampon covered in red sauce and tea out of his mug.

'Everyone looked at the thing hanging there dripping fake blood in clots back into the cup. No one in the room knew if they should, laugh, cry, shiver or fucking puke. The scene lasted a lifetime,' Jac rushed his sentence.

He continued, 'And then the poor fucking waiter walked in, all smiles and teeth, carrying a tray full of food.'

The other boys' sides were hurting, they were laughing so much.

'Then before the innocent waiter could ask if everything was OK, he saw the big man holding the thing and immediately sensed that somehow he was going to get blamed for it. All hell broke loose and the chase was on. It was like a scene from the Hare and the Hounds. It was fucking magic… wish I had my camera.'

The three boys were helpless, rolling around on the bed. Alex laughed so hard, he thought he was going to pee himself.

'I think he's still down there now, trying to smash his way into the kitchen,' Jac informed his mates. They pictured an army of waiters blocking the door.

****

Later on that day, Alex, Jac, and Kinsey walked through the lobby in the hotel and out into the bright afternoon sunlight.

'This is a great place, Alex. He played some great sounds in that disco last night,' Jac said, taking a large swig of ice-cold water.

'Talking about great things, where's Lusty?' Alex replied.

'Where do you think? He was last seen walking hand in hand with that blonde. You remember that Irish piece.'

'She was gorgeous…bit of a fruit cake, though,' said Alex, remembering how she had told him she thought she could fly.

The two talkative companions broke their leisurely stride to enquire why their Kinsey was so quiet. He appeared to be in a semiconscious state.

Kinsey didn't answer at first. He stopped and sat down on the curb. After a while he said, 'Look if you must know…I'm fucked….I can't handle all this drink. I must be getting old.'

'Drink…what about those two 'E's' you dropped? You didn't stop dancing all night,' Jac quipped, happy to rub some salt into his mate's fragile wounds. 'You were like a headless fucking John Travolta.'

'Fuck off. Anyway, I'm having breakfast then I'm going back to bed all day,' he grunted glumly.

'Billy, we have only been here for a day, you twat,' Jac laughed.

'I don't care. I'm going to bed after some food.'

They stopped to speak to Matt in the crowded street. He was wearing a baseball cap and had cut his striped brown and white pyjamas down into a neat matching long shorts and waistcoat combination.

The unusual summer swimwear was pulling some approving sideways glances from across the street. In the pretentious Café Nouvelle, the 'in' crowd abandoned their low fat lattes and were staring in pure admiration at this no nonsense fashion statement.

There were many debates raging concerning the origins of this fine cut of cloth. Many thought it was a Versace original; others a classic Louis Vitton. Some of the more knowledgeable among the fashion jet-set recognised it as an item from the daring new Julian Macdonald's Upstart of Paris collection.

They spent the rest of the day struggling to label the exciting new design, but they all agreed that 'Brown and White Striped PJ's would be the new black at this year's Milan cat walk.

Back across the street Jac told Matt that he had seen his wife and his out-laws in reception. Matt immediately turned a shade of white, pulled his baseball cap over his face, and ran the opposite way.

'You're a bad bastard, Jac,' Alex muttered.

'I know.'

The boys carried on with their quest for something good to eat.

At the far end of the street, they bumped into Lusty. He was looking fresh and remarkably sun-tanned for someone who had only been there for a day. The trouble with Lusty was he always looked fresh and he only had to read the Sun newspaper to get a tan.

He was drinking a pint of milk and wearing the same clothes as the previous night.

'Where're you off to boys?'

'Brekkie. Down by the beach in that quiet place,' Jac replied.

'Great, give me five minutes and I'll follow you down. I need to take a shower,' said the dirty all-night stop-out.

'Don't forget to dip it in Dettol, just in case it drops off.' Kinsey added, mockingly.

'Not jealous are you?' Lusty threw the milk carton into the bin.

'Of course we're jealous…you jammy, ugly looking twat.' Kinsey muttered, trying not to scowl.

They parted company and Lusty strolled back to the hotel and the boys carried on down the street full of sunburned tourists in search of grub and some shelter from the blistering sun.

They stopped and watched a busker singing a Mott the Hoople number to a small crowd.

'Won't you roll away the stone…la…la.la.la.' the strange looking musician sang. Jac threw some money into his hat and they moved on.

The next street over, Justin was shamelessly inspecting all the parked cars shoehorned in place on the dusty road. Most of vehicles were covered in dirt and had the compulsory European dents and bruises all over their bodywork.

As he inspected them in detail he wished he had brought his book of parking fine tickets with him on the trip, but he knew he couldn't chance anyone finding them and exposing his strange little quirk. Justin had an unusual fascination with cars. But it wasn't in the normal 'boy racer speeding off at 120mph' sort of car fixation. No, this was much more bizarre. Justin was a closet Traffic Warden. He was obsessed with them. He had joined a club and everything; even had a pretend uniform.

It had all started when he was young and he saw a traffic warden, professionally issue a parking ticket to his Uncle on a Saturday afternoon in the centre of town. He knew from that moment what his life's ambition would be. The power and respect these people must command is immense, he often told himself.

His obsession started on the following Sunday, when he painted double yellow lines on the road of his Scalextric track. He spent hours booking his toy cars and issuing tickets made out of post-it notes. He even sent car number five to prison for three months for non-payment of fines.

He would lie in bed, fantasising about trapping a 911 Porsche or even better, Clint's stepfather's Bedford van. He often threatened to actually stick tickets on the van to get his own back on the boy who had made his life such a misery in school. But he would always chicken-out when his mind flashed back to the tree and Charlene's Devil tattoo winking at him when she bent over.

He inspected the cars in the street to see if they were parked on double yellow lines or had an out-of-date tax disc. He was completely lost in his own twisted imagination and daydreaming of one day owning his own speed camera detector van. He didn't realise he was being watched. Alex, Kinsey and Jac followed the sad figure walking into the road pretending to take photographs of thin air.

'Justin…watch the cars!' Jac shouted out.

Justin didn't know which way to look. He dropped his imaginary camera, put his head down and sprinted back to where he started. He panicked and tripped, sprawled out in the middle of the road. He tried to crawl away from the on-coming danger, his fingers reaching for the safety of the pavement. He screamed and covered his head. When he looked up the road was empty.

'You silly bleeders. I could have had a heart attack,' Justin, hand on chest, yelled at the boys. He slowly got back onto his feet.

'You shouldn't be so fat, should you,' Kinsey wise cracked. 'And what were you doing sizing all the cars up...you fuckin' nutter.'

'Nearly killed him,' Jac said, giving Justin the one-finger salute just to add insult to injury.

'Did you know there's sixty quid in the kitty for the first person that kills or maims him?'

They all knew that sixty big ones would definitely come in handy, by the end of this trip.

They arrived at the small seaside café on the harbour.

'Welcome boys,' the café owner announced in a very poor English accent. He stood proudly welcoming his new guests into the café that he built up from sand, mortar and a drop or two of his own blood.

'Hello mate, three brekkies please?' Jac asked the proud proprietor. He peeled off his tee shirt and chucked it at Kinsey. Kinsey picked it off his head and threw it on the floor and stamped it into the ground. 'You could have had my fucking eye out...you idiot.'

'What...with a fucking dangerously sharp cotton Fred Perry?' Jac replied.

'It's got buttons.'

'You've got fuckin' buttons.'

The Café owner looked annoyed at the immature shirt throwing antics. He asked slowly, 'Bre-a-keys...what's Bre-a-keys?'

'Breakfast...you know...eggs, sausage, black pudding,' Jac spoke slowly to compensate for his lack of fluency in foreign tongues.

Alex chuckled. 'They don't have fucking black pudding in Portugal.'

'Well they have brown sauce.'

Jac shrugged his shoulders. 'Ok...not black pudding. Any beans?'

'Ah....The B-E-A-N-S.' the café owner muttered in a much slower and more deliberate accent.

'Yes...three lots of the B-E-A-N-S and three mugs of T-E-A!' replied a smart arsed Alex, mocking the over-emphasised use of words adopted by the busy vendor.

The owner walked off into the bar with a big smile attached to his greasy face. He passed Wigsy who was sitting by the bar; handkerchief balancing on his head.

'All right Wigsy?' Alex yelled across the café. 'Having any brekkie?'

Wigsy nodded his head and proudly held up a pint of lager.

'Between Wigsy and Lusty, we must have the world's best drinker and the world's best shagger,' said Kinsey, accidentally informing a passing family of the fine traits of his dysfunctional friends. The fat family hurried passed, looking like they had been grilled, boiled and then fried in a frying pan with some mushrooms and tomatoes. The lobster people ignored the world shattering news and rushed to the beach, not to miss the cancer rays that would be sizzling up their pale skin all afternoon.

The boys looked up to see a plane flying alone up in the vast motorway of the blue sky. They imagined it was taking a cargo of lost souls back to the asylum. They weren't far from wrong, it was taking a plane full of dolly-birds from Hartlepool on a hen weekend to Benidorm. It had just taken off when it had to be diverted to Portugal after the pilot refused to fly to Spain until the pilot had his trousers and Bart Simpson pants handed back.

Lusty joined his mates. He was dressed in a vest, shorts and shades. The owner brought out three big mugs of tea.

'Ah...one more B-E-A-N-S?' The café owner asked the new arrival.

Lusty looked bewildered so Alex jumped in, 'Yeah...one more B-E-A-N-S,' he told the delighted owner. 'Don't ask Lust.'

The gang sat back looking out to sea and occasionally staring at the young girls in bikinis that continued to waltz by. The sunlight bounced off the water like a million flash bulbs illuminating the opening ceremony of the Olympic Games. Fishing boats, exhausted from a hard night of trying to pull fish, lay resting on the white sandy beach. The sea seemed to be painted by a nursery child, who had no concept on how to blend colours together; a rainbow of pure transparent green with a mix of deep blue around the edges. It was beautiful, not the average British muddy grey coastline that they were used to. The only thing blue in the water around Barry Island was the freezing bodies of holiday makers enjoying the break.

Alex broke the silence by asking Lusty the one question they all wanted to ask the Welsh stud muffin. 'What was she like then, Lust? Marks out of ten.'

'She was completely insane…kept talking about how she would like to be a butterfly or something…good in bed, mind.' He knew how to drip-feed his mates with just enough information.

'Anything ummmm…kinky?' Jac snorted.

All the boys leaned in around Lusty to hopefully hear about all of the sordid details.

At that moment, the owner brought out a big plate of sausages only. He smiled a big smile and walked off. The boys were too hungry to ask. They proceeded to attack the lifeless bangers with great gusto and precision.

Jac tapped his fingers on the table top to indicate that they were still waiting for Lusty to finish off his story.

'Well,' he paused, 'the only real kinky bit was she wanted me to roll her like a bowling ball.' Lusty held up two fingers and his thumb and rotated them like the moon revolving around the sun. The others also held up three fingers, looking at them inquisitively as they tried to work out what he actually meant. Lusty knew this would confuse them and kept a serious face locked on his features as he slowly moved his digits one way then the other.

Alex was again the first to speak. 'So you inserted this finger in that bit and those two in the other one.' He was copying Lusty's hand motion.

'Yeah,' interrupted Lusty. He was dying to laugh. His mates were second to none when it came to friendship, but very amateurish in the ways of hard loose sex.

'What the fucking hell are you talking about?' Kinsey couldn't stick this game anymore.

Alex whispered in his ear. Kinsey screwed up his face; he looked at his sausage and gently placed it back onto the plate.

'Why Lust?' Jac asked curiously.

'Didn't ask her, I just went along for the ride,' replied an unfazed Lusty, who picked up the discarded sausage and wolfed it down.

'I had a girl like that once,' Alex surprisingly offered an unknown bit of information.

They all turned to listen to the next contestant in the mastermind sex-chair. Alex Davis: answering questions on the history of Native American Indians and spectacular knee wobblers behind the Station Hotel on a wet Thursday night.

Before Magnus could start the questioning, Justin walked passed the café. He stopped and said, 'Very funny Jac. I don't think so,' his comments concerned the earlier traffic incident. 'Just don't forget there's training at three o clock today and the big banquet is at seven 'o'clock. Big Ken wants everyone to be there, on time, in full club uniforms.'

'Trouble with my hamstrings,' Jac said, a pretend look of pain on his face.

'Dicky stomach,' Alex repeated, rubbing his stomach.

Kinsey didn't even bother to look in Justin's direction. Lusty nudged Alex and muttered, 'I have something wrong with these three fingers Justin.' Lusty held up his three human bowling ball fingers.

A look of panic manifested on Justin's face. He realised how important Lusty was to the team and that if he didn't play, Big Ken would be unbearable and end up taking it out on one of them.

He asked quickly, 'What's wrong with your fingers Steve?'

'Show him Lust!' Jac smirked wickedly.

Lusty leant across and held them up into Justin's face.

'Can't see anything wrong?' he said after a thorough inspection.

'Smell them...something's definitely not right with them,' Jac told him.

They were dying to laugh. Justin leant over and took a big sniff of Lusty's crevice intruders. A quizzical look came over his face and he said, 'They do smell funny. You better go see Rob about them....perhaps he's got something you can rub on them. They smell a bit like marzipan.'

Kinsey laughed so hard he spat tea all over the pavement. Justin walked off not realising he had been set up and headed for a quiet spot on the beach, to catch up on this month's edition of 'Clamping For Beginners' magazine, which he had hidden in his shorts.

'As I was saying,' Alex continued, 'I had a girl once, who always wanted me to masturbate over her feet.'

'Her feet?' Kinsey said, his voice balancing on the edge of sanity.

'Yeah. Wherever we were, I had to wank over her bare feet; in bed, in the car, even in the cinema once.' Alex relaxed back into his chair.

'What film was showing?' asked Lusty casually.

'What the fuck is that to do with it?" snapped Kinsey.

'Perhaps it was a horny flick,' Lusty replied.

'A horny flick...' Kinsey became annoyed the direction of the conversation.

The rest of the team knew that Kinsey had fallen for the bait. Alex winked at Lusty before adding, 'I think it was 'An Officer and a Gentleman.'

'What happened?' said Kinsey, regaining his voice.

'It's about a man who tries to join the elite Navy officer's squad…'

'Not in the fucking film!' Kinsey screamed at the top of his voice. 'I've seen the fucking thing, forty fucking times. It's fucking Julie's favourite fucking film of all fucking time. What happened when you shot over her fucking feet?'

'I didn't see Richard Gere doing that to Debra Winger?' Lusty played along. 'That must have been in the sequel, 'An Officer and a Foot Pervert.'

'Fuck off Lust.' Kinsey was mad. 'What happened when you wanked over her feet?'

'I think her shoes got pregnant,' Alex replied laughing out aloud.

'Fuck off you…and fuck off the rest of you cunts.' Kinsey looked away in disgust. He found himself staring at an abandoned flip-flop by the side of a rubbish bin.

'Straight up Kinsey, cross my heart and I hope he dies,' Alex smugly replied and pointed across the street at Justin.

All eyes move to Jac who was next in line for some sexual interrogation.

'Any kinky little tricks, Jac,' Lusty aimed the question straight and to the point. It was about time someone else was in the spotlight.

Jac thought for a minute, bit his lower lip and then as if hit by a bolt of lightening, announced, 'YEAH…you know Sophia…you know she used to be married to Tommy Powell. You know he went to prison for armed robbery.'

'Yeah,' they all roared together.

'She took me home one Christmas. Remember she had that big Labrador called Fudgey.'

'For fuck sake Jac, get to the point.' It was Kinsey who piped up.

'I'm getting there. Anyway, one thing led to another, and I'm on top really going for it. She's below moaning like there's no tomorrow. Then all of a sudden, I felt this cold sensation trickling down the cheeks of my arse. I thought it was an ice cube or something. Later, I found out it was salad cream, you know the ones you get in those little sachets in McDonalds.' He stopped for breathe and a swig of tea.

'That is dirty,' Kinsey said; an expression covered in disgust over his face.

Kinsey was secretly wishing this 'Tea and Tell' game hadn't started because firstly, he was next in line, and more importantly the only sexy thing he had ever done and could recall was once going down on Julie, with the light on. He remembered that he couldn't actually face using his tongue on her froufrou, so he used a piece of uncooked gammon instead. What made it worse still, was after the event his wife had cooked the contaminated meat for tea that night with a fried egg and some Smash.

He would have to make something up when it came to his turn for the sexual experienced rollercoaster.

'It got worse,' Jac continued, 'she pulled my cheeks apart, whistles twice, and then Fudgey strolled up casually, a bit like John Wayne getting off his horse, and started to lick all the salad cream off me.'

'Urgg!' Kinsey made a face like someone who had brushed his teeth with a sharp quarter of lemon. 'What? He was licking your hole?'

Jac nodded. He looked at each of his companions in turn. 'Beat that then, game set and match to Mr Jac Morgan esquire!'

'No way…what did you do?' Lusty asked. He was a touch envious of the canine sexual encounter. He had committed every sexual act in the book, but the bestiality chapter had happily past him by.

'Well, I finished with her straightaway,' Jac left a dramatic pause, 'then I started to date Fudgey. The best oral sex I have ever had.'

For the second time that day, tea shot across the table and laughter rang out across the sand.

The owner appeared again. This time he was carrying a large plate of eggs and a big stick of bread. Before he could walk away, Kinsey finally cracked. He shook his head and asked the café owner, 'Where's the rest of the food?' He was going to add a couple of 'fucks' to the sentence, but he had used up his entire ration of swear words in his last outburst.

The owner looked baffled and shrugged his shoulders in a typical European, 'I don't know what you are talking about' nonchalant type of way.

'Where are the B-E-A-N-S?' Alex interrupted, before Kinsey set about launching the shoulder shrugging foreigner into orbit.

'Ah…the B-E-A-N-S. They're coming…very good,' the café owner replied, quite oblivious to the problem which was arising. He gave Kinsey a warm pat on the back and went off to get Wigsy a top up.

Alex, who was quite relaxed about the whole episode, said, 'This is the first seven course breakfast I've ever had…or not had,' as he saw the rest of the boys tucking into the eggs. He followed close behind, bread stick at the ready.

Kinsey, who was still racking his brain about a juicy sexual encounter to share, suddenly tried to divert the attention away from his story. 'Talking about sex, did you see that programme on Sky about those shagging monkeys?' He waited for the statement to sink in.

Jac was first to speak. 'Shagging monkeys...fuck off, there is no such thing'

'Honest to God, there's this tribe or flock or whatever you call a gang of monkeys, and that's all they do all day is shag.'

'Any relation to you Lust?' Alex piped up.

'Don't start Alex, leave me out of it, I have enough on my plate without introducing shagging monkey's into the equation.'

Kinsey continued to enlighten the group 'There were males mating with females,' He made a face again. 'Bloody male monkeys bumming male monkeys. They even had adults having sex with little girl and boy monkeys'

'Dirty, hairy perverted twats,' Alex said bewildered. He spat onto the pavement.

'Lucky Michael Jackson wasn't there then.' Jac sang. 'I'm forever blowing bubbles.'

Kinsey was on a roll. 'Even women monkeys with women monkeys.'

'That sounds more like it,' Jac said excitedly, 'lesbo monkeys...did they have suspenders on and a big strap-on banana?' He turned and looked at Kinsey, who stared back, not amused.

After finally breaking away from eyeing up a beautiful Portuguese shop assistant, who was on her lunch break, Lusty entered the debate and said sceptically, 'You're having a tin-bath.'

'Straight up, Lust. I even said to my misses that when I die, I wanna come back as the chief of the shagging monkeys.'

'What did Julie say? Hurry up and die then Mr Floppy.' Jac knew this would wind Kinsey up yet again.

The remark didn't fail. Kinsey took the bait, hook, line and sinker.

'Look, I'm not Mr Floppy and secondly there are such things as shagging monkeys,' he hissed back at a smirking Jac; his knuckles white with rage.

'When I die I wanna come back as Lusty,' Alex joined in this pointless conversation.

There were several minutes of welcome silence, as they thought of who, or what, they would each like to come back as. A slightly plump, but attractive girl walked by. She glared straight at Lusty and smiled. She appeared quite smitten and slightly disorientated. She only just missed a bin attached to a lamp post, which seemed to be holding some sort of Portuguese fly convention around the entrance, but she then proceeded to trip over the pavement.

'Ladies and Gentlemen, we have a winner,' Alex proclaimed, holding up Lusty's hand. 'Lusty James knocks out the shagging monkeys in the third.'

'Shut up,' Lusty said looking embarrassed, while smiling back at the girl.

Jac changed the direction of the conversation completely. 'Look Lust, the Pozzoni brothers have followed you.'

They all glanced across at a young couple pushing a double pram, with twins sitting inside with hats and sunglasses on. They were attempting to eat ice creams.

'Hello Dorian. Hello Wayne. Need your nappies changed?' Jac shouted across at the innocent family.

The boys all laughed and became one, big, happy, insane gang once again.

'When are you going to get out of that shit hole, Lust, and what's this big plan you were on about?' Alex asked, taking a drop of tea. He checked for any odd looking pieces of string dangling out of the mug. Although he wanted to step into Lusty's single life-style, he couldn't stand the thought of going home to that cold damp flat in which Lusty survived.

'His big fucking plan should be to stop getting fucking married then fucking divorced…that would be a fucking start.' Kinsey sat back and grinned out loud, obviously fully stocked and armed with a new supply of 'Fuck' bullets.

Lusty ignored his four lettered advice.

'You wait…I've got a dead-cert way of making some serious money.'

'Do tell, Mr James.' said Alex, knowing if Lusty said serious money, he meant serious money.

'I don't know if I can trust you lot. I have been working on this idea for months now.'

'We have been fucking muckers for the last twenty-five fucking years, and you say that you can't trust us…you twat,' Kinsey snapped back sharply in a nasty voice.

'OK, OK. I'll tell you my grand plan, but not a word to anyone else!'

They all leant forward. Lusty looked right then left before he continued with his explanation. He then told them in a quiet tone that he was going to open a titty Mart. The words rolled off his tongue with immense pride.

'A fucking what?...a titty moll,' Kinsey shrieked.

'A titty mart,' Lusty lowered his voice, 'It's a place where people can go to play with tits.'

'Its official Lusty James is off his fucking trolley. You need some therapy and quick.' Kinsey slapped his leg and told the world.

'Explain some more Lust.' Alex's curiosity kicked in.

As Lusty started to explain, the group somehow seemed to get transported to the inside of Lusty's dirty mind and the titty mart. He set the scene.

'There will be a long corridor, where punters line up to pay £5 to get in.' The man in the front of the queue gave the very large bouncer money. He entered a small room with a curtain at one end. The customer opened the curtain and there was a dark corridor with flashing and revolving 60's style lighting. Beyond the corridor, they could make out a big breasted woman with no top on. She sat on a stool in a side room reading a magazine.

'Who's that Lust?' asked Jac. He was starting to get a bit of wind in him.

'Don't interrupt, you'll see.' Lusty, like a glassy-eyed, manic, hormone-fuelled Bagpuss, continued with his vivid interpretation of the inside of his Titty Mart.

They heard a bell ring, which was rung by the bouncer to indicate another customer was waiting. The bare-chested woman got up, smeared an ice-cube over her nipples and positioned them through a tit shaped hole in the wall. There were another six women, who did the same thing. Suddenly, the corridor was alive with a flock of mammary glands jigging up and down, while raunchy music bounced off each nipple.

Lusty explained there would be a big notice displayed on entering the establishment that simply stated:-

'No biting, love-bites, or photographs. Only tweaking and light sucking allowed. In bigger letters: *TITTY ROLLS EXTRA.'*

Lusty ended his fascinating business plan with a rub of his hands and a satisfying smile. He could see his mates slowly chewing his master plan over in their minds.

'You are fucking nuts with a capital N,' Kinsey finally broke the silence.

Lusty knew what type of response he would have from Kinsey; he was more concerned with what Alex thought.

'Alex, what do you think?'

'Sounds great Lust, but how and where are you going to get the women?'

'It's already sorted. I start interviewing when we get back,' he proudly announced.

'You're lying. Who would want to do such a thing?' Kinsey said suspiciously.

'Well your mother's applied. I may give her top billing. Roll up, roll up, to suck the Elephant Woman's titties,' Lusty snapped back.

Kinsey gave the handsome boy the mother of all killer stares.

'Where is this titty mart going to be?' asked Alex. He was now fully engrossed in the proposition.

'I was thinking of putting it in the old petrol station on the outskirts of town. Then the boys could use it before they go to town or if they haven't scored and need something to talk to, they could pop in before bedtime. I already got the sign made, it's based on the big M for McDonalds, but this will be a pair of big pink tits and nipples on the top.' He motioned his hands like a shooting star sailing through the night sky, as he broadcasted the name of his business venture….

'Lusty's Big Titty Experience'

'Are you going to have a drive through?' Jac said, mainly as a joke.

He thought about it for a few seconds. 'I didn't think of that Jac…nice one.' He immediately imagined a queue of cars with boys, old men and two shorthaired lesbians waiting for a turn. An old man spoke into a McDonald styled intercom and asked for, 'Two dark nipples, a portion of small titties and a can of diet coke please'

He realised this could be a real winner. He offered Jac free use of all the facilities on Tuesday nights only.

The café owner reappeared. This time with an even bigger tray with four plates spaced out on it. On each plate were the largest beans they had ever seen; they were the size of golf balls. There were four on each plate.

'Ah…the B-E-A-N-S,' the café owner proclaimed rather proudly. If there had been a drum roll at that moment, it definitely wouldn't have seemed out of place.

'Ah…the B-E-A-N-S,' they all happily repeated the words back towards the beaming proprietor.

'You...like?' He carefully laid his pride and joy in front of the boys.

'We like. They look great. Can we have four pints of lager to wash them down with?' Alex motioned.

'Its only 12.30 and don't forget there's the big banquet tonight.' Kinsey reminded Alex.

'Let's just have one or two to wake us up a bit.'

From across the street, they heard someone shouting 'Justin, watch the car.'

There was silence, and then, 'Stop that, you buggers,' came the reply far off in the distance.

They all dipped a fork into the oversized beans and started to eat. The screech of tyres and dull thud barely registered with them.

Chapter 6

'Marking the territory '

Big Ken roamed around his hotel bedroom alone. He strolled about in a similar manner to a lion patrolling his cage in a zoo. He liked the idea of being able to lock out the world and its madness. Even though he was fully aware it was only a matter of time before the madness would come knocking on his door and insist on coming in for a quick cuppa.

In the comfort of his room, he walked around with nothing covering his massive frame, except a pair of black underpants which were at least two sizes too small. His wife had bought them from Peacocks in the January sale. They didn't leave much to the imagination as they exposed a mound of curly pubic hair, which appeared to spring to life when confronted with air that, at last, smelt fresh. It looked like Mungo Jerry had snuggled into the out-of-date briefs and was chewing on a large gob-stopper.

He knew it was going to be a big night tonight. He was nervous. He needed time to relax and reflect on what was about to take place. All the great leaders needed quality time alone to devise their strategies.

Churchill, Paton, Kennedy and Kojak were all leaders he admired and tried his best to emulate.

Several years ago, when the club was struggling to attract players, he'd had a giant poster made of himself, with the words 'Your club needs you,' which was splashed all over the housing estate. Unfortunately, the only people the advert attracted were a band of over eighties, smelling of urine, carrying broom handles with bread knives Sellotaped on the end.

The butterflies that had set up camp in his stomach had slowly, but surely, started to flap their feather-duster wings, ever since the plane had touched down in the sunshine paradise.

It was now all coming together quite nicely. It was exactly as he had planned it. This was his time. In the words of the great Sinatra, 'It was his kinda' town' and nothing would rob him of his moment of rightly deserved glory.

It would all kick-off properly tonight at the official opening banquet, being held in the plush Plaza hotel. He knew the others, meaning the other committee members from the other rugby clubs would all be there striving to get their feet firmly on the first rung of the ladder to Success-ville.

He also recognised there would be lots of showboating going on at the event. There would be the usual eye-to-eye contact as each committee-man looked for any chinks in the opposition's armour. It was an extremely serious matter; life or death. Any glimpse of weakness would be cruelly exposed and exploited. It was a 'committee-man eats committee-man' world out there, and his role was to ensure his guys weren't coated in sugar candy with extra soft bits.

Spotters were even used at big functions, mainly to highlight any abnormalities in the other camp. He recalled the sad, but true, story of one of the great traditional rugby clubs of the past century, Kefny-Koed. It was a club steeped in over one hundred years of history, and it only took a simple misjudgement of one irresponsible individual to start the whole pack of cards crumbling to the ground. It was never to return to its former glory.

It all started to go wrong when an eagle-eyed member of a rival rugby club, noticed one of the Koed committee-men had slightly off-coloured white socks on at a district presentation dinner. The spotter had to look several times to make sure he wasn't seeing things.

The shame and the embarrassment were all too much to take for everyone belonging to this great club. Within two weeks, the club lost all of its sponsorship; the parents of the youth players sent their kids to other teams or bought them computer games instead. Teams refused to come to Kefny to play matches. The club closed down. Death slogans were dabbed on the side of the culprit's house. His kids were beaten up at school, mostly by the teachers. His wife accidentally had all her hair burnt off, including her eyebrows, in a freak hair dryer fire at the local hairdressers and their daughter had her labia stapled together in an 'accident' at the local tattoo parlour when she had gone in for a small angel design on her thigh.

The poor victim thought the best way out was to take his own life. He took his life by super-gluing his mouth and nose closed and locking himself in the changing rooms.

He was buried in an unmarked grave with the simple words "Please Lord Forgive me" engraved on the plain headstone. Old aged pensioners from the village would organise day-trips to the site of the grave, and take turns urinating on it.

A photographer called Melville set up a 'Slashing-booth' along side the holy ground and charged £5 for a classic 7" x 5" memento of the desecration. The Mayor, who was never shy of a photo opportunity, had a full-length snap-shot of himself taking a dump while balancing on the head-stone. He was still wearing the official chain of office and had a single red rose in his mouth. It was displayed with pride in the entertainment room in city hall.

Although Melville and a couple of other entrepreneurs became extremely wealthy, the oldest rugby establishment in the valley went to rack and ruin. The once famous clubhouse was burnt to a shell and a retirement home for overworked librarians was erected in its place.

There was a four-year waiting list to get a bed in the retirement home. This was due to two things. Firstly, the sheer amount of librarians that actually worked in the library, especially on a Saturday morning. It was a statistical proven fact that they easily out-numbered the amount of people that worked in the steelworks in the booming times. The second was that the great amount of stress the overworked librarians were under caused them to die early.

It was a story etched on Big Ken's brain. His team would never get caught flaunting the golden rules of committee-dom with such contempt. He had drilled the routines into his loyal servants. Hours and hours of practice and training disciplines had taken place. He was ready. The team was ready. This was his moment.

He did have a small concern over Justin. Although his gear was always of the highest quality cloth, he just lacked that certain 'Je ne sais quoi' to really carry it off. He had insisted Justin followed an extra strict training regime in the summer months.

He made Justin watch a great self-discipline and training video on the market, which looked behind the scenes of the stars that made 'Come Dancing' such a must see show. He had issued it to Justin along with a copy of the video and a phone number of a personal stylist, come dietician. But sadly the fat, lazy, rich twat had not listened.

He knew it was a real pity that Peter hadn't made the trip. Although well documented that Peter was a no-good weasel, he knew all the routines and moves, and his timing was immaculate. He was a very good anchorman to have at the end of the rope.

But he knew that his team was strong in every position. He was confident there wasn't a function or a presentation they couldn't appear, all 'blazered up' and ready to rumble with the best of them.

He was extremely proud of the fact that in his relatively short time as chairman, he had personally turned this rag-a-muffin bunch into one of the most feared and respected outfits in the valleys.

'If we are going to be successful, we have got to look the part,' he had told the committee in his first inaugural speech, five years previously.

'Look at Bill Hayley and the Comets! Oozed style and class,' he said while looking each and every one of them in the eye. 'Even the Beatles, before that foreign bitch infiltrated them, were kitted out in the best gear. Now compare that to those disgusting Rolling bloody

Stones; Keith Jagger and Mick Richards, and the other one who killed himself in a bucket of whiskey. All lips, drugs and ripped jeans.'

He even held up a photograph of the two rock groups to highlight the vast difference in their appearances. For extra effect he had blackened out the front teeth of each of the Stones members and gave Mick fangs and small horns on his head.

'So I ask you committee-men of this great club, which path should we go down? The road of scruffy 'I can't get no bloody satisfaction' junky pothead route to oblivion and self-destruction, or the smooth headway of smartly dressed 'rock around the clock' highway to Gold Town Successville.' As he finished his best and most important speech to date, he thought to himself that it deserved a much better audience than these numbskulls sitting in the lounge of the club munching on salty peanuts and scampi fries. Perhaps a Nuremberg style rally, or a spot at the Last Night at the Proms, would have appreciated his talents more.

He had felt the sweat of excitement flowing down the crack of his arse and settling in a large pool underneath his soaking wet balls.

There was, of course, an almost unanimous vote for the back to basics dress policy. The only person to vote against it was Gary Paranoid, who actually liked the Rolling Stones. Not long after, Gary was given a one-way ticket to Coventry and told never to drink in the club again.

At the banquet tonight, he knew they would have nothing to fear. The three hundred page report from the private detective he had hired to spy on the opposition had come back favourably. The only real competition was from the Evesham lot. The report described them as

'A well-turned out outfit; Snappy light blazers; well creased trousers; well co-ordinated. Probably shopped at Debenhams; but very beatable.'

Big Ken had planned his whole seven day offensive, with the words 'very beatable' ringing in his ears.

He made some last minute preparations. He dislodged a rather long stray hair from his nostril and yelled out in pain. A tear appeared in his eye as he thought that this must be the most painful experience known to man, other than having a 'Prince Albert' through his bell-end.

He wondered if the Nazis or the Japanese had ever used 'Nose-hair extraction' as a form of punishment during WWII.

'No, I vill not tell you vere ze top secret plans are kept,' he badly mimicked a German officer's voice as he checked his ears for unwanted wax with an old cotton bud he'd found on the floor in the bathroom.

'OK. Get the nose tweezers out of the black box over there,' Big Ken instructed the blonde bombshell in the tight fitting vest, who he had employed as his number one torturer.

'Ok, Ok, anyzing other zan zee nose tweezers.' The imaginary German broke down like a quivering jelly, 'Zee planz are behind ze painting of Hitler in a party dress, in zee drawing room.'

The sound of himself laughing at his own story, brought him back to the reality of dingy smelly hotel room. He looked pleased with himself as he removed a big ball of wax from his right ear. He couldn't help but taste the inviting brown gunk, a childhood habit, before flicking it onto the tiled floor.

He picked up the hairbrush and walked back into the bedroom and started to sing his all-time favourite tune.

"It's a one for the money ... two for the show,
 Three to get ready ... and its go kid go"

Big Ken reached across and picked up his freshly starched white shirt. He took it out of the plastic and laid it out on the bed. He struggled with the army of pins that had been speared into the shirt packaging. Mrs Moon the char lady may have had breath like a swamp creature but she knew how to iron. You could cut yourself on her creases. Big Ken just had to be careful with the pins. You never knew what you might catch.

"Don't step on my blue suede shoes
 You can do anything but lay off my blue suede shoes"

Next, he flattened out a pair of grey flannel trousers with great care and made sure that they weren't creased as he folded them onto the empty bed.

"You can knock me down
 You can sit on my face"

He picked up two cufflinks and a tiepin from beside the bed. He placed the tiepin under his nose and pretended that the cuff links were two earrings. He continued singing into the hairbrush microphone.

*"You can slander my name
All over the place"*

He completed a half turn pirouette and in the same movement unhooked the club blazer from behind the door. He placed it lovingly over the shirt. His eyes filled up as he touched the badge with great pride and a dollop of love.

"You can do anything…that you wanna do"

He then opened a drawer and picked out a pair of white socks from a drawer full to the top with white socks. He positioned them at the bottom of each leg of the trousers. Tony Hart in Art attack would be so proud.

"Oh…oh honey stay off of my shoes"

Then he bent down and from under the bed, he pulled out a new box. It contained a brand new pair of grey slip-ons. He unpacked them, placed them on both hands and slowly moved to the music. This took him back to the time he would perform the hand jive in his regular nightclub, when he was known as King Big Ken of the Teddy Boys.

"You can do anything but stay off my blue suede shoes"

The song words trailed off into oblivion, as he contemplated the last piece of the jigsaw. This was the important choice of Club tie. Big Ken held up a rack of very colourful rugby club ties, all different colours but with the same design of diagonal stripes. He picked the right tie for the occasion, a fruity mix of yellow and black stripes.

He placed the tie between his legs and pulled it back and fore, like some Brazilian tart in the 'Fantasy Lounge' gentlemen's club in Cardiff. Finally, he placed it centrally onto the white shirt.

'Elvis has left the building!' he muttered to himself. 'It's not just the clothes that win prizes, it's the whole damn experience,' he added.

He checked his watch. Still another fifteen minutes to go before he could wash off his bright, blue, aquarium fresh face pack, which covered his large face.

'Just time to park his lunch,' he thought, as he entered the bathroom, farted and kicked the door closed.

****

'1-2-3-4' Big Ken checked his watch. At exactly six 'o'clock, he opened the door to his room. He was in full gear with his hair greased back in the Johnny Cash style. He inspected himself in the full length mirror in the corridor, took a deep breath and then started to strut down the tiled walkway like a middle-aged John Travolta in Saturday Night Fever.

As he past the next door, it swung open and Keith appeared in exactly the same attire. He fell in line behind Big Ken. The pair passed the 3rd door and another committee-man joined the parade; they all sauntered down the passageway in their yellow and black ties. This went on for another two doors, until the line snaked its way to Justin's room.

Behind the 6th door, Justin was waiting. He had his ear up against the wood and was taking deep breaths, while killing time for his turn to step in line.

As the group past, he sprang out from behind the door and joined the back of the line. '*Shit!*' he thought as he looked down and realised that his tie didn't match the rest of the brigade.

'*Shit, shit,*' he whispered to himself again. '*What the hell's going on?* Small Jeff had definitely told him it was the red and white stripe tie for the initial meeting. He'd definitely been set up.

He glared at Small Jeff who was smirking rather smugly by his side. He looked at the lift then back at his room. It was too late to turn back. He gave Small Jeff another nasty look and carried on in the precession. Maybe no one would notice.

Impatiently, they waited for the lift to arrive. Keith rushed forward and did the honour of pressing the button.

He had been elected the official lift button pusher for the tour in the last committee meeting. He beat out Justin by two votes. He had been practicing for days on a make shift lift button he had rigged up at home with a cornflake box and some jelly baby sweets. For hours at a time, he would make his wife, Beryl, pretend to be in the lift of the world famous Sears towers building in Chicago, which was really their downstairs toilet. He stood outside pressing the home-made device over and over until he felt he had finally perfected his technique.

'Floor forty-four, madam. Going down,' he would repeat and close the toilet door on his wife. He religiously went through the same routine all afternoon. Beryl sat on the ceramic pan, freezing cold and bored out of her head while Keith was lost in his strange council house estate fantasy she called 'lift-world'.

Beryl's patience finally snapped after being told that the elevator would be stuck for two hours for immediate maintenance work. She had a quick piss and climbed out of the small toilet window and ran straight to the local police station. She told them that her husband had a bomb and was threatening to blow up their council house. The bomb squad was called. They knocked down the front door and took away the strange looking incendiary device with the life-like jelly babies attached. They blew it up in field killing two sheep and an asthmatic cow.

Keith was charged with terrorist activities, with possible links to the 'Burn the English Bastards' Cottages and 'Free Wales' group. He was later released and all charges were dropped when the leader of the 'Burn the English Bastards' cottages and Free Wales' group, phoned up to deny any knowledge of Keith or his plan to blow up 22 Herman Close. He explained to the sergeant that not only was 22 Herman Close, not a cottage, but that to all his knowledge, Keith and Beryl had been born in the Land of our Father.

He was let off with a severe warning, but his name was placed on MI5's blacklist of 'people to watch if nothing else was happening.' His wife had refused to give him a blow job forever more.

After what seemed like hours to a nervous and extremely anxious Keith, the hotel lift finally reached their floor and the doors slowly opened. Keith breathed a major sigh of relief and puffed out his chest proudly. The hours of practice and hard work had paid off. Some committee-men patted him on the back and shook his hand as they moved toward the lift. He couldn't wait to phone Beryl later that night; he was sure she'd be very proud of him. Hopefully she was so proud that she would relent on his oral sex famine. In reality, at that exact moment, Beryl was actually getting the locks of their house changed and Keith's toilet converted into a cupboard for shoes.

There were two boys already in the lift. They were the same boys that Kinsey had told to move to the back of the bus the day they had departed. They looked at Big Ken and then at the lift capacity, which indicated no more than five people. They looked at Big Ken again and then rolled their eyes up to the ceiling and reluctantly proceeded to abandon the lift. They pushed passed Justin, who had a smug arrogant grin on his chubby face.

The committee-men began to shuffle into the confined space of the lift. They waddled like little ducklings following behind their mother, Big Ken. Justin waited for his turn impatiently; waiting, watching, waiting, not wanting to mess up the sequence of the procession. 3-2-1, right on cue with his time, he proceeded to get in. Without saying a word, Big Ken stopped him in his tracks. He held up one finger to indicate the first point. Ken pointed to the sign with the capacity of the lift on it. Justin's eyes followed his finger. They both saw the words 'Capacity five only'. Big Ken pointed to five people that were already in the lift. He held up two fingers to denote point two. He pointed to Justin's tie and shook his large head; dandruff fell to his shoulders. At that moment the lift door closed. Justin's face dropped to the floor like a little boy who had just been told his puppy died. This was in direct contrast to the faces of the two young boys who were standing on either side of Justin who were sporting big wide 'good for you twat' grins.

On the ground floor the lift doors opened and the committee-men piled out. They walked straight into their main rival committee-men from Evesham High School Old Boys Rugby club.

It was like staring at a mirror image of themselves. The only difference between them and the rivals was the shade of the yellow diagonal that adorned their tie and their matching socks, visible to all due to the wrong inside leg measurements that had purposely been given to the mail order company by the treasurer's wife.

The hotel lobby was thick with suspicion as they filed passed each other. Big Ken and his opposite number eyeballed each other unashamedly and aggressively.

As Evesham disappeared out of sight, Big Ken had to admit that the private Dick's report was spot on. This lot were really snappy dressers, apart from the flood trousers. He was suitably impressed with the matching handkerchief positioned in their blazer pockets. It was a classy touch, he mentally chastised himself for not thinking of it. He made a mental note to add that item to the club's dress code for next year.

Chapter 7

'The second cupboard above the sink'

The official opening banquet was being held at the plush Plaza Hotel. The Plaza was not only regarded as the best hotel in the area, it was rated amongst the top three accommodations in the whole of Portugal. Everything about the hotel stank of class; from the magnificent marble lined fountain that lined the gateway of the entrance hall, to the 220 posh rooms that catered to people from the upper side of Money Street.

Every night was a lavish affair at the Plaza where every last detail and request was catered for, and tonight was no exception. These special evenings arranged by Brigadier Reginald Bracegirdle, were extremely well known for balancing on the windowsill of excellence. The lavish ballroom had been decorated vibrantly in the area's local colours. Purple and yellow were tastefully evident in every aspect of the décor. Even the giant curtains that separated the night-sky from the ostentatious surroundings within the four walls had been replaced with handcrafted, personalised monogrammed drapes of the host, BRB, and his family portraits were displayed on every wall.

The centrepiece of the large, impressive ballroom was a large white grand piano and an ice statue of the world carved into the shape of a rugby ball. The long table at the top of the ballroom was full with all the dignitaries of the region including the large breasted and glamorous Mayoress of the town in which the rugby tournament was being held.

All the Dowlais crew were there decked out in club blazers and ties, except Alex, Jac, Kinsey, Lusty and Wigsy. They were no where to be seen.

Big Ken had decided to inspect all the remaining team members before he allowed them to embark on the night's festivities.

At poolside, eighteen twenty-five sharp, he walked the line of dishevelled boys like her majesty the queen mother checking out the trooping of the colour. He had to admit, all in all, the boys had been very well turned out. Big Ken and Keith continued to march down the line of thoroughly pissed off lads. There had only been two exceptions. One of the boys was sent back to his room for embarrassingly dirty shoes and the other was pulled out for having a tattoo that was clearly visible from two hundred metres. An emergency neck-brace was rushed in from the local hospital before Matthew and his offending ink portraits were allowed to join the Dowlais entourage.

At the banquet, the committee-men were all sitting together, eyeing up the competition, cold pints of cerveja in front of them.

Brian, who was regarded by many as quite a normal committee-man, (if there was such a thing) was trying hard to appear to the outside world as if he was the sensible one. He looked across the room and muttered to Keith, 'I thought that Peter would have followed us out here after the airport police let him go?' Deep down he couldn't care a fuck. Deeper down, he wished he was watching the Marx Brothers' classic film 'A Night at the Opera', rather than sitting here, dressed to thrill.

Brian secretly longed to be one of the Marx Brothers; he often paraded around his kitchen in a curly blond wig and flashers mac, pretending to play the harp with a broom handle. Only he, his mother and a small boy called Derek, who had been living up to his reputation as a snooper and peeped through Brian's windows, knew about his kink. In the scheme of things, wanting to be a Marx Brother was fuck all on the Richter scale of weirdness in Dowlais rugby club. Even Idi Amin would have appeared normal in those four walls.

'You haven't heard what happened, have you?' Keith whispered, fixing Brian with a joyous stare.

'No!' replied Brian, with a certain interest in his voice and 'you better tell me quick' look.

'Well,' Keith paused before continuing the compelling story, 'Peter arrived back home about 11 o'clock in the night. Apparently he had been held for twelve hours, strip searched, the full works. He walked off the bus like an old man with gigantic piles and corns on his feet.'

'I bet he enjoyed that, the dirty bastard.' Brian said, remembering the rumours of Peter and the transsexual window-cleaner called Colin. Everyone knew there was something fishy going on. Colin came to clean his windows twice a month, but the dirt was still ingrained into the panes.

Keith went into great detail about the recent incident that had rocked the very foundations of Marshall Avenue.

Kathleen, Peter's wife, had fucked off to Blackpool with the girls after he left. In fact, she did it every time Peter went away on business or on a jolly and Peter never had a clue. Her usual destination was to 'Ted's Shed', aka the 'Spunk Shack' in Blackforest. There, she would attract the attention of young, virile teenage boys, take them down the local alley and milk them dry. The toothless granny gobbler would collect her winnings in a plastic container, which ensured that Peter's mushroom soup had that genuine earthy texture.

'That will put hairs back on your head,' she would tell her husband, on serving up her dark alleyway feast in her best china soup dish with two slices of wholemeal bread.

After six months, he was convinced that she was right, but he couldn't understand why a rash had appeared underneath his tongue and his ears itched.

Keith continued to enlighten Brian on how Pete had hammered on the door and when no one answered went around the back and smashed a window to get in. The noise woke up old Misses Morgan, his next door neighbour. She knew that the 'O' Neil's were away and she phoned the police. Apparently, by the time the police got there, Peter was livid because he couldn't find his passport. He had lost his temper and was tipping out drawers and throwing furniture around. The police arrived, looked through the window and saw the 'burglar', whom they thought was a fugitive butcher from the West Midlands.

The butcher was on their most wanted list for allegedly tampering with joints of meat and then selling them to his customers. There were also suspicions as to what animal the meat came from after several pet dogs had gone missing.

The coppers proceeded to sneak in through the back door as Pete was ransacking the front room. He was trying to move the sideboard with a poker as they entered the room. They told him to put the poker down and come quietly. Peter turned round, his eyes saw the local police officer, but his mind saw the airport policeman slapping on those dry, anal probing gloves.

'Apparently,' Keith laughed, 'he just flipped and started to strangle the one copper until the other one came up behind and knocked him out with his truncheon.'

Brian was wiping the tears from his eyes and rubbing his belly in fits of laughter. 'Where is he now?'

'Last reports, he was locked up in the funny farm at Bridgend. I told the slimy bastard to check his passport before we left the club.' They both burst out laughing and drunk their cerveja down in one.

A polite banging from the direction of the top table ended the hilarious story and turned everybody's attention towards the top end of the room. Brigadier Reginald Bracegirdle, the organiser of the annual and very traditional rugby competition, was on his feet.

He was an elegant sixty-year-old, with a slight hunch and a well-trimmed handlebar moustache. He stared out of gold-rimmed glasses. 'Good evening, ladies and gentlemen, Mayoress Cha'con and all of our special guests here tonight. May I extend a warm welcome to all of you here at the seventh annual Algarve rugby tournament, and if I must say so myself, the best rugby competition outside of the British Isles.'

'Hear, hear,' came back the reply from several members of the audience.

'It's good to see so many familiar faces with us again this year,' Brigadier indicated, as he surveyed the room. His eyes fixed on the group from the Evesham High School Old Boys.

'Hello Lawrence, nice to see you again. I wonder if we'll be engraving your name on this great trophy for the third year running.' He tapped the cup positioned by his side. They gave each other smug grins.

Big Ken gulped down his full pint and swore underneath his breath.

'It is a pleasure to see so many new faces here tonight. Hello HMS Gibraltar.' The major pointed his glass and saluted towards their direction.

They all stood up and replicated the Brigadier's greeting.

'Good to see you all,' he talked into the microphone.

In his mind, he thought there were definitely too many "darkies" on that team. What is the British Navy playing at these days? Why employ all these coons? In his day, they would have only been there to carry the kit or polish the white player's boots.

'Also, all the way from the valleys in Wales…we have Dallas Rugby Football Club. They will be continuing the great relationship we have had with Welsh clubs down the years,' the Brigadier said, through clenched teeth.

Big Ken puffed out his already big chest in pride.

'Welcome Dallas.' He saluted them.

Deep down the major disliked the Welsh even more than the coloured and the Irish. The only race he hated more than the 'beer bellied, always talking about the 70's, Tom Jones for King,' Welsh midget people, were the bloody Frogs. He detested the smelly, garlic, frog cowards. They should have bombed the lot of them in the war and left them in the mud to drown.

He tried to empty out the prejudices from the ashtray of his warped mind as he continued with his set speech.

'OK, I imagine that you are all extremely hungry, so I'll finish for the time being, but I would like to wish you all the best for the battles to come.' He raised his wineglass up and repeated the word 'Enjoy' several times.

What the people in the room didn't know was that the Brigadier Mayor was hosting one of his very special parties later that night, and needed to be back home by midnight or "his prey" would be getting cold.

The noise levels increased as everyone went back to drinking and chatting.

Big Ken looked across at the High School Old Boys mob. 'Look at them, smarmy cunts,' he whispered under his breath to Keith.

He still thought that their handkerchief was a first class touch. He would have to find out who their accessory advisor was and quickly.

As he looked over, he caught the eye of their own version of 'Big Ken', a Mr Lawrence Reid.

It resembled a scene from an old prison film; the two daddies of each wing, sizing each other up. Lawrence Reid nodded back in his direction.

Big Ken drifted into a daydream, a re-enactment of a scene from the film 'Scum'. He was in prison gear smashing Lawrence's head against a toilet wall. He kicked him in the balls and when he was down, said 'Oh... Lawrence. I'm the daddy now … and if you ever try that again,

I'll report you to the European rugby standards committee.' He removed the snazzy handkerchief from the pocket of his victim, turned and pushed two young babies in a double pram saying, 'I'm your daddy …who's your daddy?

Big Ken nodded back across the crowded room more in anticipation of forth-coming events, than of recognition and respect. The hairs on his back curled up and poked through his nylon shirt.

The banquet was about thirty minutes old, when there was a sudden commotion from outside the large double doors. Out of the blue, the doors crashed open and in staggered Lusty and Kinsey, half carried by a sober looking Wigsy. The drunken two found it extremely hard to stand up straight and kept falling all over the place. Wigsy spotted some familiar faces and led the two deadbeats over towards their mates.

'Oh…Fuck!' whispered Big Ken, who's face dropped to the floor.

Most of the Dowlais team thought it was hilarious and started to snigger; their shoulders shaking violently. No one had the nerve or the balls to look anywhere in Big Ken's direction.

'Get that lot out of here now Keith!' Big Ken yelled. He held up one finger and said, 'And don't tell me it's not your turn.' His face was moulded in hatred and his eyes were throwing red daggers.

But the worse was still to come in the disguise of two drowned rats following behind the initial scouting party. In ambled Jac and Alex. They were soaking wet, arm in arm, laughing and slipping to the ground. They barged through the impressive doors and due to the drunken fog that they were immersed in, took the wrong turn and headed straight towards the top table.

Halfway towards their destination, Alex spied the white grand piano and changed direction sharply. The Dowlais committee-men sat quietly, mouths open, afraid to move. Alex and Jac arrived at the piano. The room was deadly silent. Alex sat down at the ivory instrument and opened up the lid.

'Let's shake up this party,' he insisted and started to play, *"Goodbye to Jane"* by Slade.

The musical introduction was short and snappy, as he crashed head-first into the words.

'Goodbye to Jane, Goodbye to Jane
She's a dark horse see how she ran,
Goodbye to Jane, Goodbye to Jane
Dress it up like a fancy young man
She's a queen, Can't you see what I mean,
She's a queen,
And I now it's all right, all right, all right ...
I say she so young, she so young
I say she so young ...

Alex banged the keys with all his might. Jac, not to be left out, took off his shirt and started to dance like 'Baz' from the Happy Mondays. Alex liked the instinctive action of his piano playing and repeated the verse.

At the back of the hall, someone started to clap their hands. Within seconds, most of the other boys in the room, with the exception of the top table and all of the committee-men, joined in. Jac changed his dance moves to copy a young Mick Jagger strutting on stage. He climbed up onto the piano and tried to do the splits. He rolled off and hit the floor with an almighty crash, but sprang back to his feet and continued with his version of the dance.

The song finished and both boys stood to a rousing ovation. Arm in arm, they took their bow in front of the main table. While Alex was wondering if doing mad things while blind drunk constituted being spontaneous, Jac decided that he would do a handstand to complete their curtain call. He lost his balance and stumbled backwards towards the dignitaries table. Alex and the large ice statue slowed his rapid movement slightly, but not enough to stop the two boys plus the block of ice landing on the stunned guests. The ice statue landed on the lap of the Mayoress. She yelled out and tried to push it off her but it stuck to her forehead and both her hands. She rolled around, wrestling it in complete panic. Her security guard went to her aid, but he also got stuck to the powerful ice monster.

For the second time that night, the room went deadly silent.

Chapter 8

'One more time and you're out'

There was an over abundance of excitable small talk buzzing around the hotel the next morning. Even the sun had popped its head out extra early so as not to miss anything.

An area out of view of other guests had been hurriedly requested to house the inquest that was about to take place. All the committee-men were locked in the room and were perched at one end of a large table like judges in a courtroom. They were all dressed in purple Fred Perry's and dark grey slacks. This in itself indicated that this was a very serious matter. The last time they had donned this get-up was when the committee came close to banning Jac for nearly electrocuting all his team members by dropping a hair dryer into the soapy water of the old style communal baths. On that occasion he had escaped with a warning and a stern lecture from a health and safety executive on the tragic effects that playing with water could have on brainless idiots.

Strangely enough the health and safety executive later died when a steamroller rolled over him while he was conducting a risk assessment on the driver.

Although the scene was kind of dramatic, it wasn't dramatic enough for Keith. If he had his way he would have taken it to the limit, making the committee-men look even scarier. He had proposed at the annual general meeting the previous year that perhaps black cloaks and Judges Wigs should be worn when the committee were conducting matters of such a serious nature. He had even sent for samples from a weird guy in the Southern States of America who made costumes for the KKK. Although Keith had put up a very good case for the inclusion of these items in this type of situation, it was rejected because of the cost of making a special judge's wig for Big Ken's oversized head.

The inquest began. 'The five piano-playing, monkey-dancing, all day-drinking, tee-shirt wearing, piss-headed Hooligans, as Big Ken had introduced them, were at the opposite end of the table. They had their heads bowed and were concentrating extremely hard trying to not start giggling. The more they tried not to show any sign of pleasure, the greater the ball of tension grew inside of them.

A deadly silence accompanied Big Ken as he floated around the room. The whole town had been talking about the incident with the drunken piano player and his mad-dancing sidekick. They had ruined the Brigadier's special tournament party. At the door, an imaginative bouncer was paid by the hour to stop any sympathetic feelings towards the poor defendants from entering. This was punishment time, Big Ken style.

Big Ken stood to attention, hair gelled, and chest pumping. His eyes were so cold a shark would have looked away. Even the clock on the wall held its breath and tried to stop the rebellious second-hand from running amok and causing too much noise.

The adrenaline filled atmosphere was thick and the tension bounced off the wall like death charged bombs being dropped into the sea. It caused sparks of anticipation which added extra spice to the suppressed atmosphere. All eyes and minds were waiting for the storm that was surely to come; a tornado in the shape of Big Ken.

The clock on the wall ticked slowly and appeared to be getting louder, as the silence increased.

'Hope this is not going to get ugly!' Keith whispered to Small Jeff, who was sucking an Everton mint.

Keith still remembered the terrible day when Big Ken threw Nigel with a Lisp over the bar and into the beer cellar. He had been hospitalised for several months and sued the club for all his intensive dental work. It all happened because he turned up to a squad team photograph with blonde highlights and an earring.

Back in the hotel room, Big Ken finally uttered some much-needed words into the poorly air-conditioned room. 'What the fuckin' hell were you lot playing at?' he bellowed. The noise level in his sentence increased by about ten decibels, between the words 'What' and 'at'.

The room was engulfed in a mass blanket of fear and dread. In fact, fear, which had decided at the last minute, to escape out of everyone's pores, had put on a pair of welding goggles, ear protectors, safety boots and was trying to hide behind the curtains.

Alex decided to take it on himself to be the voice for the group. 'Ken…we were only …'

Alex's feeble attempt at a reply was sadly in vain. His words were cut down in all their glory by Big Ken's famous one finger in the air routine. Alex stared at the noble digit and wondered how such an object could hold such power over its fellow man.

'What the f'ing hell had you lot been taking?' The big man's eyes were staring ahead but it was clear that they were looking far beyond the confines of the four walls. What was really going on in that big Swede head of his, no one could tell and no one dared to venture to take a guess.

'I have NEVER been so embarrassed in my life,' he continued.

'What about the time he was caught in bed with his neighbour's wife?' Jac tapped Lusty's foot and whispered into his ear.

The sound of whispering unfortunately snapped Big Ken out of his trance. 'Got something to say, have you smart arse?' He sprang out of his chair. He was extremely fast for such a big man. He launched his giant hand in the direction of Jac's exposed throat. 'Shall we discuss it outside in the sunshine?'

A knock on the door stopped Ken in his tracks. Jac gulped hard. His eyes fixed on the massive hand that was only two inches from choking the very life out of him. All eyes in the room moved to the door that slowly squeaked open. They waited for an eternity to witness who had so bravely dared to come to Jac's rescue. From behind the entrance, Justin entered in a yellow Polo shirt with light grey slacks.

'Sorry I'm late,' he apologised to the stunned group. 'My alarm clock didn't go off.' He walked to the back of the room and took a seat next to Brian.

Big Ken looked at his own outstretched arm and his mind clicked back to where he was before he had been so rudely interrupted. 'Right…' he continued.

'Have I missed much?' Justin asked Brian, while rustling open a bag of Wotsits, which for some strange reason were called *'Bums'* in this part of the world. Brian sat like a statue and didn't answer.

Big Ken's face turned deep red. He swung around on a sixpence and marched over to Justin. The chubby boy started to shiver on seeing the dark cloud looming into his private sky.

'Stand up and listen here, rich boy,' said Big Ken. 'Firstly, I wouldn't like to be going to fucking war with you because you would turn up thirty minutes fucking late and then you would probably be dressed for battle in a fucking Japanese sniper fucking uniform.' He slapped the crisps out of Justin's hand and Wotsits flew all over the room. 'Now shut the fuck up Fuman…fuckin'…Chu and don't say another fucking word.'

Even Kinsey was quite shocked at the amount of 'Fuckings' Ken had squeezed into his outburst.

Justin's top lip quivered and tears filled up in his eyes. He slouched so far down in his seat that he could have become part of the stitching. In everyone else's mind he was dressed in full Japanese uniform.

During the welcomed distraction, Jac thought about making a dash for it. He got up and started to sneak towards the unguarded door. This was his chance for freedom; his chance at the great escape. He was only three-foot from the handle when he heard words that reverberated into the far corners of his soul.

'You were saying, Jac!' Big Ken focused his angry attention back towards the table of his original antagonism.

'Just saying how sorry we were Ken.' Jac took his seat next to the line of misfits.

'Sorry? Sorry? They not only wanted to throw us lot out of the competition, but they wanted to deport you out of Portugal,' he said. A bright orange Wotsit had lodged itself in his hair and made him look like a deranged unicorn.

'What... just for singing 'Goodbye to Jane'?' Alex piped up in their defence. The rest nudged him.

'You pissed in the fuckin' fountain outside the hotel, you fuckin' cretins,' Big Ken screamed. His blood was at boiling point, 'They showed us the video footage.' His veins pulsed in his neck like a neon sign outside a kebab house.

'We didn't…..did we?' Lusty said turning to Jac.

Jac looked at him and nodded in a kind of 'we fucking did' way. All the boys, including a sober looking Wigsy, fell into fits of uncontrolled laughter.

Big Ken motioned to Keith to press the video that had been set up in the corner. Keith was extremely proud. Not only was he now the official lift button presser, but he had also been elevated to the giddy heights of video control technician as well. His wife would be over the moon. Little did he realise that by now Beryl was firmly ensconced in the home of the local postie, up in his bedroom having a Greek massage followed by egg and chips.

The picture on the small screen was quite faint and in black and white. It showed the lavish fountain in the foyer with a waiter walking past carrying drinks into the ballroom. Suddenly, the five 'working-class' heroes came into view. At first they headed towards the hall doors. Jac pulled Alex back and pointed at the statue of the woman with water exploding out of her mouth. As the boys were staring at the woman, Alex undid his fly and started urinating into the fountain. This was met with great amusement and cheers from the rest of the gang. Within ten seconds, they all had their jeans around their ankles, cocks in hand and were trying to wet the Kai carp's already wet head.

Everyone in the room looked on in horror as the film showed Jac stumbling and then trying to hold onto Alex; they both fell headfirst into the fountain. This caused the watching audience to laugh uncontrollably, especially when Jac appeared with a squashed Kai carp attached to his stomach. Kinsey thought he would piss himself.

'This is not funny boys, this is serious,' said Keith. 'If it wasn't for Big Ken promising that there will be no more performances like this again, they may have kicked us out of the competition. Can you imagine the scandal? The Merthyr Depress would have a field day.'

It all went quiet as they secretly imagined what damage their local newspaper, which specialised in death, sorrow and personal pain would make of their expulsion from the sunshine paradise.

In Keith's mind he thought the front page of the local newspaper would have the heading:-

"Rugby Club disgraces the whole of Wales"

Big Ken, with head in hand, pictured the large printed words splashed across top:-

"They should be locked up forever says King Barry"

Alex envisaged the headlines in the Sunday sport reading:-

"Alex to sing at Alien wedding"

Big Ken got up and strolled around like Tyson prowling around the ring before a fight. He slammed his fist on the table. This caused the clock to jump off the wall. It landed on the head of Brian, knocking him out cold. He fell onto Justin, and pinned him to the floor. No one moved a muscle.

'Well, what have you got to say for yourselves?' he boomed.

'Look Ken, we are sorry, nothing like this will ever happen again, we promise,' said Alex, who crossed his fingers underneath the table.

In the background, Justin was struggling to free himself from under the unconscious man.

'OK … apologies accepted but you are banned from going out tonight.' He looked at each of them in the eye. It felt a bit like trying to out stare King Kong who had been out all day drinking tree stumps full of Strongbow and black.

Lusty objected. 'That's unfair,' he said, jumping to his feet.

'Unfair...unfair.' Big Ken's voice was at fever pitch 'The poor Mayoress had to have that fuckin' ice rugby ball surgically removed from her fuckin' forehead, and you talk about being unfair. Fair should have been you lot on a plane back to sunny Wales.' His stare was cold.

'Now there will be no arguments...there's a big game tomorrow, and it will not do any of you any harm for one night to stay off the drink and all that other shit you lot take.'

Alex kicked Lusty under the table. They reluctantly agreed. They got up and left the room, their eardrums ringing with the outcome.

Big Ken clapped his hands. 'Right, let's go down to the beach.' He walked over to Justin, who was still being held under the weight of a lifeless Brian. 'It's the brown costumes and the big fluffy yellow towels today. Have you got that, kinky boy?'

They all filed out behind the master and headed towards the lift. Some of the committee-men picked up Brian and followed in line. Keith moved to the front, his lift button finger cocked and ready for action.

Chapter 9

'I think we are talking Crossed wires'

It was early evening, and the warmth of the night sky had pulled up a chair and was sitting next to Alex, Kinsey and Jac on the balcony of their hotel. A large joint of wacky backy was never too far from the action and several bottles of red wine helped to lubricate the conversation.

Since they had been banned from going out, they had decided to relax and watch the world go by. Radiohead's song 'Street Spirit' was playing in the background. It had been Alex's choice.

They noticed Justin crossing the crowded street below them. They also spied Matthew hiding behind a dustbin; the spider in PJ's waiting for the chubby fly. As Justin ambled towards the hotel out jumped Matthew and yelled out, 'Watch out for that car!'

Justin went through the same panic-stricken routine as he had done during the previous attempts to drive him out of his sanity.

'You stupid bugger,' came back the reply from Justin. His language was quickly deteriorating every time someone tried to frighten him to death.

The world carried on walking past, completely unaware of Matthew's failed attempt to put his greasy fingers on the prize money for killing the overweight committee-boy.

'Life is good,' Alex said warmly on viewing the comical scene unravelling in the street below.

'Have you got anything less depressing than this? It reminds me of back home on a pissing down Wednesday,' said Kinsey, pouring another glass of wine while passing the spliff to Jac.

Alex appeared disappointed with Kinsey's attack on his choice of music. 'This is a Classic,' he said firmly, 'and what do you know about music? You thought that Shaking Stevens was the lead singer with Bad Company.'

'Ha fucking ha …it's a classic fucking depressant.' He started to rifle through the mountain of CD's, placed on the dressing table. 'Have you got any Marley or Steel Pulse or at least something a little bit more exciting than four middle-class zombies on fuckin' Prozac?. Oh this is more like it.' He took his seat back on the balcony. Suddenly 'Place your hands' by Reef blasted out.

The fearless guitar riff that accompanied the song spat out pure aggression with every note. Alex had to admit it was a good selection. He wished he could stop the world at this very precise moment and encourage everyone in the vicinity to sing along to the chorus. He looked below at all the people rushing about in the sun and concluded that life was too short for all this nonsense.

He didn't know if it was him speaking or if the drugs had taken over completely. He always got philosophical while under the influence of mind-bending substances. He drifted off and pictured the world as one big juke-box; with himself the 'soul' owner of all the fifty pence pieces in the world. He imagined the music machine jammed packed with all of his first choice songs and everyone else was sitting on a large comfy settee, singing along like it was the last night of the prom but without the Union Jack flags and the stupid upper-class, chinless grins.

He started to feel a bit peckish and went off into the bedroom to search for some nosh. This was another habit he acquired, while floating on the magic carpet of marijuana. He came back onto the balcony, sucking on a minty tube of fluoride toothpaste.

'Oh fuckin' hell, Confucius is thinking.' Kinsey informed the world about Alex's present colourful state of mind.

There was a sudden knock on the door. It was loud, sharp and full of impatience. Jac got up to answer it. He steadied himself and slowly turned the handle. Lusty burst in to the room at a hundred miles per hour, carrying a large white bag.

'Come on you lot…ain't you ready?' Lusty enquired.

'Ready for what Mr James? Ready for what?' Alex replied, struggling to concentrate on what he was actually trying to say.

'To rock this town…Paint it red; New York, New York and all that other bullshit.' Lusty took a puff of the joint. 'Hey that's some good shit.'

Kinsey snapped back like an alligator with a toothache. 'Haven't you forgotten, Big Ken and his warning from the lost ark,' he continued in a deeper voice, 'you scum will not go to the ball!'

'Fuck that,' Lusty said eagerly. 'Anyway, I just saw them all going to some party in Albufeira. A committee-men bonding session whatever that means, probably getting ratted on the kitty money, but anyway they won't be back until late tonight.'

Lusty's words were the reality pill they wanted to hear; it was a real live action news report about a major ground breaking story. His words sounded like a poem about a brand new bunch of flowers on a hundred year old gravestone; there was suddenly colour back in their lives.

'Are you sure, Lust?' Alex asked excitedly, as the drug haze began to subside. It was replaced with the joyous anticipation of another night on the town.

'Yep ... and because I am a bit sick of you losers not pulling any gash, I decided to give you all a chance.' Lusty put his hand into the bag and proceeded to throw out three wrap-over Sarongs to each of them.

'What the fuck is this?' Kinsey commented, holding the item up. He thought it was a flowery shirt.

Lusty modelled the sarong. 'Look...if Mr Beckham can wear one so can we. I am telling you these are 100% guaranteed to get you laid.'

Kinsey realised what the piece of material he had in his hand was and threw it across the room in disgust. 'Fuckin' laid...by who...Transvestite fuckin' Trevor?'

The others laughed.

'Where did you get them, Lust?' Jac said, sizing himself up against one.

'Don't fuckin' worry where I got them from.'

'Well, I am not wearing one of them. We'll look fuckin' ridiculous.' Kinsey was outraged.

'You will be giving yourself another Barclays Bank tonight then, will you?' Lusty used the 'self-mutilation' card on Kinsey to defend his choice of evening wear.

Alex was nodding. 'Let's give them a go; I need something to help change my luck. I've got blisters on my hands the size of rucksacks.'

'OK, give us twenty minutes,' agreed Jac. He aimed an additional harmless question towards Alex. 'Have you phoned Claire yet?'

'No...not yet...have you?'

Jac nodded meekly, Alex turned to Kinsey, 'What about you Kins?'

'Only about three times,' he replied, staring out onto the balcony.

'Only three times? Who are you? Busby the telephone freak?' Alex snapped.

Lusty pretended to look confused, 'What? You've phoned his wife three times?'

Alex told him to fuck off. He closed his eyes and imagined his wife wearing an enormous frown as Kinsey's wife told her all about the long loving phone calls she had with her loving husband.

'Thanks boys, you could have told me,' he said. 'You know what she is like. Lusty can I borrow your phone?'

'No probs.' He threw him his mobile phone and jokingly added, 'Ask her is she missing me?' He stuck his long experienced tongue out and moved it very fast. It didn't miss a single beat.

Lusty and Jac left the room. Alex splashed some water on his face to ensure he was drug-free and in control for the awkward questions which were to come. He dialed the number. She picked up within two rings.

'Hello Baby,' he whispered.

'Oh, you've decided to see how we are at last, have you? It's about bloody time!' Her opening words were spat-out with real venom; he could taste the poison down the line. 'Billy has phoned Julie three times already....three times.'

Alex looked at Kinsey and mouthed the word, 'Wanker'.

Kinsey shrugged his shoulders. This really irritated Alex. If he had a knife, he would have stuck it in his smirking so-called friend. Not all the way, just enough to pierce the skin and show him what a wanker he really was.

Alex decided to ignore her opening rant and continue, 'How're the kids?'

'They are bloody hard work as usual. They are sleeping down your mothers tonight.'

'Oh...so you are going out are you?' Alex's voice leaked suspicion.

'I'm only going down to bingo with Helen.'

Helen was standing in the room. She started to motion with her fingers that Claire's nose was growing like Pinocchio.

Helen was Claire's mate. Not her best mate, but one she called when she was lonely and needed a good night out on the tiles. She had the reputation of being 'one hell of a good time girl'. Some of the stories about her exploits could actually turn hairs grey. Helen's name was never too far away from people's lips in the village and usually for all the wrong reasons.

'You are not going out with that slag.' Alex was quick and direct in his response.

Claire tried to cut him off before Helen could hear. 'What's the place like?'

He paused. 'Oh...it's very quiet. It's in the middle of no-where really. All we've been doing is training and playing cards; boring stuff. I can't wait until I come home to see you and the kids. I miss you so much.'

Kinsey pretended to put his fingers down his throat and mouthed, 'Liar, liar pants on fire'. Alex laughed.

The mood and the chit-chat between the long-distanced married couple began to flow smoothly. In the background Kinsey held up Alex's shirt. He gave him the thumbs up. He then held up the sarong that Lusty had bought. Again Alex nodded his approval.

Across the ocean, many miles away, Helen seemed to be repeating the exact actions of Kinsey. It was as if they were identical clones, but she was minus his anger and his two meat and veg.

She held up a blouse. Claire nodded. Helen held up two skirts; one short, the other extremely short. Claire didn't need time to think about her choice. She immediately pointed to the very short one.

'Any other news?' Alex enquired.

'You must have heard about Peter,' she said, applying false tan to the inside of her thighs.

'Yeah...good enough for him...in the nuthouse ain't he,' he replied.

'No he escaped,' she added.

'No way...escaped!'

'Yeah...apparently they caught him walking on the M4 towards London with no shoes on, carrying an airline ticket, a machete, and a frozen chicken! They say that he's lost his marbles. He spends all day in a straight jacket, dribbling like a baby.'

'Fuckin' good enough for the slimy twat,' Alex yelled.

She also went on to explain how Father John had gone missing and that an Indian tracker called Fluffy Muff had arrived at the empty church, sniffed around for a bit, then ran barefoot into the sun set, followed by a posse of Arch-bishops on horseback armed with Holy water-pistols.

Kinsey held up a pair of boxer shorts. Alex thought about it, before he put his hand over the phone and said in an upper class voice, 'I'm going to swing in the wind tonight, Billy, my old boy.'

At that precise time, Helen held up two pairs of knickers, one skimpy pair, and one of the thong variety. Claire thought about it, before putting her hand over the phone and said, 'None…I feel lucky.'

Both girls giggled wickedly.

'I've got to go now Love…its Lusty's mobile.'

'OK darling…Anyway I'm going to be late for the first house if I don't go now. Bye love…Don't forget I love you.'

'Bye love.'

Alex was very pleased that he'd somehow managed to overcome a very difficult situation and escape with flying colours.

The two girls took a long look in the full-length mirror. They were pleased with what they saw. They were dressed to the nines and it was still only seven 'o' clock. They bolted back their Bacardi Breezers and, arm in arm, closed the door and sashayed down the rain soaked street, singing,

"It's raining men… Hallelujah … It's raining men"

****

The gang of four were assembled in Alex's hotel room. Sarongs covered their modesty. The last act before they departed was to have an early evening livener. Four large white lines were separated on the bedside cabinet. A note was rolled. One big snort and they strolled out into the red night sky. Each of the boy's right eyes was watering.

John, the club captain, stopped them in the reception. 'Where the hell are you going? There's a big game tomorrow.'

'Only going out for a short walk,' Lusty said ruefully.

'Come on boys, there's plenty of time for going out tomorrow after the match,' John moaned

'Sorry John ... But don't worry we'll be back in about sixish,' blurted out Jac, who was already starting to feel the hair on the back of his neck standing to attention.

Then, like four missiles on a deadly mission, they shot out of the comfort of the hotel cannon and headed towards the war zone of disco lights. They walked down the lively night-strip, some boys cheered them and girls whistled and shouted for them to give them a flash at which Alex duly obliged.

Jac wiped his weeping eyeball with his hand and informed the party that perhaps Lusty had been right about the skirts. They all agreed as goose pimples the size of goose-gogs walked up their spines towards the back of their exposed necks.

Two hours later, the boys were lost in seventh heaven. Their treasured nightclub was bouncing and the music was driving hard into their very soul; it made the walls breath in and out. Sweat was dripping off the bricks and mortar and, for the gang, chewing bubblegum had all of a sudden become an Olympic sport. Alex's overactive jaw was doing a fine impression of a young Carl Lewis, while Kinsey's was limbering up for a rerun of a hundred meter sprint in the land of uncut speed.

The raw music and uncut speed made a perfect husband and mistress partnership; the type of sexual relationship that was locked in a firm embrace in a downtown Chicago motel room on a hot Tuesday afternoon.

Alex, Lusty and Kinsey were all drinking Buds and leaning on the bar. Jac was dancing with a pretty, mousey haired girl who was built like a gymnast and dressed like a schoolgirl. 'The perfect combination in any situation,' he said to himself.

'Lust, give us another dab. I think I'm coming down' said Kinsey, whose tongue was orbiting around in his mouth similar to a hamster on a wheel.

Lusty opened up a small bag. Kinsey licked one finger and rammed it in the bag. It appeared again, covered in white powder, which he proceeded to rub around his gums. He repeated the process several times.

'Slow down Kins, you'll be flying until next Tuesday. It's base, not the usual crap.'

'I'll have a little go at that.' Alex eagerly followed Kinsey's lead into the little white bag of happiness.

Lusty packed the powder away and headed off to the toilets. The boys looked across to Jac, who was now kissing the little gymnast schoolgirl quite passionately.

'It must be the bloody skirts,' Kinsey implied.

'We'll see, it's not working for us though,' said Alex. Then from across the room, Alex noticed a dark haired girl, looking in his direction. He smiled back.

Lusty came out of the toilet, but before he reached his destination two lovely looking girls, sitting at one of the tables, stopped him.

'Hello handsome …got anything under that sarong for me?' said the girl with the blond hair, eyes glistening.

'I've got something for you…and you.' Lusty slowly pointed at each of the girls in turn.

'Well, sit down and tell us more.'

Lusty sat down and started to work his magic. The conversation was electric; sparks bounced off every syllable. He could sense that he was on a roll. He pointed to the first girl and enquired, 'I would say that your name is Wicked' and pointing to the second girl, 'and your name is Evil.'

The two girls produced the most evil and wicked grins that ever had the misfortune of appearing on such pretty faces. Even the devil himself would have argued ferociously to have first bagsy pick on those infamous smiles.

'Look at him.' Kinsey pointed towards Lusty. 'Why can't I do that?'

'Because he is a sex god and you are an ugly twat,' Alex quickly replied.

Jac walked past, hand in hand with his girl and said, 'Don't wait up boys. I may be back in time to catch the plane. I am going to help her with her homework. Don't worry I have a rubber just in case she makes a mistake!'

He put his hand around her and headed for the door. As he walked out he bumped into John the captain and some of the other team members, who were in make shift dresses, entering the nightclub.

'I thought that you lot were staying in to discuss tactics,' Jac said, surveying the strangest array of semi-transvestites in town.

'And leave you lot to have all the women,' John commented, as he motioned his arm and they all piled into the wall of sound and unadulterated sweat.

Alex felt someone close to him, trying to squeeze in by the bar. He turned around and was face to face with the dark haired girl who he had smiled at earlier.

'Sorry,' he said, 'I'll move over a bit.'

'It's OK. I'll squeeze in here. It feels quite nice actually.' The dark haired girl, whose name was Laura, replied.

She was with her best friend, who was an attractive blonde haired girl named Danielle. They didn't make a habit of picking up strange men, but it had been a hard and tiresome week. There had been many creeps and weirdoes in such a small place.

'What is your name?' she asked quietly.

'Alex...and this is Kinsey...oh arrrrr...Billy.' He thought that he would bring his friend into the conversation at an early stage.

'I'm Danielle, hello Billy or is it... Kinsey.' She eyeballed Kinsey, who stopped chewing immediately.

'It's...It's...its Billy.'' Kinsey stuttered badly.

They both gave themselves a little 'not bad, seen worse' type of smile. Kinsey turned and subtlety spat his chewing gum out. The chewing gum was distraught. It had been excepting a long and full night of jaw crunching. Perhaps, even a bubble or two. It was just about to consider it's next plan of bubble gum attack, when a size eleven loafer, accidentally ended its short but now, fruitless life.

'What are the skirts for?' Danielle enquired.

'It was his idea,' Kinsey pointed to Lusty.

'Oh ... we saw him earlier ... good-looking boy ...but I bet he folds his clothes!!!'

'What does that mean?' Kinsey asked, wishing that he hadn't been so hasty with his chewing gum. He replaced it with a long swig from his bottle of Bud.

Danielle waited for the music to stop before she explained what she meant. 'I bet he's married. Haven't you heard that expression before?'

'No,' both boys answered.

They looked worried and slyly tried to slip off their wedding rings.

'No, he's divorced...Are you married?' Kinsey tried a bit of reverse psychology with the aim of deflecting the spotlight off the two guilty married criminals, who were on the verge of getting caught red-handed.

'No chance...I'm too busy enjoying myself for all that marriage crap.' Danielle slowly moved to the music. 'What about you two fine, young men?'

They both replied 'NO!' simultaneously.

Their response was so quick and loud that it had 'Lie' written all over it; guilt leaked out of every pore in their bodies. But unknown to them, she didn't really care about his answer. She could see in his eyes that he was a decent type and probably that meant that he was married or just divorced, but she was going home soon and she needed some male company and some quick fun.

After some general chat about the weather, the cold sea, the drink and the weather back home, Laura suggested that they all went and sat in the corner, where it was less noisy. The boys agreed and stayed back a while to order a fresh round of drinks as the two girls headed off for the table.

It was decision time for everyone concerned; the sixty-four thousand-dollar question. Was every thing going well or were they stuck with the monsters from the deep? Danielle gave Laura the thumbs up, which was a relief for Laura because Danielle was not easily pleased with many men, but she had found Billy rather cute. This was great news for Laura, because she had the hots big time for Alex.

Kinsey was tingling all over. He was in lust. His eyes were in love and his mind was made up. His heart was out on Main Street, covered by an umbrella and dancing to 'Singing in the Rain'. This was better than the real thing. Alex was slightly cooler than his friend, but suitable warm enough to feel a good night ahead.

'It's going well. I'll get the drinks in and you go and see if Lusty wants one,' Alex told Kinsey.

The speed and the prospect of a little roll in the hay had taken them to a cloud that was above the number nine. 'Thank god for women and chemically induced highs,' Alex prayed to the Lord of Adultery and Pleasure for it to always continue.

Kinsey walked over to where Lusty had Miss Evil and Miss Wicked in stitches and hanging on his every word.

'Ha…Ladies. Let me introduce you to Mr Kinsey. He's got balls the size of Peru,' joked the handsome Lusty.

Kinsey looked embarrassed. The girls looked inquisitive. 'Don't listen to him girls,' Billy replied.

Their curiosity soon turned to an obvious look of disappointment.

'Hey…Lusty do you want a drink?'

'Sit down for a second Kins. I was just teaching these fine creatures how to speak Welsh.'

'Go on say that again…. Steve. It's making me come over all fanny,' Miss Wicked gestured coyly, living up to her newly adopted name.

Now Kinsey had known Lusty since they were both ten years of age. He knew everything about him. What made him tick, what got him angry, what his strength and weaknesses were. Due to this vast amount of hidden knowledge about the person in question, he could categorically state, that Lusty could not speak a single word of Welsh. He knew this because Lusty never went to Welsh classes. He believed that learning the Welsh language was a complete waste of time.

'What's sexy about Welsh?' the good-looking stud would ask the teachers. 'Now, French is another matter all together. That's a language that can peel off a pair of panties from a woman from two hundred paces.'

So instead of trying to learn the language of his forefathers, he would bunk off the morning session and go and serve morning coffee with biscuits to the married women's Bridge Club, which took place at Mrs Richards' house.

Due to the high stakes and the handsome waiter, they had a waiting list of three years to get on to that bridge table. So Lusty left school without an idea of Welsh, but a first class honours degree in the workings of older Welsh women.

Kinsey whispered to Lusty, 'You don't speak Welsh.'

'Shut up Kins, watch and learn.'

He turned to the goggle-eyed ladies and whispered softly, 'OK are you ready for this.'

They nodded. He left a small pause, then in a deliberately slow 'rounding the words around his tongue' sort of way, he casually pronounced, 'Heolgerrig via Troedyrhiw', which wasn't actually Welsh but it was two small villages outside his hometown, linked together by a simple 'via' and a stretch of smelly canal.

'What does that mean?' Miss Wicked had been had hook, line and sinker by the made-up language from King Lusty's lips.

With a glint in his deep brown eyes, he replied, 'It means…Your eyes melt my heart.'

Even though the music in the room was drumming on everyone ears, those simple words had a sound and eloquence all of their own. There was a noise exclusion zone around the table.

'That is lovely. Say something else.' Miss Evil jumped straight into the net.

Lusty thought for a second, then continued, 'Maes-y-Cwmmer ain't it Ystrad Mynach'

Again, there was not an ounce of Welshness in the meaning, but it had the same winning ingredients as his previous success.

'What's that?' Miss Evil was like a little girl caught mooching around a sexual healing sweet shop.

'Darling, you shine like an angel on a dark night.'

The girls physically wiggled on their seats.

'It's starting to smell like a fishmonger's armpit around here,' Kinsey thought to himself, wondering if someone had slipped a kipper behind the radiator.

'One more…it sounds so sexy,' Miss Evil panted.

'Nantyffyllon,' he replied slowly in his best Richard Burton accent. He looked so gorgeous in the light of the disco that a nun would have ripped her extra itchy knickers off and put them in his mouth.

He whispered what it meant in Miss Evil's ear. Her smile gave away any mystery about the actual content about his explanation.

'Anytime…Anywhere!' She murmured it into the inviting ear of Miss Wicked. She also grinned and agreed.

Kinsey now knew what it felt like to be a spare prick in a wedding. He grunted, 'Do you want a fuckin' drink or not, Lust?'

Lusty was trying to concentrate on other sexy Welsh towns. He already had 'Machynlleth', 'Llandrindod Wells', and the mother of them all, 'CwmRhondda al a Turk' in the bag,

He replied, 'I'll have a …..'

Before he could finish giving his order, Miss Wicked butted in, 'No…He's OK. He's coming with us.'

She grabbed his hand and the three of them rushed out of the disco. A pack of cats and seagulls followed them all the way back to the hotel. The confused creatures all sat on the fence waiting in hope that the handsome fisherman would throw some scraps over the side. They walked or flew home in the early morning, empty handed and very hungry, except for a nasty ginger tom, which had eaten two seagulls during the overnight ritual.

Back at the disco, everything was going to plan. The two couples were sitting at the table. Alex and Laura were getting on like a house on fire. Kinsey and Danielle were going at a slower rate. This was due to the fact that Kinsey was not a very chatty person unless someone mentioned wrestling or boxing. But to be fair, the couple's conversational plane was starting to taxi on the runway of getting to know each other.

After about ten minutes of trying to explain to Danielle the merits of living in a place that always rained, she interrupted him while he was half-way up mount thunderstorm. 'I always wanted to go to Wales. I think that the language is so sexy. Do you speak Welsh?' she asked.

Kinsey was just about to say no, when he remembered the success that Lusty had. Kinsey was well known for his terrible chat-up lines. 'You don't sweat much for a fat girl' and 'Can I just play with your titties, for a bit then?' being some of his better attempts. So perhaps a new approach was just what the doctor ordered.

'Yes, of course I do. Would you like me to say something in Welsh?'

Alex, who was sitting close, stopped to listen. Alex knew that Lusty was the only person in the world who was worse at Welsh than Kinsey. Lusty, of course, had a good excuse. It was a case of either learning the Welsh alphabet, parrot fashion, or servicing the many frustrated houseflies that buzzed around the town. There had been no contest, especially for a fifteen-year-old with an eye for the crack. Even Willie Welsh from Welshpool, studying Welsh for a living, would have agreed that Lusty did offer a grand alternative. But Kinsey's only excuse for his lack of fluency in his mother tongue was his inability to pronounce the word correctly and his greater inability to stop losing his temper when Mrs Price poked fun at his feeble attempt to conquer his foibles.

'My granddaughter could pronounce the word better than that, and she's only four years old,' she informed Kinsey one bitterly cold December morning in room 2A.

The class laughed. Mrs Price joined in. She had noticed the slight anger building up in his eyes, but sadly for her, she had completely missed the textbook aimed at her head. Regretfully, no one realised how much damage 'How Green was my Valley' (Hardback edition) could inflict on someone of that age.

Kinsey was expelled, yet again, and dropped Welsh from his suite of subjects. Mrs Price never fully recovered. She was forced into early retirement after she refused to take off the crash helmet and gum-shield she insisted on wearing during lessons.

She died tragically several years later, when a bookshelf at the local library collapsed on top of her as she tried to abseil down from the non-fiction section. The librarians who had been on duty that sad day had major trauma, and were also forced to retire early. Luckily for them, a brand new retirement home had just opened on the site of an old disgraced rugby club. The retirement home had been designed by some bloke who had been to Disney and included many fun rides. The librarians loved the one where they would ride on a magic novel and had the opportunity to blow the heads off sneaky book thieves. There was always a large queue.

'Yes, I would,' muttered Danielle 'but I must warn you mind that I may not be able to contain myself. Me and foreign languages are a deadly concoction.'

Kinsey prepared himself. He took deep breaths and then blurted out, 'Heolgerrig via Troedyrhiw.'

It was supposed to sound like a young Tom Jones. It came out more like a strange mix of the Krankies and the fat controller from Thomas the Tank-engine.

'That sounds nice, what does it mean?'

'Your eyes melt my heart. Would you like some more.'

She nodded politely, trying hard to hide the laughter that was building up inside of her.

'Maes-y-Cwmmer ainty Ystrad Mynach.'

Gone was the Krankies and the fat controller, it was replaced by an impression of Alan Ball on helium. He went on to explain that it meant 'You are my angel in this dark time.'

Alex was surprised and impressed. The sneaky bastard must have been revising when he got expelled, Alex thought.

'Tell me something rude and sexy.' The hotness in her voice sent shivers in his direction.

Her words hit the panic button within Billy. He couldn't remember the third name that Lusty had said. He thought long and hard. After struggling for the right phrase he nervously muttered, 'Merthyr Tydfil.'

Alex stopped nibbling on Laura's ear. He was not only curious about the choice of his hometown as a sexy Welsh word, but the strange Russian peasant accent, which his mate had now started talking.

There was quiet. Kinsey felt that the whole disco was waiting for the next instalment. He sputtered out, 'Merthyr Tydfil....Benefits Office.'

Alex spat beer all over the table and doubled up laughing, repeating the words, 'Merthyr Tydfil Benefits Office'

Danielle, who had controlled her feelings quite well up to this point, asked sarcastically, 'What does that mean, Billy?' She then burst into laughter.

'Come on Darling, explain what that means then,' Alex squawked loudly, tears rolled down his face.

'Oh fuck it... who wants a fucking drink.' He stormed off, wishing that he had stuck to the safety of boring her to death about the fucking weather.

****

An hour later, the two couples were walking hand in hand on the beach. A large hole had appeared in the dark sheet of the night sky and the moon was trying to stick his head through it. It had got stuck halfway. Lights from the distant nightlife were blinking away. The heavy beat of the bass line drifted along on the beach. A crab scurried alone on the sand. It stopped suddenly in the glare of a spotlight. It did an energetic type of sandy tap dance before heading back into the ocean with the intention of trying to shag a minx of a mussel or a nice pouting prawn.

Laura held Alex's arm tight. She turned to him and said, 'I've had a great night. I haven't laughed like that for ages. He's crazy.' She pointed at Kinsey.

'I know he is. I've had a great night too; it's a pity it needs to end.' Alex tried his romantic approach, to see how far he could push the boat out.

'It doesn't need to end just yet,' she replied.

They started to kiss, the waves splashed over their feet. A crab, in a large shell-like cowboy hat, bucking a prawn rolled over his foot while trying to get back towards dry land.

'Can I tell you something?' Danielle asked.

Alex nodded

'I haven't had a man for about two years…I just didn't feel the need…but I do now…will you take me home?'

She didn't tell him how she had been hurt so badly by the last man. It had been so dreadful that she had considered ending it all and becoming a social worker. How someone could turn into such a no-good bastard, was beyond the realms of bastardom. Physically, she had kept herself in good nick, but mentally, she had been cut to bits. When she finally walked out, sporting two brand new black and blue eyes, she could hardly see properly but she never looked back.

They kissed some more. This time the kiss had a very different feel to it. There was passion, pure lust, while their tongues danced with each other. Alex thanked his lucky stars. He also thanked Lusty for the skirt idea.

They caught up with Kinsey who was telling Danielle about the moon and the stars and how they revolved around the world. It was another one of his famous crappy, chat-up one-liners.

'What's all that shit, Kins? Hurry up; we are going back to the girls' apartment.'

Laura's bedroom was bursting with sexual tension. The light was off, and the moonlight was shining through the curtains. As Alex walked into the room, Laura was already in bed. She slowly moved back her blankets to expose her beautiful formed body.

'Come and get some …my Welsh tiger'

Alex growled as he climbed onto the bed.

Next door, Danielle had gone to the bathroom, to slip into something more comfortable. Kinsey was nervous; he didn't know what to do. He scanned the room. He thought that the layout was all-wrong and it was not making the most of the space that could be available. He thought that perhaps he had been watching 'Changing Rooms' too much.

He snapped out of it, then realised that time was running out. He decided to get undressed. He neatly folded his clothes over the chair and posed on the bed.

He could feel the pressure building up inside him. Danielle would be back soon and that would mean 'performance time.' He scanned the room again. It seemed that all the objects had sensed his fear and ganged up to take the Mickey out of him. The lampshade resembled a throbbing member, which had been unleashed and was about to lay siege in a nice, hairy tunnel. Even Danielle's stiletto shoes were lying on their backs, high heels erect like John Holmes in one of his famous porno flicks. 13 inches of leather manhood, laughing at his limp slug.

'You can do it!! … You can do it!!' he told himself.

He recalled the two times in his past when he failed to rise to the occasion. Once was before he was married, and the other was on a business trip to an electrical conference in Dublin. These failures had scarred him deeply. He had needed a good run to get his confidence back.

A year later, he decided that a stag weekend in Amsterdam was just the ticket to banish the memories of those poor performances. During the second night in Amsterdam, he sneaked off from the rest of the boys, who had been transfixed by a classic film concerning a donkey and an 19th century fiction character. It was called 'Mary Pop-it-in'. He headed for the redder light district.

He eyeballed the many girls behind the glass doors. Then with a certain case of intrepidation he picked out a "made-to-mate" Mexican girl. She washed him, rubberised him and went down to inspect the merchandise.

Kinsey closed his eyes and prayed that it would not be third time unlucky.

'Three strikes and you're out,' he could hear the God of Erection hovering behind him with a baseball mitt and face protector on.

'Fail this time and its Erectile Dysfunction City for you, butt,' the devil pitcher pitched in with some seriously serious advice.

The prostitute whose name that night was Sabrina, opened up her legs to reveal her flower. She took hold of his still limp weapon and guided it into her silky walls.

In his mind, he found himself on the canvas, his manhood visibly shaken. A boxing referee was standing above the bed, counting to ten.

'One' the referee started the count.

'Come on you can do it,' he told himself.

'Two' – 'Just clear your head and concentrate.'

'Three' – 'Not too hard … Just relax.'

'Four' –'Come on my boy … get up onto your knees.'

'Five' – 'A little bit further….yes … yes.'

'Six' – 'Oh-no… don't slip back down… quick look at those tits.'

'Seven' –'Concentrate … concentrate... Relax. .. Get up'

'Eight' –'Hi….Oh what's that?… Oooohh.'

The referee didn't need to continue the count. Sabrina the hooker, who knew every trick in the book, and had even invented one or two of them herself, had gently inserted her finger into the paying client's trap door. She had done this a thousand times, and many drawbridges had risen up.

'Continue fighting,' the referee indicated, after finally seeing Kinsey start to stand to attention and sprang up off the canvas.

The bout didn't last long. It was a clean fight, even when Kinsey sent through a rabbit punch and a very low blow that ended the contest after thirty seconds of the restart, which nearly shot the top of Sabrina's head off.

They were no losers in the room that night. Kinsey walked from the semen-stained ring, like the champion of the six and a half inch welterweight division. Sabrina, after tax and pimp charges, had pocketed twenty five Euros towards building a new life back in her beloved Mexico. Now she only had another thousand more days of her clocking-in and 10,989 new clients to continue cocking-in, before she was free. She just hoped that her petal or her middle digit finger would not wear out by then.

He heard the light going off in the bathroom, he saw his clothes all neatly folded and remembered that it was the sign of an old married man. He rushed up and threw his clothes all over the room and jumped back on the bed, just as Danielle walked into the room. She was only wearing her bra and knickers. She tripped over his shoes that he had just thrown on the floor. She climbed onto the bed. They started kissing each other.

He could hear the bedsprings moving violently next door and Laura moaning like she was being murdered. The pressure was mounting on him. He was very nervous.

Danielle went down between his legs; after a while her head popped up and she said, 'Is everything OK?'

'Great,' he lied.

He tried to think of everything sexy that he could imagine. Big tits swinging in Lusty's Titty mart, black lesbians, bald beaver, the works…but instead all he saw was his wife and kid crying, sitting in a big bath of Brussels sprouts.

'Are you sure you're OK?' Danielle asked; her jaw was starting to ache.

Kinsey thought about asking her to do the same as Sabrina had done with her magic finger. But he decided he didn't know her well enough. Could he possibly do it to himself, without her seeing? He thought the idea was disgusting and physically impossible.

He cursed the people who controlled his lower functions. He imagined them, at this moment, watching some bloody Disney video in the control room of his loins. Could he send someone in like the guy from that film 'Inner-Space' to insert a bluey into the machine? That would do the trick. It always worked for him and Julie on Sunday afternoons, when the kids were at the mother-in-laws.

He decided that he was going off his trolley and just pulled Danielle up towards him and asked her, "Can we just cuddle for a bit?"

Danielle appeared to be disappointed, but reluctantly agreed.

From the next bedroom, it sounded like there was a sex marathon going on. Alex was on course to win gold, silver and fucking bronze, in a New World record time, as Billy's overactive mind played dirty tricks with the situation.

'Fuck it!' Kinsey said to himself, wishing he was far away.

'Fuck it!' Danielle said to herself, wishing he was far inside her.

Thirty, awkward, minutes later, she fell asleep while Kinsey lay there wide-awake cursing the redundancy of his under active loins. Next door, Alex was shagged out, relaxing on the bed, Laura in his arms. He heard lots of banging and dragging of furniture coming from Kinsey's room. 'That's my boy…that's my boy.' He too fell asleep.

In the morning, Alex kissed Laura goodbye and knocked on the other door. Kinsey was already dressed and was waiting for him. They started walking home. There was no eye contact.

'Fancy some breakfast? All that shagging has given me an appetite,' Alex said, as they stopped at a small café.

'That was an amazing night…Lusty was right about the skirts,' he continued, 'you know, she was sex mad… told me she hadn't had it for two years. She taught me a trick or two. I'll have to put my balls in a saucepan of ice cold water when I get back. How did you go? Heard some strange noises from your room you dirty little man,' he nudged Kinsey.

'It was OK.'

'What do you mean OK?...It sounded like you were running the Grand National in there. You're a fucking dark horse.'

There was an awkward silence. Kinsey was half expected his new sexual failure to become front-page news. The weight of guilt and expectation or just plain sadness was too much to bear. 'I couldn't perform,' he whispered sheepishly.

Alex, who was tucking into his breakfast asked, 'What do you mean, you could not perform, Red Rum?'

'I couldn't perform … you know … OK I couldn't get a hard on… OK now. I kept seeing Julie and Little Josh sitting in a bath of Brussels sprouts.' The words slid slowly out of his mouth.

'Brussels sprouts…what was all that noise then?' He was confused.

Kinsey shrugged. 'When she fell asleep, I decided to rearrange the room a bit.' These words came out even slower, covered with pine-cones, which got stuck in his throat.

'What the fuck for?'

'To make some more space for her to put her clothes and things, it was completely the wrong design. Look Alex please don't tell anyone… Jac already calls me Mr Floppy.'

'I promise, but I think you need help. Perhaps you should start by going to Changing Room Anonymous.'

This intended joke completely fell flat.

'Another thing … I feel so guilty … I don't know how I am going to face Julie when I see her again. I feel like I've cheated on her.' Billy put his head in his hands. 'Oh no…what am I going to do when we go to her Mother's house for Sunday Dinner?…She always gives us brussel sprouts.'

'What are you going to tell her? Look, Julie, when I was away, I carried out some interior design in some girl's bedroom…she'd fucking divorce you on the spot…when's the last time you did any DIY in your own home.'

'How am I going to face her when I get back? I won't know what to do.' He considered crying.

He made the same pathetic noise that poor Charlie the Grass had made just before the Pozzoni brothers sliced the underneath of his tongue with a razor blade.

To be fair to Charlie, he was not the one who had dobbed Wayne Pozzoni in to the pigs over the grand ivory graveyard robbery, but he got mistakenly blamed for it and paid the price.

Half way through his breakfast, Alex slammed his knife and fork down on the table and confronted a whimpering Kinsey. 'I'll tell you what you are going to do. You are going to do the same as men have been doing for the last two hundred years. When you get home, you make sure the kids are not there, then you knock on the front door. When she answers you look deep into her eyes, drop your bags, take her in your arms, kick the door closed, unzip your trousers, rip her knickers off and give her one, right there in the hallway. Now, that's what you are going to do. So finish your breakfast and let's go and play rugby for King and Country.'

Kinsey nodded.

'Rearranging her fuckin' bedroom,' Alex shook his head and pointed a sausage at him and continued, 'you fucking idiot.'

They both started laughing. Deep down Kinsey thought that it was about time he went on another research trip to Amsterdam. This time he would take more 'erection' money and a single red rose.

Chapter 10:

'White Riot ... I wanna riot on my own'

Everyone on the team knew this sad day was coming, but it was still one hell of a big culture shock when it finally arrived.

Now, to all of the boys, playing rugby on a lopsided field in the Welsh valleys in the driving rain with someone shooting a double-barrelled shotgun in the air was quite natural. But attempting to run about in shorts in the sunshine, in a country that was knocking on the door of paradise, was completely alien to them all.

The Dowlais team walked with a great deal of reluctance towards the gates of this place known as Purgatory. It was the morning of the first day of the big rugby tournament and the moment most of them had dreaded. To make matters worse, it was an extremely hot day more suited to relaxing activities like drinking and more drinking than attempting any kind of physical exertion. They walked slowly around the perimeter of the rugby field. If life had been a big remote control device at that moment, then the fast forward button would have been deployed to skip straight passed the main feature and stop at the non-rugby adverts, probably at a beer commercial with some chicken wings on the side.

There was already a game underway. Evesham Old Boys had just scored another try against one of the poor, local sides.

'They look good,' Kinsey commented to Lusty.

Lusty wasn't watching. He hated watching other teams. He saw what he was looking for at the far end of the field. He waved to his two girlfriends. 'We'll see,' he answered Kinsey. 'They haven't played anyone with any fire in their belly yet.'

They walked up to the far end of the pitch, threw their bags on the ground and settled down to catch a bit of sun and perhaps watch the opposition. Lusty wasted no time in heading straight towards the wonderful sight of Miss Evil and Miss Wicked.

At the opposite end of the field, Lawrence Reid unpacked his binoculars from out of his brown leather briefcase. He always carried his brown briefcase everywhere he went. He had convinced himself that it was a symbol of sophistication and manly power, and he just knew it had a devastating effect on the fillies.

'I'll just see what the opposition are up to,' he suggested to Neville, his second in command and the guy who designed and hand-made all of their ties and handkerchiefs.

Neville was a wizard with the old needle and cotton. He was very much in demand and was often being poached by local clubs to come and design for them. One club even sent him a brand new Singer sewing machine with variable speed control and vibrating foot-pedal as a little tempter. On seeing the sewing machine in Neville's front room Lawrence Reid went berserk. It had a large red bow and a card attached. It was from those sly, underhanded bastards from Wyre Piddle. After throwing the unwanted present in the canal, he reminded Neville that he still had the photographs of a younger Neville, in kipper tie, star jumper and eight button flares, while dancing at a family wedding, and he wasn't afraid to show them to people. What a fashion shamer! Blackmail was a powerful tool when wielded in the right hands.

Of course, Lawrence had no intention of spying on the opposition. He had seen some lovely looking creatures joyfully parading their tight wares up near the changing rooms. If only he had his Triumph Stag with him at this moment. How easy it would be to roll back the soft-top, cruise up to the two exquisite looking bits of totty, and ask them to come for a spin. They would be extremely impressed. In fact they would be knocked-out. His sports car was nothing short of a guaranteed 'fanny' magnet, and with him sitting like the cherry on top. It was no contest; even Ladbrokes would not have accepted bets on such a dead cert.

'I'm now good enough to eat,' he told himself daily.

Ever since his wife left him he felt the urgency to slow his life right down or even try to reverse the process for a while. It was now more important that he looked his best, since the rules of his life had suddenly changed. Although he was pushing fifty, he still looked after himself. He always ate the right stuff and exercised everyday. But age was now starting to mug his face, so he had paid privately and invested in a little bit of Botox treatment, but only around the eyes where the wrinkles had taken root, and his forehead.

He had almost forgotten the day when the bitch had left him a note stating that, *'She didn't love him anymore and she needed to spread her wings before she was too old to fly.'*

The insult and the shame of her leaving him, the man who had dragged her up from the gutter, was too great to deal with. To make matters worse and the cuts to run even deeper, she had left him for a bloody woman. And not just any woman, no it had to be Mandy, the loud-mouthed, common barmaid from his local golf club.

'No wonder your bloody handicap wasn't improving,' he screamed at her, when she had come back for her clothes. 'You spent too much time trying to get a hole in one at the nineteenth with that dirty mouthed lesbian whore.'

She listened, and then slammed the door in his face and on his life.

It had made him physically sick to think that his wife was a dyke, a muff muncher, a cock dodger. He just hadn't seen that coming. He couldn't believe that Mandy and his wife were two saddlebag chompers. That was the last time he saw her, or, indeed, her saddlebags.

It took a couple of months for the shame and the twisted whispers to die down. He decided that he would get back up, dust himself down, and go conquer the world. He had always been considered a major catch and a bit of a playboy before he got married. He started to hang around his old haunts again. He appeared daily around the circuits where once he was so popular. The squash club and tennis set were now his favourite watering holes. He modelled himself on the Lacoste man out of the Grattan catalogue. Bright coloured shirts with a yellow cardigan strategically positioned over his shoulders were the height of his fashion statement.

Of course he stopped going to the golf club. Especially after the security camera video had mistakenly recorded Mandy and his wife romping around in the locker room showers, playing gynaecologists and nurses. The DVD was an overnight sensation. It was copied, pirated and sold under the counter at the local butchers.

'2lbs of tongue and faggot sausage with two slices of liver,' was the secret password used by the customers to obtain a copy of the horny illicit lesbian encounter.

At one point in time there was a queue of men in raincoats that stretched a mile around the small family-owned slaughterhouse premise. They were all waiting for the opportunity to purchase some local delicacies. In the end the police raided the little shop of porno. Along with extensive DVD copying equipment, they also discovered two YTS scheme teenagers frozen to death and hanging from the meat hooks with giant erections.

Mandy and his wife moved to Brighton. The butcher jumped bail and was last seen on a bus in Bristol carrying a shoulder of lamb and a pig's head.

This strange chain of events not only plunged Lawrence headfirst into a mid-life crisis, but a fully signed up middle-class, mid-life crisis. At first it took its toll. But after a while, he finally started to get his life back together and then there was no stopping him. OK, so he dyed his hair a little and touched up his pubes, just in case. He didn't think it was proper for young girls to be going down and seeing a big forest of grey pubic hair surrounding his lollipop. 'That would be disgusting,' he told himself.

In his eyes, he became the height of cool. He even had his own stool at the local wine bar. His oldest daughter told him to start growing up and find someone his own age, but he didn't want anyone his own age. He wanted to feel young again. The Peter Pan of the middle age set was ready to take on the world.

He became one of the rugby boys. Saturday nights saw him indulging in some harmless fun with his new rugger club chums. He liked this way of life. He wouldn't change it for the world, at least that's what he told his companions, and his reflection, on a daily basis.

Back on the field, he spied the two beauties leaning provocatively over the fence through his binoculars. He was just thinking the time was right to strike, when he spied a rather handsome, dark-haired boy strolling up to them. They proceeded to kiss him and one even grabbed his arse. Lawrence turned away and immediately focused his attention and lens back to his original target, the pack of stupid Welsh blockheads. He viewed the band of fat no-hopers, who appeared to be more interested in catching some sun rays than preparing for the game, which was kicking off soon.

Suddenly, he saw one of them taking a strange substance out of a bag and threw it to one of the other sunbathing boys. This brought the rest of the tribe to life. They were like dolphins leaping out of the sea trying to catch fish.

'Quick, they are all taking drugs. Steroids I think. Let's put in a complaint. Let's have them all drug tested. That fat one must have eaten about twenty of them,' he screamed at Neville, and passed him his binoculars.

Neville stopped unwinding a ball of wool and surveyed the scene. After a short while, he turned and said, 'Those are not drugs.' He passed the glasses back to Lawrence. 'Those are pork pies, I can see the wrappers.' He packed up his knitting pattern, wool and then stormed off.

'Pork pie's...Bloody pork pies. They are playing a game in fifteen minutes, what are they doing eating pork pies?' He thought he would make an official complaint anyway. That was definitely not in the spirit of the game. This was supposed to be a professional sport. 'Whatever next,' he muttered, 'Fish and chips at half-time.'

Big Ken felt his heart racing as he surveyed the immensity of the tournament. People were everywhere. Players in brightly coloured shirts walked around the fields or went through light routines at the edge of the pitch. Referees in green shirts were dotted throughout the crowd. But these were only secondary distractions in the eyes of Big Ken. The primary objective of his quick scan was to have first hand viewing of the opposition. And what a sight it made! Gangs of different committee-men of all shapes and sizes were out in force. It looked like a scene from 'West Side story' combined with a touch of 'The Phantom of the Opera.' The air felt thick with intensity. He knew that this was where all the talking stopped and the walking began.

'We are playing that Army side first and then two of the local sides after that,' Keith informed Big Ken. 'If we win all three, we'll get into the final on Friday. Heard the army side are quite useful, so we better get the boys well prepared before they go on.'

Big Ken looked across at his boys. They were all lounging around or fighting over pork pies. 'What a shape to be in', he thought to himself.

He informed Rob, the Physio, to start getting the boys warmed up. Rob, who was all track-suited up, was on his feet in a second and marched over to the flock of beached whales.

Rob was not really a physio. In fact he worked as an embalmer in his uncle's funeral parlour. He never really wanted the position, but it seemed to find him by accident. It had been the same story with his job at the embalmers. He only went to see his uncle about sponsoring him for the Christmas badger hunt, but ended up helping him, to stick back together and bandage up poor Mrs Rogers, who had died when a toilet pan had cracked and nearly split her in two at the local social club. It took five hours and ten firemen with breathing equipment to finally get her out from behind the toilet door of the social club. In the end, they had decided to form two teams. Each team went in to the adjacent cubicles to see who could get her out first. Unfortunately, both teams caught hold of different parts of Mrs Rogers and pulled at exactly the same time. She came out in two pieces from underneath the cubicle. It was not a pretty sight.

The toilet had never been used since. The strange thing was that every now and again, especially when someone won the jackpot on the bandit, the toilet system would some how flush, followed by a horrible scream. The world famous 'Bog-busters' were asked to come and check it out, but they refused, saying that they only dealt with ghosts in urinals or cold spirits in the washbasin.

The main reason Rob had been given the title of physio and main blood and guts doctor of the club all came about when he was the only person who could actually spell 'Physician' at the Boxing Day family quiz.

He was told on accepting the role that his main responsibilities would include making sure the teams were warmed up before a game; making sure the teams were cooled down after a game; making sure any injuries were correctly diagnosed and the correct recovery programme was implemented. He was also offered lots of training and development programmes to help him carry out his tasks.

The actual tasks that he carried out were far different and a lot less sexy. They included carrying the water bottle and sponge, checking that no one stole any of the Paracetamol and Codeine out of the first aid kit and, finally, washing the kit. At least it stopped him from playing with dead people at the weekends.

'Come on boys, let's warm up.' Rob started to perform stretching exercises in front of them.

'You must be joking,' replied Jac, 'It's fucking boiling already. We should be cooling down.' Pork pie crumbs shot out of his angry mouth.

When Rob had first taken over the job, all the boys thought that he was a nice chap and didn't pinch any thing out of the first aid kit. After a short while, they collectively decided that he was a prat and not only started to pinch stuff out of the first aid bag, but even pinched the first aid kit itself.

At that moment the Army side who they were about to play came piling out of their dressing room. They were all in identical kit, greased up and looking ready for action. They set themselves up opposite the Dowlais team and started to go through some warm up routines. The valley boys were oblivious to all the commotion, they didn't move or acknowledge them in the slightest. They just continued to lie back with shades on, listening to Reggae music, which was blasting out of their cassette.

'That's what we should be doing, let's get ready.' Rob tried everything to get the team wound up.

'Hey, Rob,' Alex piped up. 'Move out of the way, you are blocking the sun.' He turned over on his back and placed his shirt over his head.

Rob felt like screaming out loud or shaking the lot of them into some reaction.

'Have you got any cream, Rob?' Jac propped himself up on his elbows.

'Of course I have.' Thank God for that, thought Rob. At last, his positive attitude was having the desired effect. With face beaming he continued 'What do you want? Vaseline? ... Ralgex? ... White oil?'

Jac looked at him for a second, then towards the sun, then back in his direction, and said 'Have you got any factor fifteen…my fucking shoulders are burning.'

Rob looked at him in pure disgust. It didn't matter how hard he tried, he would never understand what made these idiots tick. He found it easier to hold a sensible conversation with some of his dead clients, than he did with this bunch of brainless morons. In fact most of his dead clients were more agile than this lot. Poor Mr Grey, who had no legs and had been found stone dead in his garden, a week after venturing out to the shops for some milk, could stretch further even in his dead state than Wigsy ever could.

He finally decided that he was fighting a losing battle and reluctantly threw some sun cream to Jac. 'Hope rigor mortis sets in,' he yelled and stormed away. He couldn't wait for the day when he would get his own back. It wouldn't be long until they were on that mortuary slab. He would be in control then. There would be no sun cream that day; just him, a dead, stiff, ex-rugby player and a big jar of embalming fluid. 'Roll on,' he muttered to himself.

He was completely ignored as he walked off. If it hadn't been for the arrival of the sun-cream, no one would have realised that he had been trying in vain for ten minutes to get them warmed up. He was like the man that never existed; the unwanted ghost with the stretching routines; the poltergeist with the smelling salts.

'Oh Jac, me next. My shoulders are red raw.' Wigsy stretched his hands out for the substance.

All the boys start to apply sun cream, except for the ones who were dancing to Bob Marley or sleeping. 'Stir It Up' belted out the battle cry. The Army boys appeared to all be in the zone and were training like wild animals in need of red meat.

The clock at the far end of the ground indicated that it was nearly time for the game to get underway. The sunbathing had finally stopped, but not until Jac had decided to perform a little bit of nude streaking across the field. There had been a great roar as he walked upside down on his hands for the last twenty seconds.

The team now started to make last minute preparations. It involved necking down cans of Red Bull, having their last fag and taking copious amounts of Effergene tablets. There were American troops in the Vietnam War who could not have prepared with greater precision.

Every last detail was to clockwork. There had been many years of going through this routine.

Next door the Army side were screaming like men possessed. Their captain swore at them. He slapped their faces and punched them in the stomach. After finishing an earth shattering count to ten, they exploded onto the field.

The expression 'chalk and cheese' had never been so aptly used to explain the difference between the two camps. To the Army side, this was not just a game; this was all out war. On the other hand, the Dowlais team saw it completely differently. This was an eighty-minute punishment that they needed to get over, before they could start to piss it back up.

They strolled out, talking and laughing onto the ground. There was a reasonable sized crowd to watch this game, including the Brigadier and his followers. All this unprofessional attitude and sheer unadulterated tomfoolery had not been lost on the Brigadier. He hoped they would have their come-uppance. He had even taken a little wager on the Army boys defeating this lot of useless, overweight, working class scum-bags.

The game kicked off to great interest from every corner of the ground. The Army team were really up for it and piled into the opposition. During the opening exchanges the Dowlais boys realised that perhaps a three-day strict fitness regime based on drinking large quantities of liquor and taking hard drugs for twenty hours a day was not the best preparation for this type of activity. In fact they quickly appreciated that if they continued to run headfirst into the headlights of the oncoming traffic in the fast lane, they would not only run out of petrol, but almost certainly collide with a large, fuck-off, petrol tanker.

The first scrum of the game proved a much-needed break and a chance for both sets of forwards to see what each other were made of. After a quick water break, both front rows eyed each other up, while the referee told them to engage. Two deep breaths and both packs smashed together.

'Good God, it smells like a brewery in here,' said one of the Army boys.

The scrum half tried to align the scrum so he could put the ball in and save his team from suffering the fumes of lager. Suddenly and without prior warning, Wigsy farted so loud, two policemen in the square of the nearby town, dived onto the floor, thinking that the anti-sunshine terrorist group had detonated a car bomb.

Both sets of forwards immediately got up, holding their noses. People in the crowd thought that a full-scale fight had broken out.

'Did you see that? He was punched on the nose,' an onlooker indicated on witnessing the sudden emergence of the both sets of front rows. 'Fight...scrap...bloody hell...they all were,' he cried in disbelief.

'Fuck me, Wigsy what did you eat last night,' Alex shouted at a smiling and slightly red-faced boy.

'You should have a fuckin' medal for that,' another Army boy added disgustedly.

'Yeah, the Victoria fuckin' Cross,' Jac stated. 'Or the Bombay Curry Badge of Honour.'

All the boys were still holding their noses, when one of the Dowlais boys started to heave. The sight of a fountain of yellow liquid flowing out of every facial orifice of the poor victim opened up the floodgates. It proved to be a catalyst for an explosion of liquids of every possible colour and thickness from various players on the field.

'Come on you lot.... Let's pack down.' The referee tried to encourage the boys to start to make a game of it.

'You fucking pack down ref. We are not going anywhere near that,' the Army boy said, pointing at the large pool of larger and chicken piri-piri vomit.

'OK... let's move the scrum over there.'

He had found a solution and they all moved about ten yards to the left. The referee called the Dowlais captain over. 'Look...anymore of that behaviour and he's off.' Everyone agreed.

Fifteen minutes into the game, and Dowlais were losing fifteen to nil. The outside half for the army team was having a belter. He controlled the game beautifully and was destroying them all by himself.

After another score, John the captain stared long and hard at each player behind the goal and angrily said, 'OK, fun's over. We did come here to play rugby. Now we need to sort that fucking outside half out and fast.'

John hated losing. 'Coming second best' was not in John's vocabulary. That's why he had been selected Dowlais Captain for the fifth year running. He was the type of person who had an inner strength that could bond people together and make them overcome most obstacles.

He continued 'Kins, next scrum you and Lusty just do him.' Kinsey nodded and produced a psychotic smile. 'The rest of us, just get ready for when it kicks off.'

They all slowly nodded and replicated a set of old familiar valley-style evil grins across their faces.

At the next scrum, Kinsey eyed up the Army outside half, who was now strutting around like he owned the place. Kinsey was balanced on the edge of the scrum, breathing hard, fists clenched and definitely very unbalanced. His world just moved into slow motion. In his mind this was not a rugby game anymore, this was survival and honour. The Army boys won the ball. It was passed to the golden boy, who in turn kicked it, way down field. As he was watching where the ball bounced, Lusty caught him and turned him around in one movement. The boy shrieked as the runaway train in the form of Kinsey headed straight at him. The human locomotive landed a right hook straight onto the poor boys jaw. As he fell, Kinsey followed through and fell on top of his victim, ensuring that his knee connected firmly with his exposed groin.

All hell broke out. Some of the Army boys who had seen the attack started to retaliate but the Dowlais boys were ready and waiting. What took place in the next five minutes was not pretty. In fact it was downright ugly. It was so ugly that even innocent bystanders shook in terror. They fought in two's. They fought in packs, some even fought with weapons. The Army didn't know what hit them.

To be fair, the Army boys had only been training to fight world terrorists for the last three years. The Dowlais boys had grown up fighting all of their lives. Even world dictators like 'Sad-Ham Insane' would have found it difficult to survive on a council estate built upon a foundation of weekly knee-capping and daily witch dunking. Sad-Ham's moustache would have made him an easy target for the barber gangs that roamed the estate after dark issuing unprotected short back and sides to anyone who stepped on the cracks in the pavement.

They all served a long and arduous apprenticeship in street fighting. It started when they were five or six years of age, scrapping for bonfire territory. Sticks and fire-lighters were the preferred weapons for the toddlers of the day. Then, there was the 'rival school' death matches in the yard, and finally, the blood-stained gladiator gang-land brawls with the bouncers of the infamous Brandy Bridge nightclub. This exposure to violence served them very well when it came to bust-up's on the field.

They fought like savage dogs. They jumped out of trees and slithered out of the drains. These were the real professionals. Fifteen John Wayne's in rugby boots and one common goal…destruction with a capital D.

The ref blew his whistle several times and waved his hands frantically over his head. Some supporters and committee-men raced onto the field, to either join in or stop the mayhem.

Wigsy walked through the chaotic throng, towards the cocky outside half who lay face down, writhing in agony. His objective was to finish off the poor boy by performing his famous 'belly' flop routine on him. He mastered this routine after years of practice, swallow diving on the opposition. His success rate was extremely high with his victim normally being stretchered off, never to return. Dale Murphy from Wattstown not only retired from the game after being on the receiving end of Wigsy's calling card, but was also unable to father children. This was really a godsend, considering the fact that there had been a history of battery-hen style interbreeding amongst the Murphy clan. This already left most of them born with only three toes on each foot and an unnatural obsession for custard creams.

The only real failure that Wigsy had experienced was in a local derby when he lined up Skinny Jones, for the mother of all belly flops. Unfortunately for Wigsy, Skinny moved out of the way just before contact. Wigsy hit the ground with such force that it measured 3.4 on the Richter scale. He landed face down in the mud and was unable to move. It was only because of the quick thinking of a youth, who fed a tube (which he was using at the time to siphon diesel from buses), into the ground, so Wigsy could breathe, that his life was saved.

The sharpest tool in the box that day was Lusty. On seeing the face print embedded in the mud, after the forklift had hoisted Wigsy up, Lusty devised one of his money-making plans. He rushed home, got some quick drying Polycel, and filled the hole left by Wigsy's face. He then produced an imprint of Wigsy's bomb face, and sold them to children for Halloween masks. He made a small fortune.

The ironic outcome was that four criminals used the masks when they held-up the local post office. It was screened on Crimewatch, and Wigsy became an instant hero. He and Skinny became big mates, until the police arrested Skinny for his part in the robbery. They also arrested the youth with the life-saving siphon tube for the same offence.

Wigsy reached his destination and like a Mafia hit-man carried out his assignment with chilling precision. The King was King no more.

When calm was finally restored, the outside half got stretchered off the field, still unconscious and very, very pancaked.

The game started again. This time Dowlais and especially Lusty rolled the Army team over quite easily and ended up winning thirty points to twenty. After this show of strength and aggression, mixed with a little bit of skilful teamwork, they went on to destroy the other two teams, who appeared to be more concerned with the underhand guerrilla tactics that would emerge than trying to follow the ball. The team they played last spent all of the game in a circle waiting for the mad Welsh Indians to attack. Dowlais beat them 60-nil and just for good measure, left their Captain with five arrows in his hat.

Behind closed doors, there had been uproar. The chairmen of all the other competing teams had gathered at a meeting with one item on the agenda, the disgraceful tactics of the Dowlais team. They insisted that Dowlais be dismissed from the tournament immediately.

After two hours deliberation by the Brigadier, it was decided that a final warning would be handed to the team and its supporters.

On the advice of the referee, Wigsy was banned from eating curry and pork pies before kick-off. This was a major blow for Wigsy, since he perfected his pre-match energy giving ritual over many years and was concerned that the local food maybe somewhat lacking in guff power. He need not have worried.

****

The after-match dinner was organised in a large room of the local rugby club. There was a stage at one end and a long bar at the other.

The entire tournament's competing teams were there, sitting around the room, nursing their bruised and battered bodies. Some individual's bodies were bruised and battered more than others.

As usual at these functions there was a bit of a singsong brewing. It was started by the host team. One of their members had just finished singing a typical rugby song about 'a girl called Bertha from Merthyr', who for some strange reason had a fanny on top of her head.

When it finished the compere asked someone from the Evesham High School Old Boys to give a song. The captain of the team got up like a shot and started to sing a very boring folk style ballad. All of the Old Boys joined in with great gusto.

'I hate this song…why do people like singing this shit?' Alex grunted to the rest of the group.

He remembered the story his grandfather once confided in him. He told him that there was a government intelligence top secret white paper that told the real reason behind the troubles in Northern Ireland.

'It was nothing to do with religion, m' boy!' he told him, as Alex wheeled him around the park on his Sunday visits.

'The real reason for all the bombing was that Ireland was trying to rid its shores of all their terrible folk-singers. If you examine the evidence, everywhere they placed a bomb, there was a folk singer topping the bill that night.'

The IRA apparently worked in conjunction with the British government to try to achieve the goal. They're biggest mistake was the night they blew up the Cardigan Arms in Londonderry.

On stage at the time, and regrettably blown to smithereens, was Seamus 'Fiddlesticks' Murphy. He was a larger than life character, who had a big mop of white hair and long beard, which covered his jolly face. Allegedly, he could play the mouth organ and sing at the same time. According to surviving witnesses of the blast, he had apparently been in the middle of one of his famous fifty-five minute banjo solos, when the bomb went off.

All involved with the assassination believed that the elimination of the Father Christmas of Belfast would end years and years of people singing depressing protest songs and wearing waistcoats with 'save the whale' badges attached.

Alas, the opposite happened. Seamus 'Fiddlesticks' instantly became a folk law martyr. Within a week, two thousand freedom folk fighters were not only born, but were restringing their fiddles and tightening up their Bodhran drums.

'The IRA and the Loyalists admitted defeat,' his grandfather sullenly said 'and the rest is history!'

'Why was it all linked to religion then, Grandpa?' Alex asked this wise old man, who was sitting on a park bench eating a beetroot sandwich.

'It was less complicated to blame something like religion, m' boy. Did you know that folk singers outnumbered Catholic's by ten to one in Northern Ireland and that's not counting the folk singers who just practice in small groups in their bedrooms?'

Alex listened to the manic warbling of the boy on the stage, and he cursed Seamus 'Fiddlesticks' Murphy and his memory. He looked around and sadly saw all of the Dowlais committee-men joining in the song.

'Give us a line, Lust,' Alex demanded.

Lusty produced the ball of white powder and all the boys on the table helped themselves to a giant lick.

Big Ken bellowed out the words to the song. 'I love this. This is what rugby is all about….communal singing.' He turned to Keith. 'I'm going to the bog; I have a turtle's head touching cloth. I'll be back in a minute.' He got up, unpicked his pants from the crack of his arse and walked into the toilet.

On entering he caught two of the younger boys lighting up a joint. 'Oh…. Give me that,' he bellowed at them. 'Now get in that bloody room, put your jackets back on and join in the singing.'

He went into the cubicle, he sat down, lit up the joint and started to get ready to play his favourite game of 'dirt bombing the U-boats'.

Back in the main arena, the terrible singer finished his song to the great relief of most of the normal people in the room, which had unfortunately been decreasing in numbers as the singing and the drinking progressed. The compere took the mike back. He looked around the room at the faces of the nervous team members who had not had the chance to pollute the airways yet.

'Thank you Howard, that was great,' he lied. 'Now how about having one of those lovely ballads from one of the Welsh teams…Dallas! We have seen today that you lot like to play your rugby hard but we know that you lot can all sing like angels. Can we have a singer please?'

It was around that same time, the Army outside half finally woke up in the ambulance, not knowing where or what he was, with several cracked ribs.

'Let's have Animal,' Jac shouted out.

'Jesus…Please no,' thought Keith. He looked violently around for Big Ken. He had panic written all over his face.

It was too late. Suddenly, all of the boys piped up for Animal like some mad, power-crazed lynch-party in the Deep South.

Animal, whose name had nothing to do with his love for God's species, was sitting alone by the bar. If the truth were known, other than his three bull-mastiffs, who were the ugliest dogs in the world, he detested all types of animals including humans. He had no friends. That was mainly by choice, not by design. He lived with his parents in a small two up, one down council house. He was a very private, deep person, who just happened to frighten the shit out of everyone, mainly due to the fact that he was six feet seven inches tall, had a huge shaven head and was the size of a small mountain. He has 'LIVE' tattooed across his forehead. It should have read 'EVIL', but he did it himself with illuminated Indian ink while looking in a mirror.

His dogs were his life. He ate, slept and talked to them every day. On special occasions he would buy six kittens from the local pet stores and they would all go up to the 'Council field' and play 'Survival of the Fittest'. Only the same four ever came back.

He had fallen into rugby by chance. It happened when Lusty saw him knock out the Pozzoni brothers, plus their fake Father and all of their cousins (which was a considerable number) one night during the annual council estate 'Heroin dealers reunion' weekend.

Next morning, Lusty was thinking what a great body guard to have, and tracked him down. After purchasing four lamb vindaloos, which Animal and his canine fiends ate together from one large dish, he talked him into doing something a bit more constructive with his life. A week later Animal became a member of the infamous club.

Over time he turned out to be quite a decent player. He would turn up, tie his dogs to the goal post and do whatever he needed to do. After the game, he ate faggots and peas, had two pints of shandy and walked home with his dogs. It was normally in the pitch dark, and poor pedestrians in the estate would move to the other side of the street, not to come face to face with the snaring pig dogs or the Frankenstein monster with the words on his head shining out like a lighthouse beacon. Then, after one particular game, Animal ate ten faggots, consumed four pints of lager shandy and for some reason sang a 'Sham 69' song, before walking home with the dogs. No one knew why. No one asked, just in case. This was his new routine after each game, even if no one really wanted to hear him sing.

'Animal…Animal…Animal.' The chant from the boys stirred the soul. People from other teams joined in.

'Mr Animal…the stage is yours,' the compare indicated, placing the microphone into the stand.

'I can't watch this,' Keith quipped and got up, looking for the safety net that was Big Ken.

Animal jumped onto the stage to a great roar. He whispered something into the compere's ear. The compere looked slightly confused, but went along with the suggestion. Animal walked slowly to the mike and the room went deadly quiet.

Big Ken had just about finished the last of the joint, but was struggling to get to grip with his air-raid plan. He sat there grunting and groaning, his head spinning wildly. A couple of piles popped out with all the strain going on. 'Bugger' thought Ken. He'd left his suppositories back in the room and the Portuguese toilet paper was like sandstone.

The compere knocked off the stage lights. Animal was motionless in the darkness. He slowly looked up, to reveal the illuminated tattoo on his forehead. There was a sudden loud gasp from the unprepared audience.

'This is going to be magic,' said Jac excitedly and necked back his pint.

Animal started to sing 'My Way'. But not Frank's version; no this was the full-on Sidney Vicious version. With anger in his face which was only matched by the pure aggression in his voice, he started to belt the tune.

'And now the end is near and so I face the final curtain….
You cunt I'm not a queer, I state my case, of which I'm certain.

He was standing very still, his words shot out from the darkness. He continued standing motionless until in his mind the guitar kicked in. The compere switched the stage lights back on. Animal was like a man possessed. He was pogoing around, legs kicked out and arms flailing. All of the Dowlais boys joined in, banging the tables. Half way through the song he stripped off his tee-shirt, exposing another home-made tattoo of three dogs wearing Doctor Martins on his back. His mother had done it with a knitting needle, while Animal was asleep. It was a treat for his twenty-sixth birthday. She told him that the tattoo fairy had visited in the night.

A giant roar went up from the crowd. He was having fun. It was nearly as good as watching his pride and joys ripping a badger apart.

He stepped out of his shorts without missing a key and continued the song in the nude. His todger was like a small python, about two feet long. Screams were heard from the area where all the wives and young children were seated. The Mayoress fainted, fell backwards, crashed against the chair behind her and somersaulted over the table.

In a grave in East London, Sidney Vicious opened one eye, smiled to himself and rocked the coffin from side to side.

Animal finished the song by jumping up and punching the air. Both fists went through the tiles in the ceiling, sending dust and debris down on top of his bald head and the rest of the stage. He put the mike down, walked off the stage, still in the nude, and sat down and finished his pint of lager shandy. The Dowlais boys congratulated him with cheers and pats on his back. The rest of the room was in complete silence, except for the moans of the Mayoress and the distant noise of bombs splashing onto their toilet targets.

'Thank you, Mr Animal. That was...umm...interesting.' The compare struggled to find the right words. A piece of ceiling tile fell and hit him on the head. 'Can someone please give Mr Animal his clothes back? I think that is enough singing for one night...goodnight.' He walked off the stage and straight to the bar.

Big Ken re-entered the room, quite pleased with the results of his toilet moonlight-bombing raid.

'Did I miss anything?' he asked Brian.

Chapter 11

'We'll need a bigger boat...Quint'

Kinsey walked back from the pool-side bar carrying four vicious looking drinks. The drinks really should have belonged in high heels, sauntering down the street of the Rio de Janeiro carnival. They were full to the brim with bright rainbow coloured-liquid, bird feathers, sparklers and umbrellas with plenty of attitude.

Alex, John and Lusty stared in amazement as he handed one to each of them to sample.

'Oh...I'm Spartacus, so when in Portugal, do as the Roman's do,' he said to the inquisitive recipients of the 'Coco-Cabaña' cocktails.

They all realised this was what touring was all about. Relaxing and talking bollocks with friends in a beautiful country with beautiful weather and a mug full of exotic beverage.

The temperature kicked its way to the top end of the thermometer. For some reason, the man who operated the sun had the four bars of its gas fire on and the central heating at full blast. It was hot. Even the workmen opposite filled the pool of the unfinished hotel and were jumping in and out, in between bouts of moving empty pallets from one space to another. It was the day after Animals solo performance and everyone had been taking in the sun's rays to the maximum at the edge of the pool.

Big Ken had summoned Keith and Brian. They had gone for a long walk to try to clear Big Ken's mind. It needed to be a long, long walk.

Kinsey tried to machete his way through the forest of items in his drink. His straw finally reached liquid and he sucked at the juice. 'Hey....not bad,' he said 'Anyway where were we? Oh yes, have you seen that girl, Christine, lately. What a bloody mess…looks like she's been to a health spar at Auschwitz.'

'I didn't fucking recognise her when I saw her last week,' Lusty replied, covering his body in sun-oil. 'She must be about three fucking stone. She had to walk around the drain in case she fell through. She's a right smackhead. I have been told that she was even giving blowjobs to school kids for their dinner money.'

Alex thought this through for a minute, and then added 'Can you imagine a line of school kids with boners in their trousers, queuing up outside a place with a sign over the top which said Christine's Tuck Shop.'

He painted such a vivid picture that even John joined in by adding 'Yeah, and she could replace the 't' in tuck for a big 'f'.' This took a few seconds to sink in, but was well received when it finally reached its target audience.

'Imagine that at dinner time. "A gobble please Miss and five black jacks," Alex said sharply.

Roars of laughter filled the afternoon air.

'I can't understand how someone can take that shit,' Lusty frowned, half way through rolling a joint. 'Just the thought of sticking a needle in me makes me faint.'

'What about that shit, then?' John pointed to the large spliff taking shape between Lusty's fingers.

'Big difference. This is natural shit, it's all that chemical shit that plays tricks with your head,' he replied. 'Remember that Sammy Sticks character; in his last few months he just turned into one of the living dead. It was no surprise when they found him dead in the toilet in the precinct with the needle still in his thigh…Poor bastard.'

'Poor dead bastard,' Alex added.

'Poor thin dead bastard,' John chipped in.

They could all recall the photograph in the local paper that showed the poor skeletal, shadowy figure jacking up in the bus station toilets; not a decent vein left to inject his deadly poison in to. His loyal dog lay by his dead master's side.

Kinsey explained to them all how a girl called Judith, who worked in the chemist, told him that there were about sixty people in Dowlais alone taking Methadone. Some of them were so fucked up, they were pretending to swallow the stuff, going outside, spitting it back up and selling it.

'What chance have we got?' John poured more fuel onto the depressing grey clouds that their conversation had inadvertently produced. Gone was the earlier light-hearted conversation that beamed a ray of bright sunshine. All their talk was now in danger of free falling into an environment of rain and thunder, which, if they didn't stop immediately, could lead to chat of work, or worse still…marriage.

Suddenly, there was a barrage of wolf whistles echoing around the pool. The boys looked around and there, walking towards their table, dressed in the smallest bikinis that had ever been manufactured, were Lusty's two companions from the night-club. Everyone, including the waiters and the builders, drooled out loud, eyeballs on springs. The sight of these two beauties, appearing to fall from the heavenly skies, quickly extinguished any further conversation about big, black Heroin clouds.

Gone was the drug addicted mood; it was replaced with two angels with slightly dirty expressions on very dirty faces.

'Hello Ladies,' smiled Lusty, who pulled up two chairs. He turned to the boys and introduced Miss Wicked and Miss Evil. The boys just smiled nervously, eyes facing the safety of the floor. The girls said 'Hi' in return.

'Where have you been ladies?' Lusty asked.

Polly, who was an extremely attractive brunette, answered in a very cockney Eastend type of accent 'We've been doing a bit of shopping, we're going home tomorrow.' She bent towards Lusty and whispered into his ear, but just loud enough for the boys to hear, 'And we just had two all over body waxes…just for you.' Her tongue darted in and licked his eardrum.

One cheeky builder, with good eyesight, fell headfirst off a scaffolding pole and lay pole-axed on the ground. No one bothered to help him.

Alex, and especially his earlobes, was extremely jealous. He tried to change the subject to save his ears from exploding. 'Where do you live, ladies?'

'I live in South London,' replied Sarah, who was also a stunner; a six-foot blonde with ice blue eyes and a body that could start and probably finish the third world war. 'And Polly lives just outside in Croydon.'

'What do you do?' Alex continued the interrogation. Every part of his anatomy was standing to attention.

Polly got up and bent over to take off her shoes. John's face was about twelve inches from her bottom. It was a bottom that armies would have been privileged to die in battle for, and mild mannered gentlemen would have camped out all weekend just for the brief opportunity to glare at its unnatural, magical beauty.

John got up immediately and dived into the ice cold pool. From the very moment his toe hit the water, he knew it had been a mistake. It was freezing. It sent his average sized penis into full retreat back into the warmth of his loin region. What a catch-22 situation to be in? Jump straight out of the pool and be called Mr 'no John Thomas'; stay in and possibly lose the use of his John Thomas for good (which was quite funny, since his name was actually John Thomas in the first place). So it didn't really matter which option he picked. He decided to jump out and lay face down on the sun lounger.

'I work for Virgin Travel,' said Sarah, 'That's why we are out here, checking out the hotels …and the talent. Polly works in marketing for the Mars Company.'

Kinsey had not said a word but suddenly burst into life. 'A Mars a day helps you work, rest and play.'

Everyone turned to stare at the advertising wizard in the checked Bermuda shorts. Kinsey got up and jumped in the pool. His name was not John Thomas, so he decided to suffer the icy cold water biting at his lower regions.

Polly whispered in Lusty's ear again. This time Lusty nodded his head and smiled at the two girls. A single wink from his dark brown eyes indicated he fully agreed with the ladies request. He called the waiter across and whispered into his ear. The waiter looked at Lusty, and then at the two beautiful girls, shook his head and walked off, talking to the sky.

No one said much. The sexual tension was all too much to bear. John got back up and dived back into the pool. The waiter returned with a bottle of champagne and three glasses. There were actual tears rolling down his face.

'Thank you, my man.' Lusty handed him some money, stood up, picked up the drink and glasses, signalled to the two girls and the three of them walked off arm in arm towards Lusty's bedroom.

Around the pool, you could have heard a pin drop. Everyone was frozen to the spot. Only their sad envious eyes moved. Tongues lobbed out like freshly caught fish that had been released from the nets and were break dancing on the deck of a fishing trawler. Boys, waiters, and builders followed the sex kittens who headed to their love nest. Only the water from the fountain in the pool moved. It jealously poked its ugly head out and shot arrows into Lusty's back. Lusty didn't notice or even if he had he wouldn't have cared a flying fuck anyway. He had a feeling this was going to be a good afternoon.

The waiter, who was crying earlier, wondered what the hell he had done wrong in his life. He had been married to his childhood sweetheart and they were together for over thirty years. But their sex life had never been that adventurous. In fact, the movement of the bedsprings in his house was now down to once a year. That was every Tuesday before Lent.

On seeing the handsome boy pluck the two lovely looking things up on this hot, sticky afternoon, something snapped inside him. It was like a bolt out of the blue. He decided that he would rush home and make mad passionate love to his wife, even though it was May 22nd and he officially still had another three hundred and thirty-four days and twelve hours to go.

He ran the two and a half miles home, planning his every move. He was excited. Passion seeped out of his pores. He heard noises from upstairs and rushed through the bedroom door. He found his beloved wife on all fours being back scuttled like there was no tomorrow by Malmo, the goat herder. At first he couldn't take it all in, especially the bell that was placed around her neck and the sight of Ralpho, Malmo's prized Billy goat, tied to the side of the bed. All year he had been waiting for his one-day to make mad passionate love to her, and while he was on yearly rations, a man who made soft goat cheese for a living was shagging her to death. At least that explained the reason for the constant mountain of cheese in the fridge and why all his flowers had no petals.

In a fit of rage he stabbed Malmo to death. He made his wife give him oral sex, and then stabbed her through the heart. He skinned the goat and then hung himself from the town's clock. A police sergeant cut him down. He didn't need to check his watch to clarify the time of death. The timepiece had stopped dead on 4.16 pm. The sergeant thanked his lucky stars that it was Tuesday and not Monday, or perhaps it would have been him laying dead in the waiter's bedroom, along side his pet Iguana.

Unaware of the poolside romance, which was taking place, Jac walked in carrying a crash helmet. Everyone was still frozen to the spot. Jac looked confused as he meandered between the boys and stopped at Alex's table.

'Oy...What's wrong with you lot?' Jac muttered.

Before Alex could reply, there was an almighty splash as all the builders jumped into the pool to cool off.

'He's amazing,' Alex answered but was not really listening. He was imagining what could possibly occur in that bedroom. He knew Lusty had a very sexually open mind, and the two girls looked like they could feel at home hosting a very naughty late night Italian game show. What a combination? It was a mix of whiskey, water and four tit-shaped ice-cubes.

'Who is?' Jac was still baffled and was starting to get slightly irritated with the zombie treatment he was receiving.

'Lusty, but you really don't want to know anyway.' Alex finally snapped out of his trance. He saw the crash helmet in Jac hands and asked, 'Where have you been?'

'We hired some mopeds...me, Ceri, Russell and Milky. We've been all around the town. It was magic. You should have seen Russell; he couldn't ride to save his life. He's crashed about forty times. We left the twat in a ditch about three miles away.'

Alex held out a rain forest drink. Jac took it and relaxed on a sun bed.

Out in the wilderness, Russell was in Panic Station City. He was desperately trying to get back to the hotel. The scooter seemed to be possessed. If he could have found a church and could have stopped the bloody contraption, he would have taken it in for a full exorcism and perhaps a set of new front brakes. Every time he tried to turn left, it would go right. If he beeped the horn, the lights would flash. If he actually tried to stop, it would keep going but only faster.

He found himself on the wrong side of the road. He just missed a waiter from their hotel, who was running in the opposite direction with one hell of a smile on his face. Russell hoped that the waiter would get what he wanted. He tried to wave to him, but wobbled badly. Cars, shoppers and tourists were coming at him at high speed. It was all a blur. He was the central character on the streets of 'Wacky Races' and a town called "Accident-ville" was just around the next bend.

Suddenly like an oasis in the desert, he spotted the flagpole of his hotel in the distance. He swung the bike across the road into the path of an oncoming bus. The bus screeched to a halt sending all the passengers somersaulting forwards towards the enraged driver. Russell apologetically nodded and wobbled again. The hotel steps were coming to greet him at a pace of knots. Just when he thought he had beaten the beast and tamed the scooter, the devil somehow pinched the handle bars and snapped the brake cable. Panic set in again, big time.

Inside the reception area, new arrivals were waiting to book into their rooms. Russell closed his eyes and tried to beep his horn. Of course, the lights flashed. The scooter mounted the steps and continued its journey through the reception, smashing through the new arrival's suitcases and continuing through the double doors and into the pool area. Everyone started to jump out of the way. Justin was standing with a flock of committee-men talking about yesterday's game. Most of the committee-men saw the runaway bike and jumped out of the way.

'Justin, watch out !!!!' Jac shouted out.

Justin was having none of it. He was pissed off with all this childish behaviour and it was about time he put his size five feet down. He placed his hands on his hips and replied in a loud voice. 'Who do you think I am?…I am sick and tired of these childish pranks. OK, come on car …hit me…come on hit me,' he screamed at the top of his voice.

Unexpectedly, he heard a noise behind him and turned around, just as the scooter, and Russell, smashed into him. The impact sent them hurling twenty yards through the air, plunging the pair head first into the deep end of the pool. There was a loud hissing noise.

Jac, who still had the straw in his mouth said, 'Well if you don't want my advice…you can fuck off then, you fat twat!!!!!!' He turned away and sat back on the sun-bed.

Everyone else rushed to the edge of the pool. The bike was at the bottom, Russell was swimming to the side, his crash helmet full of water and Justin laid face down floating on top of the icy water.

'You've killed him,' Kinsey said looking at Russell, 'you bastard … You won all the money.'

All the boys looked at Kinsey, and then looked at Russell who was smiling as he took off his head protection. They all dived into the pool and dragged Justin out. No one could manage the kiss of life, so they just turned him on his stomach and jumped on his back, until he coughed his way back to life.

'Throw the chubby fucker back in,' Jac demanded.

Big Ken, Keith and Brian were walking down by the sea front. Big Ken was overloaded with thoughts, most of them aggressive. Behind closed doors the Brigadier had given him a full dressing down regarding the appalling behaviour of his team. He needed to get out of the intense environment at the hotel in order to sort his throbbing head out.

They paddled in the sea with their trousers rolled up, eating three mint Cornettos.

'I'm getting too old for all this. I'm going to give it all up at the end of the season,' Big Ken announced to the other two.

'Don't be silly, Ken. You are the best chairman that we have ever had. There's no one else who could or probably would take over,' Keith replied.

'These boys are driving me to an early grave. They are getting worse. I like a bit of fun, but my hearts not in it. I realise there is more to life than rugby. There's so much Carol and me want to do.'

Keith's ice cream fell from the cone and plonked into the water. Brian tutted and Keith asked. 'What are you thinking of doing Ken? This club is your life.' He watched the dollop of ice-cream float away.

'I don't know, but something really exciting like getting an allotment or buying a caravan down Trecco Bay, something other than bloody rugby clubs. You can become Chairman, Keith.'

Outwardly Keith frowned. Inwardly he really liked the idea. 'Keith' He could see it up in lights; 'The new (and best) chairman of the rugby club'. Then things would change, he thought. Beryl would be so proud of him. He would start practising to take over as King as soon as he got back. He already put a down payment on a throne from IKEA, which he intended to have placed in the corner of the lounge.

Brian didn't like the idea of Keith becoming chairman, not one bit. He thought that he was an obsessive arse licking creep, who would wrap the club up in more red tape than it was already in now. He piped up, 'You'll have plenty of time for all that retirement stuff Ken. But you will miss all this and they are a good set really. Just a couple of rough diamonds, but every club has got its fair share.' Hopefully he could persuade the big man to hang on in there.

'A couple of rough diamonds? They're all fucking nuts. There's not a sane one in the whole group, probably including us,' interrupted Big Ken. 'I'm afraid to think what they are up to as we speak?'

'You worry too much. They are all probably just sunbathing or sleeping by the pool,' Keith said, just before a wave knocked him off his feet.

Big Ken looked at Keith struggling to get back up from the surf and thought 'What chance have we got?'

Brian, who read exactly what Big Ken was thinking, said 'If you go and leave the club in his hands ...No fucking chance!' He licked his ice cream and headed towards dry land.

Back at poolside, it appeared that the hotel was surfing on a wave of 'Benny Hillness'. It was manic. All that was missing was a little bald headed fellow being chased by some tarts dressed up as nurses.

A pick-up truck pulled the dead motorbike out of the dark depths of the water. Russell was positive the bike had spoken in foreign tongues before the impact. He was also sulking in the corner because he was

£60 poorer. An ambulance crew was strapping a much alive but delirious Justin onto a trolley.

Now with all the high spirits around the pool, it really should have been enough excitement for one day. In fact, if excitement had taken the form of a small child, he or she would now be tucked up safe in bed in fresh new pyjamas and a belly full of warm, hot milk. Unfortunately, it was not a small child. It was not even a glint in its teenage father's eye yet. So just when everyone thought it was safe enough to go back into the water up popped Matthew with a massive, blonde American GI soldier.

Now if there was ever a time not to introduce a strange character into the scene, it was at that precise moment. People were very unstable, because they were finally realising that abnormal people can not live in each other's pockets for longer than was absolutely necessary and the tour was dragging on.

'What's the?...Who's the?' Matt tried to ask on viewing the devastation before him.

'Russell nearly won the 'Killing Justin' competition,' bemused Alex.

Kinsey eyed the Yank with suspicion and asked, 'Who the fuck is that? Herman, the fuckin' German?'

'This is Dan the Marine-man,' announced Matthew, in a very proud 'I found him, he's mine' protective coating sort of voice. 'His ship is in port for a couple of days. I met him in a bar in town.'

'What a gay bar?' Jac asked.

'No, a bar bar.'

'You sound like a fuckin' sheep,' Kinsey added.

They all eyeballed the big Yank. He was big. He would have made Arnie look like one of the Teletubbies. He must have been six foot five, and nearly the same size in girth. His shoulders would not have been out of place on a big grizzly bear. He had blond close-cropped hair, cut to perfection and a massive desperate Dan chin protecting a set of brilliantly white teeth.

He informed his new mates he had been in this part of the world for three months. His ship had been patrolling the seas around these waters, keeping them safe from all the Arab terrorists. His voice was New Yorkish with just a touch of Southern, which made it very robotic. The boys circled around the good-looking marine like Indians around a wagon train, bombarding him with all sorts of irrelevant questions.

'Seen any action? Jac asked, his eyes lighting up like a Christmas tree.

'Plenty, man,' explained Dan 'Done some time in the gulf. Fucked those mothers up for good, kicked their arse all over town.'

He continued to indulge in boasts about his war activities for about ten minutes. He told them how he fought the Iraqi army single-handed and how he once escaped certain death by jumping out of an aeroplane. Due to the lads open mouthed inquisitiveness, this continued for a further twenty-five minutes. In the beginning it sounded quite good and fairly convincing but as the stories started to get more unbelievable, eyebrows started to cock up. They were all starting to wish he hadn't jumped from that bloody plane.

'I wish you fuckin' left him in that bloody gay bar,' hissed Jac.

'It wasn't a gay bar…it was a bar bar.'

'Fuck off black sheep,' bleated Kinsey. He could see straight through this bigheaded faker from the very first bullet shot from his star and striped tongue. Unlike Jac, he was not impressed one bit and he was going to make his point. 'Killed any allies recently, any friendly fire?' Kinsey taunted, trying to impersonate a tough American accent. It sounded more like Jim Wayne, a pipe fitter from Cardiff, than the famous John Wayne from Hollywood.

He continued his taunt. 'Look, there are some of the goods guys over there…lets go and blow them to bits.' He rolled about pretending to have been shot.

They all stared at Kinsey.

'Who are you all looking at? Warmongers…fuck them,' he protested his innocence.

Jac jumped in quickly, noticing that Dan just realised that these nasty remarks were aimed in his direction and he was beginning to flex his considerable muscle. 'Don't worry about him…he's having a bad day. Tell us some more stories. When are you going back into battle? How many guns do you carry?'

'Normally, when I'm in battle, I carry one rifle on my shoulder, one gun in my holster, and one gun in my boot.' He acted out the scene.

Kinsey took a long toke on the spliff and slowly said 'But you only got two fuckin' hands, mate!'

This was the switch that finally ignited both men's fuses. They jumped up and stared at each other. To be fair to the short Welsh man, this was one big beast, but Kinsey had fought and beaten big beasts all his life.

'What's your problem, man?' Dan asked, looking down at Kinsey.

'Look, cool down, Kins.' Jac was quickly between the two. 'Fuck off Kins and get the drinks in.'

Kinsey turned and headed for the bar, but only after bumping his shoulder firmly into Yank-boy's stomach.

As he walked out of earshot, Jac explained. 'He's been under a lot of stress recently; he's not normally like that. He's a bit of an anti-war protester, if you must know. His grandfather died fighting for King and Country.'

This was complete and utter tosh; his grandfather died from a spider bite while pinching bananas from the docks, but it was all Jac could think of that could possibly defuse this British/American incident.

Dan nodded politely but the veins in his arm and neck throbbed like a neon light over a strip joint.

Kinsey was livid. Fuck the American and fuck his mates if they listen to all that propaganda shit, he said to himself. He walked past the bar and went straight up to his room. 'Now we'll see how hard General Patton is,' he told the servant lady who was trying in vain, to clean their room.

He returned to the bar with a small bottle of cloudy white liquid and an evil grin on his face.

Lusty was by the bar with only a small white towel on, ordering some strange items from the bemused waiter.

'Hello Kins…what's that?'

'It's what I call "my American magic mushroom concoction" on the rocks.' He smiled and quickly asked in return, 'How's your day going?'

'Not bad, I have had worse,' Lusty replied. His eyes searched the shelves behind the bar.

He turned to the waiter and asked in a calm, clear voice for a large glass of ice-cubes, a large bowl of ice cream, and some fruit; preferably an orange and two bananas.

Before he left with his stash, he turned back and repeated, 'Give me a straw and two spoons.' He grinned and headed on his way.

'What's all that stuff for, Lust?' asked Kinsey. Deep down he was not afraid to ask the question but was more afraid of the answer he would receive back.

'Instruments of love, Kinsey, m' boy…instruments of love. I'll explain it to you when you are old enough.' He shrugged and turned away.

The waiter and Kinsey looked on in disbelief.

'Jammio Twatio,' the waiter hissed under his breath.

Kinsey asked for four bottles of the local lager. He drank some out of one of the bottles then poured the mushroom juice in. He headed back to the table and was just in time to hear the end of how Dan rescued the President single-handedly.

He handed over the spiked bottle to Dan, and offered him his hand in friendship and apologised for his earlier behaviour. Jac was impressed and thought that the doctor's medicine must be finally working. Dan went on to prove that he had skin like a rhino, by exploding straight into another tale about the time he captured some Moslem Fundamentalists in a canoe off the coast of Mexico, with only a balloon, a jelly fish and a dart.

After a long fifteen minutes, the boys started to notice that something was not quite right with Dan the Marine-man. In fact he seemed to be going completely pear-shaped. The noise from the workmen's equipment across the street seemed to be playing tricks with Dan's mind. The sound of the pneumatic drill transported Dan back to his days in the Gulf. His movements started to get twitchy; he constantly looked over his shoulder and rubbed his hands to warm them back up.

All of a sudden, Dan saw the waiter with a towel over his arm and all hell broke loose.

'He's got a knife,' he screamed and launched himself at the waiter. He knocked him into the pool. He grabbed another in a headlock and held a broken bottle to the poor waiter's throat. 'Quick men, you take the tanks and I'll hold our position on the beach…run…run!' he instructed loudly.

'Lets get out of here…he's gone mad,' shrieked Kinsey. 'He's fuckin' bonkers.'

'I can't understand,' Jac looked confused. 'Go and sort him out, Matt, he's your gay friend.'

'He's not gay…he's American,' Matt protested.

'He's probably on something. You know what these gay war veterans are like, addicted to drugs…and cock.' Kinsey was dying to laugh as he played along.

'Fuck that,' Matt said, just as a bottle thrown like a hand-grenade landed at their feet.

They all headed for the relative safety of the bedroom. They pulled up some seats on the balcony to survey the battlefield below. Kinsey, who was really enjoying his moment of triumph, put on 'Ballroom Blitz' by The Sweet on the CD player. The music added to the manic events below.

The carnage was like a scene from the Alamo. Dan barricaded himself in at the far end of the pool, hiding in between overturned tables and chairs. He had a headband on and his face was camouflaged with jam from the breakfast bar. He had a waiter tied to a chair. Empty lager bottles were strategically placed all around for the attack that was soon to come. The waiters and management of the hotel were trying to surround him. They used chairs as shields and threw fruit in their defence. The hotel manager and two waiters took off the tennis net and decided to charge Dan. Dan was sharp and he knew it was coming. He picked up two bottles and rushed the enemy.

On the balcony 'injury betting' on the battle beyond was taking place. The money kept coming in thick and fast.

Dan tried to swing across the pool, but slipped by the edge and the group led by the hotel manager snagged him in their net. The sound of police sirens broke the afternoon air. The police and waiters carried Dan out to the waiting van in the tennis net. He was upside down like a freshly caught tiger in the jungle.

Big Ken, Keith and Brian were walking to the hotel. Keith was still soaking wet. The police cars went shooting past and came to a screeching stop outside their destination. The men looked at each other and then went running up into the lobby.

They were met at the door by the sight of a big blond mountain of a man being carried in a tennis net, drooling from his mouth and covered in raspberry jam. The local flies were having a 'pay five Euros and eat all you want' party on the big man's preservative covered face. The big American beast was kicking and howling at his captives.

Big Ken leant onto the wall, waited until his breath had caught up with him and humorously said, 'Thank fuck for that, for the first time on this bloody tour, it's nothing to do with our boys.'

Keith sat down to wring out his socks.

Chapter 12

'Double, Double-Dealing'

The sound of the door being knocked was loud and booming. It reverberated for a lifetime around the old mansion. Nothing seemed to be disturbed except the elderly butler who treaded the old familiar pathway to the giant wooden door.

Lawrence Reid, the chairman of Evesham High School Old Boys Rugby Club, had been summoned to the residence of Brigadier Reginald Bracegirdle.

It was an impressive mansion over-looking the ocean. The butler showed Lawrence into a large study, where two other gentlemen were sitting in big leather chairs, smoking cigars and sipping cognac. Lawrence sat down in a similar chair and the butler offered him a cigar and a drink. They all acknowledged each other with a polite nod but no one said a word. They stared at the giant clock while waiting and wondering why the Brigadier called this strange array of gentleman together on this dark night.

The Brigadier was still soaking in the hot bath. He heard the loud knock but decided that he would leave his guests waiting for a while longer. He was still in the middle of his power nap. It had been a long productive night and he still had a smile on his face.

In his dreams, he imagined moving quickly through certain parts of his life. He studied at Oxford. Well not so much studied, as messed about for four years and then his father payed for some meaningless qualification. He had been born into rich stock. His father made millions during the shipping crisis of the early 50's. Lawrence had been a member of the rowing team, and of course, the captain of the dark blue rugger team. His greatest triumph was leading his team to victory against the light blues of Cambridge on that memorable day at Twickenham in '62.

He moved to Portugal for personal reasons, after his father made him a non-board executive of the company and caught him in a stationery cupboard with the office junior called Stuart. This basically meant that he would turn up for the annual general board meeting, drink some one hundred year old brandy, bang the table a few times, and take his large stakeholders cut without breaking into a sweat.

He decided that a good old-fashioned English title would open up doors in his newly adopted country. *'The Earl of Sherriff's Lench'* gave him the credibility that ensured his induction into European upper class circles would be impeccably smooth.

Pretty soon he became known to all of the in-crowd. He would ensure that the pockets of those people were lined with silver and their every need was catered for. This included lavish dinner parties, usually ending up in some form of sexual orgy involving whips and Gestapo uniforms, which delighted the movers and shakers of the rich set and soon cemented his growing reputation and power. His power was growing at a very unhealthy rate.

To the watching world, he was the well-respected gentleman of this society. But the Brigadier, like most people of standing, had a much darker side. What normal people didn't know was that he was the high priest and grand master of the werewolf underground. His mansion often held full moon festivals where goats were sacrificed and blood poured over the wriggling naked bodies of his guests, who howled at the moon while making love and howled even louder during mutual ejaculation.

It was a very secret club. Invitations made from human blood were hand delivered by servants to the high-classed clientele. The Brigadier would view all the midnight debauchery from a specially imported throne made from Maldivian palm bark, until it was his time to deflower the local village's fifteen-year-old virgins, be they male or female. He ensured that this had been written in to the constitution.

There was nothing better than deflowering a young tight fifteen-year-old while dressed as Lon Chaney in a hairy mask and hairier gloves.

Questions were soon being asked about the authenticity of the Brigadier and his title. A German Count, who was not really a Count but the son of an immigrant sausage maker, was the main catalyst behind the rumours. His nose had been dramatically put out of joint with the introduction of this upstart from Britain. A month later, the Count was mysteriously found floating in his swimming pool? His body was covered in human bites. All gossip about the Brigadier had been buried with the remains of the Count.

He decided to start the rugby tournament to keep up with his links to the past, and open doors to his future.

In the bath the Brigadier opened his eyes. He finally decided to reward his guests with his presence. The butler was already waiting by the throne with a glass of port and a lit cigar.

'Hello, Lawrence old boy, thank you for coming at such short notice. This is Police Chief Fernando.'

They shook hands. 'And this is Mario; he owns the café by the beach.'

They also shook hands. Lawrence now recognised the café owner and commented on how nice his food was.

'I heard about the tragic events at the town clock. Such a shame about Ralpho, I was looking forward to working with him,' The Brigadier added; a picture of the goat's bare flesh covered in hot sticky blood flashed into his mind.

Lawrence looked puzzled and tried to lighten-up the situation. He asked, 'Had an accident, did he?' with reference to the sad demise of this person called Ralpho?'

'It was skinned,' replied the Brigadier, whose slate blue eyes felt so cold on Lawrence's skin, that he developed an ice-burn on his chest.

The Brigadier sipped his drink and continued with his introductions. 'I have called this meeting tonight to discuss the big match on Friday. Before I continue, I would like to give you my thoughts, so you may understand the reasons as to what I am going to ask you to do.' He spoke in a slow deliberate manner and relaxed into the soft leather chair.

'This is *my* competition. It was *my* idea to start it seven years ago. It's been a success, mainly due to *my* hard work and I have enjoyed every minute of it…except for now.'

The audience looked on with deep interest, afraid to take their eyes off the man. They all heard the rumours and mentally decided that they would rather be a friend, not a foe, of this powerful man.

'What I am about to tell you, I hope will stay in this room.'

Of course, they all automatically nodded.

'I feel it is extremely important that this bunch of inter-bred, drug taking, half-wits from Wales do not, under any circumstances, win *my* tournament and get their dirty, beer stained hands on *my* trophy.'

Lawrence was sure beams of red light escaped out of the corner of those powerful demonic eyes.

'No need to worry, Brigadier, we'll beat them hands down.' Lawrence was quick to jump on this prudent bandwagon.

'But I am worried. When they actually play rugby, they are quite good.' The Brigadier was even quicker off the draw and firmly made his point by jumping out of his chair before adding, 'Although I have every confidence in your team, Lawrence, I do not like taking chances. I didn't get all of this by taking chances.' He signalled at the luxurious expensive finery around the room. 'And if I am going to take a chance, I would like to make absolutely sure that it is a dead cert. Do I make my self clear?'

'Crystal clear, Brigadier,' the police officer replied, 'but what do you want us to do?'

'Right Lawrence, I want you to ensure me that your team will be on top form. That means no nights out, drinking until the final…and feed them raw meat if you have to…but just make sure they are ready.'

'They'll be ready and waiting for that lot, Brigadier, you can be assured of that.'

The Brigadier then turned to the Police Chief and talked in Portuguese for several minutes. The Police Chief nodded in agreement and slammed his clenched fist into his hand and grinned.

Then Reginald turned to the café owner. Again, he talked to him in his native tongue.

The café owner smiled and replied 'Ah…no PROBLEM…the BEANS.'

'So we all understand what needs to be done to ensure success.'

They agreed, and then all relaxed back into the comfy leather chairs.

Lindo, the butler, topped up their glasses. He then went back to cleaning last night's blood out of the cracks in the cold stone floor.

Chapter 13

'Here comes ... Deputy Dawg'

It was an extremely quiet morning. For a change there had been nothing peculiar happening to write home about. Most of the party had gone to the local shops for some present buying. Keith, who didn't always act as dull as he looked, decided to purchase a couple of dodgy items at the last minute from Lusty. They were all wrapped and labelled up back at the ranch.

For the first time on this tour, he found himself with some quality time on his hands. Times like these were few and far between, so when it did accidentally come along, he grabbed it with both hands and sometimes both feet.

He liked to spend this time indulging in his favourite pastime of sipping back gin and tonics and losing himself in one of his many cowboy novels. Today was no exception, as he pulled up a sun lounger and sat down with a large G and T cocktail and a book entitled *'Gun Fight at the Last Stop Saloon'*.

Before he started turning the brand new pages, he wanted to analyse his performance concerning the lift-button duty that he had been given responsibility for. He surveyed a graph that he produced, which showed his performance against target. It concluded that it had been a great success so far. Out of ten attempts, nine actually found their exact destination, with only one miscalculation to speak of. He could not believe how Brian had made so much out of the twenty minutes that they had been stuck in the basement instead of being in the penthouse suite. Accidents do happen and he was sure this had nothing to do with his finger control, but the faulty wiring of these foreign lifts.

Just to make sure, he got up at three 'o'clock in the morning and rode on the deserted lifts until dawn. He randomly picked floors and depressed the buttons. He only experienced one mistake, when he had fallen asleep and found himself surrounded by cleaning ladies, with mops in hand, who were heading for reception. Satisfied that he mastered the art, he went to bed, only to be sharply awoken by Big Ken who had been sleepwalking.

After about an hour and three cocktails later, Keith started to nod off. All the sun, the booze and the stress had taken its toll. He floated into sleep and started dreaming straight away.

He suddenly found himself sitting in a Western style Sheriffs office. He was confused but secretly delighted with his new surroundings. He examined his cowboy clothes and grinned. He was wearing a red and black check shirt, leather breeches and white cowboy boots, which had his initials protruding from the front. A large black Stetson hat was balanced on his head.

A noise in the jailhouse made him turn around sharply. There was snoring coming from one of the cells in the jailhouse. After further investigation he saw the town's alcoholic sleeping on the threadbare mattress. The drunk looked a lot like Wigsy. How long had he been in here? What right had that no-good bum to jump into his dream; even if it was a small, no-talking role?

The door to the jailhouse burst open and in ran a cowboy, who resembled Justin.

'What the hell is going on?' he thought.

'Deputy Keith, Lusty James and his gang are in town and they have just shot up the sheriff. I think the sheriff's dead,' said Cowboy Justin, who was dressed in a strange mixture of cowboy outfit with traffic warden accessories.

'Quick, they are in the saloon having a drink. They said that they were going to rob the bank next and steal all the drugs and pretty girls.'

Deputy Keith picked up his pen and red book and headed for the door.

'You will need your gun as well, Deputy,' Cowboy Justin reminded his superior.

He saw the belt in the drawer and began to attach the holster and guns around his waist. It felt good. He took a large swig out of a cocktail glass which included a small fake umbrella. He headed out of the door with Cowboy Justin in hot pursuit.

The small Western town was strangely quiet. A large sign on the side of the drug store announced 'All presents for the wives and kids inside. Come on in'. Some tumbleweed rolled down the dusty street.

Deputy Keith could see the body of the sheriff lying face down in the dirt in the middle of the street. Deputy Keith was nervous. This was normally out of his comfort zone. The sheriff would always sort out this type of disturbance. He looked at Cowboy Justin who was egging him on. He could not turn back now. With heart pumping he finally reached the sheriff and turned him around.

The sheriff was actually Big Ken. He had a large bullet hole in his large head. In the hand of the deceased was a claim for a small caravan up near the cemetery.

'He wouldn't need that,' thought Keith. He tucked the deeds into his shirt pocket.

Cowboy Justin arrived and slowly took the sheriff badge off Big Ken, made the sign of the cross and placed the shiny badge onto Deputy Keith's chest.

'You are the sheriff now…Go and sort those James' boys out Sheriff Keith. Go and sort them out for the sake of the club.'

The pin of the badge pierced his skin. Deputy Keith slapped Cowboy Justin across the head. 'You stupid rich prat,' he shouted, tears welling up in his eyes.

Keith, the newly appointed sheriff straightened up and slowly walked in the direction of the last chance saloon. He touched the badge. Beryl would be so proud of him. Now perhaps his in-laws would treat him with the respect he deserved. If they didn't he would throw them in the slammer with Wigsy until they did.

From the corner of his eye he saw something moving. He quickly turned his hand on his pistol. He breathed a visible sigh of relief on seeing Matt dressed as an Indian. He had war paint on his face and he was wearing cut off pyjamas. Lines of similar dressed people were parading behind him, like some Indian tribe catwalk. The sheriff and the Indian acknowledged each other.

He continued on his journey. As he got nearer the saloon he swore that he could hear 'Goodbye to Jane' being played on the piano.

Suddenly from out of the swinging saloon doors, stumbled Lusty James and his gang, Gold Tooth Alex, Quick Fire Kinsey and Black Hat Jac. They saw the new sheriff and stood in silence.

'Lusty James, you are under arrest for the murder of Sheriff Big Ken.' The words from Sheriff Keith's mouth made his heart beat at a million times per hour. If he survived this, Beryl would be very proud of him; so proud in fact she may even give him a blow-job (without her teeth in).

Lusty laughed out loud and added menacingly, 'Deputy, you'd better go back to making up rules for each committee meeting and leave this to real men.'

Sheriff Keith started to walk away. He looked at Big Ken lying there on the floor. What he would have given now for the support of the big man. Brian, the owner of the bank, was at the window shaking his head in disgust. All eyes in the town were now fixed firmly on his every action. To his great surprise he found himself turning back to face up to the gang.

'You're talking to the new sheriff now Lusty…so you'd better come quietly.'

The tension in the air was heavy. The five men stood face to face. They waited anxiously to see who would make the first move. Quick Fire Kinsey, who was only living up to his name, decided to go for his gun, but Sheriff Keith was too fast and drew his gun and fired.

When the smoke from the gunfire cleared, Lusty James and his gang were all laying face down, dead on the ground. There was a silence, and then all of the town folk came rushing out of the shops and doorways. They picked Sheriff Keith up on their shoulders and paraded him around the town. He wished Beryl was there to see it.

They headed for the town's brothel, which had a Jacuzzi outside with two bare-chested, corset wearing saloon girls, relaxing in it. They waved for their new hero to come and join them.

Back in the real world, Keith was unaware that Lusty and his gang had arrived back at the pool. They saw Keith dozing on the sun-bed and decided this was too good an opportunity to miss. They picked him and the sun lounger up and were slowly edging towards the swimming pool.

Back in Golden Nugget town, a smiling Sheriff Keith was gently being lowered into the steaming hot Jacuzzi with the ladies of sin. Perhaps he wouldn't tell Beryl about the last bit.

In reality, Keith was thrown feet first into the ice cold Portuguese swimming pool. Dreamland met reality-city. Keith woke up sharply and was startled by the sheer coldness of the water. He swallowed gallons of the stuff, and splashed and spluttered towards the edge of the pool. He clambered up onto the side. He looked up and standing over him licking a 'Fab' ice-lolly was Big Ken.

'I leave you in charge of the fort for two bloody minutes and the natives have stormed the fuckin' castle already.' Big Ken turned away thinking that he would never be able to leave his club in the hands of these idiots.

Brian stood there shaking his head in disgust.

Back in the swimming pool, the paperback novel floated on top of the water next to a large black Stetson hat.

Chapter 14

'Do you need some plastic lovin?'

The four boys were back in their favourite nightclub of the tour. The hours were now quickly ticking down towards the final game. Another drink and drug-free curfew had fallen on more deaf ears and even dryer throats. The entire room was buzzing yet again. Half of the occupants were high on the innocent excitement of the music and its rhythm. The other wilder side, were happily being induced by the chemicals that exploded psycho toxic flares into their minds. Of course, the gang of four weren't content to take just one side only. They continued to bounce back and fore on either side of the trampoline of fun.

Lusty was perched by the bar, chatting away to a beautiful coloured girl. His two original beauties had already flown back to the fair country, so it was time to try to unwrap some dark chocolate and see if he could sample some of her Curly-Wurly. He was certain to be spilling some of his Milk Tray.

Jac was on the dance floor with his gymnast, their tongues sword fencing at ten paces. Alex and Kinsey were sitting at the back of the room, with the Scottish girls, whom they had taken home a couple of nights before. They were all laughing and enjoying themselves. Bowie's 'Young Americans' blasted out of the speakers.

'Billy, don't drink too much tonight,' Danielle turned to Kinsey and whispered quietly.

'Who are you? My mother,' Kinsey snapped back, nearly letting his true colours slip. 'Don't worry about me… I can hold my drink.'

He necked his third southern comfort without it touching the sides.

'I'm not worried Billy.' She lowered her voice, 'I want us to make love tonight…I am going home tomorrow and I want to feel you inside me before I leave.'

These words sobered Kinsey up immediately. A panic bolt shot straight across the emergency door that protected his closed mind. He shook, and then plunged headfirst back into that bath of Brussels sprouts. This time it was even worse. In his mind's-eye, he pictured his child crying in the bath of green vegetables. Also his mother-in-law was sitting in their pointing at him, along with some white haired priest, Maxy the Tramp, and for some reason, the fat, sweaty bloke who worked in the petrol station in the high street. It was too bizarre for words.

He made some excuse and he headed to the toilet. He quickly gestured for Jac to follow him immediately. Jac rushed in thinking that perhaps Kinsey had a spot of aggro.

Before he could speak, Kinsey, who looked like he had seen a ghost, asked, 'Have you got that liquid Viagra with you?' His hands were shaking and he was acting very peculiar.

'Yeah!' He handed him the bottle. 'I don't need it…she only needs to look at me, (with reference to his gymnast) and I get a hard on like a nuclear sub. But don't take too much,' he warned his mate before heading back to the direction of the music.

These last words were lost on Kinsey. He was only concerned with getting out of the imaginary pool of impotence, and getting all the weird people out of the Brussels Sprout bath in his head, and finally acquiring an enormous hard-on.

He went into the cubicle to examine the bottle. It looked a bit misty, but in his life he had drunk things that made this look like Earl Grey tea. He winced when he remembered the time he had drunk out of the toilet bowl in Sticky's house, during the water strike of '85. That was the wrong night to have experimented with Amphetamine fish cakes.

He then examined his old boy. 'This stuff needs to be top-drawer,' he thought to himself, and then just to make sure, he downed at least three-quarters of the contents. He put the rest in his jeans and went back to join his girl with the self-confidence that his flute would soon be playing any tune, in fact, a three to six hour symphony.

They continued talking for about fifteen minutes; Alex and Laura were on the dance floor doing some strange karate dance movement. Lusty left arm in arm with his prize. Ebony and Ivory would tonight be playing in perfect harmony. Jac was by the bar, watching his girl bend over to touch the floor. X-rated thoughts raced through his mind.

Kinsey started to feel strange and lost all colour in his face. His throat felt dry and goose pimples the size of lemons, in jack-boots, marched all over his body. He tried hard to get a grip.

'Are you OK? You look terrible.'

He wished she told him something he didn't know.

'Yeah... I think so,' he started to slur his words.

The music had somehow actually got inside his head and was shaking his senses to bits. 'Can we go and get some fresh a....' The words stopped with a worrying thump and Kinsey suddenly slumped to one side, foaming from his mouth.

He was unconscious. The scream from Danielle's pretty mouth was loud enough to cause the record on the turntable to jump.

'He's dead, he's dead .... Billy ... Billy.'

Alex and Jac ran over quickly. It all felt as if they were moving in slow motion. The scene was just too difficult to comprehend with their best mate out cold and in obvious trouble.

'What have you given him? What has he taken?' Danielle screamed back at Jac.

He wished that Lusty was around. He was one cool fucker in situations like these. He often wondered if it was because of the times that Lusty would return home from school and find his mother in the clutches of yet another suicide attempt. A slit wrist or a trail of sleeping tablets was often her way of crying out to the world for help. Lusty, being the only man in the house, had to deal with shit like that and then carry on with his life. He never complained or shouted at his poor mother, he would clean her up, put her to bed and then make his own tea. What a hero!!

'He just fainted. I only told him I wanted him to make love to me,' Danielle told the whole pub.

She was out of control. 'He's dead. Billy's dead!' she screamed.

'Shut up, you stupid bitch ... Shut up!' Jac was in no mood for all this crying malarkey.

Alex was well aware of this, and asked Laura to take her friend outside for a while. He then started to slap Kinsey's face.

'Kinsey, can you hear me. Come on Billy, wake up. Can you hear me?'

Jac rifled through his jeans and found the almost empty bottle of Viagra.

'Oh fuck, he's taken all of this.' He nearly poked the bottle in Alex's eye.

'You are only supposed to take a little bit, you idiot.' Jac started slapping him, more out of frustration than pity.

A bar man came over to check his pulse. Alex looked at Jac in disbelief. A worried look appeared on the man's face. He told a woman behind the bar to phone for an ambulance and quickly. Pandemonium broke out. Girls were screaming, Jac was crying and trying to wake him up. Alex sat down in silence.

The ambulance finally arrived. It had only taken a few minutes, but it seemed like a lifetime to the two distraught friends. The paramedics checked him over and placed an oxygen mask over his face. They gingerly lifted him onto the back of the vehicle. Alex and Jac climbed on board. The medic went to tell them that they couldn't ride in the ambulance, but one look in their eyes and he knew that wild horses would not have dragged them off.

Before it sped off, Alex shouted to Laura to find Lusty and tell him what happened. Normally he wouldn't have allowed a girlfriend go anywhere near Lusty James. That was not because he didn't trust

Lusty. He trusted him with his life. It was the females he didn't trust. But this was different. This was an emergency.

The A&E waiting room was cold and clinical. It reminded Alex of a thousand waiting rooms, which he had unfortunately sat in over the years. They were all the same throughout the world. White tiles with polka dot dark red bloodstained wallpaper; a medical McDonalds, but with surgical gloves and doctors, instead of cheeseburgers, Ronald McDonald and spotty teenage waiters.

Jac and Alex sat in silence. A Portuguese family were crying rather politely in the far corner of the room.

'I've killed him Al, I've killed him,' Jac cried.

'Don't be so stupid, he'll be OK,' Alex said more in hope than optimism.

'What if he dies? I've known him since we were three. We grew up together. What if he dies? What I am going to tell his mother and father, Bernard and Mary.' Jac turned and punched the chair.

'Look, he's not going to die.'

Jac started to cry. Tears fell straight onto the floor. He added, 'I love him to bits, what am I going to say to his brother?'

He tried to wipe away the droplets of emotion around his eyes. 'Oh what about his dog Lucky?…he loved that dog.' He broke down sobbing uncontrollably. 'What about his sister, Denise? And his goldfish, Harry?'

Alex reached across and squeezed his mate's hand tight.

Loud footsteps echoed down the hallway. They both looked up, hoping that it would be Kinsey bouncing towards them, swearing like a trooper, or maybe Lusty coming to the rescue. It was neither. The footsteps belonged to a young looking chap in a white coat. He was carrying a clipboard. For some reason they didn't think that he could be the doctor. Perhaps it was because of his age or it could have been the fact that he had a pair of training shoes on.

They were both very surprised when he introduced himself in perfect English, as Doctor Manolo.

'Are you Mr Kinsey's friends?' His voice was soft and seemed to somehow belong within the surroundings of the hospital.

They both nodded.

He stared straight at them and continued 'Do you know what Mr Kinsey has taken?'

'Yes Doctor,' replied Jac. He wished he could have answered 'No' to the doctor's question. 'I was told it was supposed to be liquid Viagra.'

Although he spoke good English, the doctor struggled to recognise and understand the meaning of Jac's reply. 'What is this liquid Viagra?' he asked rather befuddled.

If Jac thought that the first question was hard to answer, there wasn't a college or university in the land, which could have prepared him for the latter. He thought long and hard before answering. He was acutely aware that part of him wanted to ask the doc 'Why the bloody hell hadn't he heard of Viagra?' Was it because every man in Portugal's muscle pecker was in excellent working order? He had heard many rumours that it was something to do with the olive oil or because the swimming pools were so cold.

He resisted asking the doctor the question until a more appropriate time.

'Who gave it to him? And what does it do?' More questions which were piling emotional straws onto the already overburden back of Jac's invisible camel.

'It's this doctor.' Jac showed him the bottle, which contained the remains of the stuff. 'I gave it to him. I don't really know what it's supposed to do? His last sentence appeared like a noose around Jac's neck.

The Doctor's eyes gave away his thoughts. Jac felt like taking the pencil from out of the doctor's pocket and piercing them, so he could escape their glare. Jac thought that the doctor was lucky that Kinsey was not in the hot seat, or he would be wearing an eye patch before he could say "stethoscope". He wanted to laugh, but he didn't.

The Doctor took the bottle, 'I need this.'

Before he departed to get it tested he turned and added purposely, 'Call yourself a friend. Imagine giving him something when you don't know what it is or does. I don't know why I bother to waste my time.'

Alex jumped feet first into the discussion to try and deflect some of the pressure off his mate, 'Will he be all right, Doc?'

'He has not regained consciousness yet, only time will tell.'

He walked away. The two boys felt as though they had been smacked around the head by a baseball bat swung by one of the New York Yankees. Jac couldn't feel his legs. He broke down again, but this time even the family in the corner could feel his grief.

Lusty came sprinting into the room, a concerned look spread over his usually chilled-out face 'What the hell happened? Laura said she thinks he is going to die.'

Even Lusty appeared stressed, which was never a good sign.

'I've killed him, Lust,' Jac muttered 'It is all my fault. If only I'd got that bloody speed instead of Viagra. I'm going to kill Danny for giving it to me.'

His mind flashed an image of Danny, the estate drug supplier, handing over the bottle and explaining how the liquid was the latest craze, which was taking Cardiff by storm.

Why did he take it? What the fuck did he think he was going to do with the fuckin' stuff anyway? Sniff it up his fuckin' nose. He vowed at that precise moment that he would give up all this shit. No more drugs. No more being the village clown. Better still, no more the village clown on fuckin' drugs.

'He drunk all of the liquid Viagra and he just collapsed,' interrupted Alex gravely. 'It doesn't look good, Lust.'

They went back to sitting in silence. They were staring at everything except each other. Hearts longed to hear the manic, aggressive yells of Kinsey throwing a wobbly. But their minds were too busy thinking the worse.

'What if he dies? What are we going to do?' Jac just couldn't let it go. His over-emotional mind was cart wheeling out of complete control.

There was another pause. 'We will have to change the shape of the coffin for starters,' drawled Lusty.

The rest of the boys looked up in surprise.

'Look,' he continued, 'if he did drink all that Viagra and he does die, I bet he's got the biggest hard on in history. They'll never get the coffin lid closed.'

One of the main reasons why the four of them had been such great friends for all this time was their ability to laugh in the face of despair. Even though one of the team was lying on his deathbed, the other three were imagining what the funeral would be like. Especially, the sight of them carrying the coffin, with a big phallus shaped extension on the top. Although there were many who would have found the humour bordering on the boundaries of bad taste, it was a priceless moment in their world.

'Come on lighten up,' instructed Lusty. 'He's not going to die; he's as hard as nails. No pun intended.'

They all burst out laughing. The family opposite muttered something about 'British' and 'Crazy horses', then went back to their own private grieving.

The artificial joy was short lived before Jac started to cry like a baby again.

The hourglass moved slowly during the next couple of hours. The conversation consisted of lots of small talk followed by more small talk, followed by no talk at all.

Alex hummed the song *'Drug's don't work'* quietly to himself. Jac curled up into a ball to block out the nasty, nasty world. His mind wandered back to some of the good times that Kinsey and he had been part of.

He remembered the first time they had really become mates. It was an under seven's football game. A boy with a latent talent for kicking smaller kids booted Jac up in the air and ran down the wing. Within a second, Kinsey had slid into the boy, sending him flying into the fence. The boy never kicked a ball or someone's ankle again. In fact, he grew up designing children's soft toys for Argos. Kinsey winked at Jac as he held out his hand to pick him up off the ground. It was friendship at first fight.

He smiled at the memory of having their first fag behind the sports centre and getting caught by the fearsome Mr Lee. Kinsey tried to hide the lit cigarette in his uniform pocket. It burst into flames as they entered the head-masters office. After the compulsory six of the best from Mr Lee, Kinsey's mother made him wear the holey blazer for the entire term. He had more fights in that period than Larry Holmes did in his entire career.

He glanced across at Lusty and Alex and his thoughts travelled back in time to when the four of them put on their first punk record. It was *'Neat Neat Neat'* by the Damned. No one in his mother's front room that day ever forgot the experience. They pogoed around to the same song all afternoon. By the time his sister came home from school, they had transformed themselves into home-made Punk Rockers on a mission to change the world. That night they all smashed up their collection of Deep Purple albums and their life was never the same again. That first in your face 'fuck the world' lick from the guitar proved to be the bloodline that made them life-long brothers, forever. Those were great times, never to be replaced.

His happiness switched back to sadness when he played back his best man's speech at Kinsey and Julie's wedding. He looked so uneasy in his top hat and tails. The priest nearly came a cropper when he asked 'Do you William '2 amp' Kinsey take this woman to be your lawful wedded wife.' If looks could kill, Kinsey would have been on a manslaughter charge that day for murdering a holy man.

It all turned out great in the end. He did marry Julie and they were living happily ever after, until his best man had bloody well killed him. Tears flowed again, but this time much faster, until the boys all dropped off to sleep on each other's laps.

Alex felt a tap on his shoulder. He slowly awoke from a deep sleep. Through a pair of throwaway eyes, he found himself staring at a face populated with blond hair and a big handlebar moustache. He recognised him from somewhere. It finally occurred to him that it was the busker they had passed earlier in the day. He wondered why he was at the emergency unit in the first place. Perhaps his plectrum had accidentally lodged underneath his fingertips or his guitar wire had snapped and gashed his face. On further inspection he noticed no blood or bandage. Next question that popped into his mind was why was he waking him up? Was it because he hadn't put money into the busker's hat? If he had been perfectly honest, he didn't think that his singing or his strumming merited him parting with his hard-earned cash.

Suddenly, the mouth underneath the busker's big moustache spoke 'He'll be OK, have faith.'

By the time Alex rubbed the sleep from his eyes, the busker was already walking away, strumming on his guitar. He sung loudly, 'You have got to have faith, faith, faith,' as he marched out of the exit door and disappeared.

Alex lay there without moving, wondering what to make of the guitar playing vision with the encouraging, but encrypted message.

A set of new footsteps woke the other two boys from out of their slumber. A man, who looked like he made a good case for being a priest, came out from behind the hospital ward door. He must have been about two hundred years old. He was kitted out in the usual black attire with a single white neck brace. On his feet he wore a pair of running shoes.

'Was there a clear-out sale at the local shoe store, or was it the normal work-wear of the white-collar workers of this area?' Alex thought to himself.

He sat down next to them. His face was solemn with lifelines that could probably tell a thousand tales.

'Can I have a word with you boys?' He looked worried and added, 'Is he a Catholic?'

The safety and hope that their earlier comfort sleep had given them was suddenly shaken out of the boys and replaced with a bed of sharp nails and home truths.

'Yes, Father. He is.' Alex was first to respond.

'Do you know if he's practising?'

'He comes training twice a week and goes for a run on the weekend,' Jac replied without really listening or making sense of the question.

'He doesn't mean that.' Alex jumped in again for the umpteenth time that day. 'Don't know Father. Why do you ask?'

The priest fumbled with the figure on the cross that hung from his neck. The many lines on his face had all joined up into one, which made him appear as if a tractor had unearthed a deep furrow in his forehead. Perhaps Russell and the Devil scooter had somehow driven into the room at that moment and diverted across his face.

Even though he said these words many times over, it didn't make it any easier. 'I need to administer the last rites'

Jac exploded into an avalanche of snot and tears. He sunk to his knees and reached out to hold the priest's large honest hands. He expected them to be cold, but they were warm and very sweaty. Alex immediately stared at Lusty. He needed Lusty to show him a sign that it would be OK! Lusty was normally a rock. 'The rock with the cock' he often called him. But this time he saw fear in his mate's eyes. Now he felt scared.

He asked, 'Last rites, Father? Can we see him? Please, Father please?'

'I'm sorry boys I don't think so, but I'll ask the doctor…I promise. Now lets all get down on our knees and pray.'

They all joined Jac on the floor. A circle of hands were made with their prayers bonding together their grief. Tears rolled down all of their faces.

'Come on, let's be strong.' The priest tried his best to ease the situation in this difficult time. 'Let's be strong for him. Let's pray together. Dear Lord…we ask you to spare our son…you can see all the love in this room…his friends need him, please make him get up and walk back to us. Please do not take Emilio, please let us …'

'Emilio...Who's Emilio?' Alex stopped praying. His eyebrow lifted towards the ceiling.

A petite nurse, who had a pair of normal shoes on, came rushing up to interrupt the prayer ceremony. She whispered to the priest in Portuguese and pointed to the family in the other corner. The boys could just make out the words 'Emilio's family are over there, Father'

The priest jumped up dramatically to his feet. He bowed his head, which was now the colour of scarlet and announced, 'Sorry boys, hope your friend will be all right.'

He walked towards the crying family, his face changed from deep red to 'I have bad news' pink.

Alex was first to react to this revelation 'Nurse, how is our friend Billy Kinsey?' he asked, a faint smile cut across his face.

'I will go and find out for you,' she said pleasantly and disappeared.

Kinsey found himself being led to a rather uncomfortable looking chair by a person who was a cross between a bag lady he knew from Sheffield and Liberace. She looked strange, but he felt even stranger. He scanned his new surroundings. He was sat at a large roulette table, which included a massive roulette wheel and betting mat.

An even more bizarre array of people sat motionless around the table. They were all shapes, sizes, colours and ages. Including himself, he counted at least twelve faces staring out at nothing. All the seats were occupied except one on the left-hand side. He was mystified. Where the hell was Alex? Where had the Scottish girls gone? They were no-where to be seen. Was he dreaming?

A small commotion from the end of the room broke out and disturbed his thought process. A tall, athletic man entered and took the last remaining seat. An Asian boy, who was sitting by his parents and his younger sister, rushed over and asked the new arrival for his autograph.

'That's Hugo Pulkda,' said the old woman in the seat next to him. 'He's the new Portuguese football goalkeeper,' she added majestically.

Kinsey thanked her for supplying that much needed titbit of information, but recoiled sharply away from her, due to the sight of a hideous sore that was taking over one side of her once beautiful face.

'Welcome Ladies and Gentleman,' announced the smartly dressed croupier, who appeared like a genie from a bottle. 'I would like to thank you all for coming along tonight; some of you at such short notice.'

He produced a red rose from the inside of his jacket and handed it to a pretty but drawn looking girl sitting on his left-hand side.

He continued, 'Tonight we only have six spins of the wheel. That's only six chances to change your life forever.'

'I feel lucky tonight,' the old lady informed Kinsey and squeezed his hand tightly. 'I've been coming here now for the last couple of weeks and I haven't won anything. Not even close.'

Kinsey felt the sadness in her words.

The croupier went on to explain the rules of the game. There were thirteen spaces on the roulette wheel. Everyone was asked to pick a ball with a number on it, from the bag that was paraded around by the beautiful assistant called Angela. Kinsey was fourth in line and extracted the number two from the silky black bag.

He also felt quite lucky tonight and wondered what the prizes would be. Perhaps it would be like the Generation Game, where the winning contestants would sit by a conveyor belt and try to remember as many objects as possible in sixty seconds. 'Cuddly bear, food processor, cement mixer,' he giggled to himself as he thought back to those days when all his family would sit around the gas fire, which was never on. They would collectively scream at the winner who could not hear their ranting because not only was he two hundred miles away in a BBC studio, but it was highly likely that the contestant was probably watching the pre-recorded programme himself from a cottage in Devon.

'Have you all got a number,' he asked. He knew they had. 'So let the games begin.'

A drum roll sounded out from no-where and the wheel was spun in an anti-clockwise motion. The plain white ball was tossed into the arena to start its journey for a place to lay its head. It skipped and jumped around unable to make its mind up on the revolving track. The crowd were mesmerised by its movements and gasped as it finally settled in the position marked up with a seven.

'Number seven' the caller's voice was loud.

All eyes darted from their ball to each of the contestants fixed in their seats. A rather well-to-do gentleman slowly held his counter in a shaky grip. When the rest of the competitors double-checked that their ball did not match the number being shown, the caller said, 'Well done Sir. Mr Longooly, isn't it?'

The gentleman nodded. 'Please can you go with the lovely Angela, she will look after your every wish.'

He was lead towards an extremely grand door at the far end of the room. As he walked through, Kinsey could just make out lots of different people milling about on a thick red carpet with a brightly-lit chandelier above their heads. That snap shot of victory had started to wet Kinsey's appetite for at least one of the last five places.

By the time he looked back to the confines of the gambling table, the number seven space had been turned off and a new game was already underway.

The next number to be called was one. Again, all the attention was focused on who was the lucky winner of the second roll of chance. Strangely, from out of what appeared to be a pram, a small-deformed baby's hand became visible, clutching a rattle and the correct numbered ball. Angela wasted no time in taking the ball, unlocking the brakes of the pram and pushing the unfortunate infant through to the winner's enclosure.

Kinsey was seriously wondering what the hell the age limit was to enter this game. Unlike Britain, where you must be eighteen years old to do anything, he knew that the European law was a little more relaxed, but this was downright crazy. That young child could never compete against the clock and remember all those items on that conveyor belt. It may know what a cuddly toy was but would he have the experience to understand what a set of steak knives looked like, or a portable car vacuum cleaner?

He smiled at the pretty girl who had received the gift of the flower earlier. As she unconvincingly smiled back, he noticed the bandages around her wrists and the bottle of sleeping tablets that she had been feeding on. That's all he needed, another fucking junky, he thought.

'Number eleven' the call went out.

Now it was getting really exciting. There was a scream from beside him, which nearly made him fall off his stool. The little old lady with the mangy face quickly raised her arm to show the rest the magic number.

'Well done...Well done.' Kinsey congratulated her.

He was genuinely pleased for the lady he had just met. Perhaps now she could get a doctor to examine that nasty wound that was obviously affecting her quality of life. Unfortunately, she kissed him on the cheek and told him to pray hard and if he believed, his number would come up. She promised to keep him a seat next to her in the big room. Before he could ask her what she knew and what type of seat it was, she had gone through the door as happy as a sand-boy; she never looked back.

Kinsey closed his eyes to pray to God. He hadn't really done this for a long time. In fact, it was about three years ago, when he had actually got down on one knee and asked for guidance. He hoped that this would not have the same result, since his horse had finished third on that occasion and he had to go home to face the music, minus half of his pay packet. What made the matter worse was that he lost his temper and broke his knuckles punching the betting office wall. He had to fork out an additional £30 to get it fixed and missed four weeks off work.

He concentrated hard, but kept imagining Jac's earlier tale concerning the congregation jigging down the aisles with Pope Masks on to Rory's pipe music. 'Shit' he thought, he would never win at this rate. He cursed Jac for poisoning his mind with those unclean thoughts, so he decided to just cross his fingers and legs instead.

Next number out went to another old lady who claimed the number five and was ushered away.

'Ladies and gentlemen there are only two more rolls to go,' the croupier explained.

They all gripped their counters even tighter. The next ball danced on top of the compartments on the wheel and then somehow came to rest on four different spaces at the same time.

'Numbers four, twelve, ten and six,' shouted the caller.

'What was going on?' wondered Kinsey. 'That must be a fix!'

He was about to start to throw his toys out of the pram, when he saw that the Asian family had all the correct numbers.

'What are the chances of that then? It must be a miracle!' Kinsey spoke to the bandaged girl.

She ignored him and swallowed another couple of Smarties. He watched the happy family skip merrily towards the door. He wished it was him and his family going on that trip, but he was never that lucky in life.

It's crunch time. Last roll, last chance. Five people left and only one winner. The wheel turned in slow motion. The white ball was even more mischievous this time. It took great pleasure in springing in and then out of all the survivors' spaces. It moved around the wheel for the last lap and bounced between the numbers two and three. Two….No...Three…no two…wait three. The wheel started to find its final resting place and the ball of fate landed on the number three.

'Bastard, trust my fuckin' luck.' Kinsey jumped up and yelled miserably. He threw his ball onto the floor.

The good-looking goalkeeper held up the right number ball.

'Trust him, the arrogant prick,' Kinsey said under his breath. 'He knew he was going to win it. Bet he wins everything and I bet he's got a fucking gorgeous fucking model fucking wife and fucking perfect fucking kids. Fuck it.'

He watched as the last winner followed Angela into the room. 'I'll bet he'll fuck her as well,' Kinsey whispered to himself.

'Hard luck, ladies and gentlemen, but we will see you all again. Don't worry your time will come,' the caller muttered. It was followed by a great puff of smoke and he disappeared.

Kinsey opened his eyes. This time he found himself in a hospital bed with nurses busily rushing around. He tried hard to remember what happened? Where was he? What about the roulette game? He looked across the ward. Most of the occupants were asleep or talking to visitors. In the far corner, a TV set was playing to itself. Suddenly the news caught his attention. The reporter was at the scene of a horrendous car crash. It appeared that a BMW had smashed headfirst into a tree. Kinsey dropped the cup he was drinking out of when he saw the photograph of the Portuguese goalkeeper flash onto the screen with the caption underneath 'Hugo Pulkda 1982 – 2001'

Kinsey went cold. He needed to talk to someone. He turned to the bed next to him and in there, fast asleep, was the girl from the wheel of fortune game. She still had the bandages on her wrists. On her bedside cupboard was a bottle of tablets and a single red rose. The respirator by her side indicated that she was doing fine. Another image on the television forced him to watch more. A fire in the capital city had killed an entire family of Asians. The photograph of the little boy and his sister was too much and Kinsey fainted and fell off the bed.

When he came to, he was flat out on the floor with his three mates surrounding him. He had a confused look on his face and his front tooth was missing. 'Am I still alive?' he said more to himself than to the three angels from his past.

'Of course you are, but you frightened us to fuckin' death, you tosser,' Jac barked, still wiping the tears away from his eyes.

He caught around Kinsey, picked him up and held him tight.

'How do you feel?' asked Alex

'A bit light headed. They thought I swallowed my tooth, and they've been X-raying me all over to try to find it.' Kinsey answered. 'Boy, I had the weirdest dream. I can't wait to tell my mad Aunty Veronica.'

Aunty Veronica was the official secretary of the Druids section of the social club. She had an uncanny knack of predicting who would be axed next from the various popular soap shows being shown on TV. She stated that it was due to her ability to analyse dreams and study the tealeaves. She conveniently forgot to mention that her ex-lover worked as a sound technician on the sets of most of the TV shows.

Alex produced the missing tooth from out of his pocket and explained that when Kinsey went unconscious, he thought that he would swallow it, so he put it in a safe place. Jac still hadn't let go of his mate and kept repeating that Kinsey was a bastard and he would get him back.

'I have got to show you this,' said Kinsey mischievously. He pulled back the covers, to reveal a massive erection underneath his hospital gown.

'Fuck me, wouldn't mind one of those myself,' Lusty muttered.

'They advised me not to wear trousers for a couple of days until the swelling goes down.'

Jac finally wiped his eyes and announced, 'I could murder a drink.'

'A drink…I could murder a Fuck,' roared Kinsey, waving his old boy at his mates.

They all burst out laughing including the woman in the next bed with the bandages on her thin wrists.

The four all-conquering friends arrived at the nearest bar; Kinsey still in his hospital gown. The morning sun was just about breaking into a warm smile. The barman was pleased to serve them with four of his coldest large beers as long as it meant that the cash register was ticking over.

An Indian in full war paint walked across their field of vision. He approached a door opposite the café and sniffed at the wood for several moments. He stopped and spoke into a mobile phone.

All of a sudden from a side street, two police vans pulled up. A large black limousine quickly followed them. Out jumped several policemen from the van, and two guys who looked like Will Smith from 'Men in Black' jumped from the Limo. They proceeded to knock down a door to the house opposite, and they ran in to it en-masse. Seconds later, the two 'Men in Black' characters walked out holding the busker from the street. The Indian scout was sniffing the man wildly and bouncing on one foot. One of the men removed the busker's blond wig and false moustache to reveal none other than …Father John.

They were screaming at him in Latin and jumping up and down. They bundled him into the black limo and drove away at maximum speed.

Kinsey turned to the rest of the gang and asked 'Are you sure I haven't died?'

They all drank their pints down in one, ordered four more and a bag of ice for their mate's throbbing member.

Chapter 15

'You ain't nothing but a hound dog'

Big Ken had fantasised about reaching a cup final ever since he saw Bobby Stokoe, the manager of Sunderland, race across the field to hug their goalkeeper in the 1973 FA Cup Final at Wembley. He would daydream for hours about what it would feel like to walk his team out of the tunnel in front of seventy-two thousand adoring fans. The atmosphere; the passion; the cream suits with dark blue shirts.

He had it all planned to perfection. He had a speech ready in case they won, a loser's speech in the unlikely event of losing, and a speech just in case the game had been disturbed by a sniper in the crowd who had shot the Queen and Prince Phillip.

No rock was left unturned.

In his mind he replayed the scene a thousand times. Each time it was slightly different but each time a little more special. It would always kick-off with a morning bonding breakfast session with the entire team and committee-men. His head told him that the entire entourage would be wearing purple v-neck jumpers with grey stay-press trousers. It seemed to him to be the only natural thing to wear, but his heart raced at the thought of the more daring black polo necks with matching slacks and brothel creeper shoes. What a sight! What a fashion statement!

It would be no ordinary run of the mill breakfast either. It would be the full works, including black pudding and potato waffles, all paid for by the club.

After the grub, it would be a quick debrief and a change of clothes. There would be no expense spared, money was only an object that he would require to mould his team into the ultimate fashion warriors.

Even the supporters and the player's wives would have to sign a loyalty agreement, which would consist of them following a strict dress code. He would make it top priority that if there was no signature on the agreement, then there would be no ticket allocation for the occasion. He knew it was a tough stance, but perfection never won any friends in the popularity stakes and he was adamant his team would not go back to being named 'the polyester brigade from the place with the smelly tip.'

Now all those hours of minute planning and the years of trying to achieve his goal had finally come to fruition. His first ever cup final. Ok, it wasn't at Wembley or the Cardiff Millennium Stadium, but a rugby field in Portugal was a start.

But sometimes even the best plans can go wrong. Fate has a nasty habit of dealing hands that are so bad that even Willie Wander, the card shark, who could make a small fortune out of high-stake bluffing, could not conjure up a simple pair never mind a diamond flush. Today, as it happened, turned out to be one of those days.

Down in the hotel lobby, the team, or what was left of the team, were sitting there helpless. Keith already explained to Big Ken that it appeared the team had been decimated for all manner of reasons. To his credit, Keith in his wisdom had an oxygen mask and extra bottle supply brought over from the hospital before he even attempted to go into the precise detail of the nights events with his leader.

All eyes anxiously watched Big Ken, who was sucking on the oxygen like some pregnant mother during childbirth.

Keith went on to describe how John the Captain and Pinchy had been arrested and were locked up at the local jail.

It all started to go haywire at about 10 pm the previous night. John and Pinchy were in the main square, minding their own business, eating a portion of gravy and chips. Pinchy, unknowingly, dropped a chip on to the sidewalk and continued on his way back towards the hotel for a good night's sleep before the big game. A police car pulled up to the kerb with a loud screech. Two policemen got out. They were fully armed and shone a torch into the boy's eyes. They were told in no uncertain terms to drop their weapons (meaning the carton of boiling hot chips and gravy) and put their hands up. These coppers were prepared for the unexpected, unlike their unfortunate colleague who tried to apprehend a car thief and ended up with a mouth full of steel bar.

The two boys were pushed violently up against the bonnet of the car, their legs spread-eagled and then searched.

John, who thought that it must be some sort of sick joke and was sure they had been set up, tried to turn around and asked, 'What's wrong, officers?'

The question was completely ignored, either due to the language barrier or the fact that the two knuckle headed policemen were following some sort of well rehearsed script.

'Where are you from?' demanded the smaller of the two.

'Dowlais flats,' replied Pinchy, 'next door to Mister and Mrs Roberts.' He was nervous. His only experience of the law was watching repeats of the Sweeney on cable TV.

John started to laugh, but stopped suddenly when a truncheon in the small of his back helped to remind him that it was not a laughing matter.

'Sorry Sir'' he commented, getting back up on one knee. 'My friend didn't understand the question; he's from Wales you see! We are staying in the Dolphin Hotel, over there.'

The second policeman, who had one extremely long eyebrow and appeared to be reading his lines from a piece of paper said, 'It must be a Welsh thing then, throwing all your rubbish onto our streets, smashing glasses, kicking over dustbins.' He decided to ad-lib the last two points. His colleague winked at him in admiration.

Both John and Pinchy laughed nervously. John added 'You must be mistaken officers; we have only just come out for something to eat.'

Before he finished his explanation they were dragged into the back of the cop car and thrown into a cold jail cell. The Police Chief was informed of the success of the first part of the plan.

In the hotel reception, Big Ken was now lying on the floor with a cold flannel on his head. Keith picked his timing with great care before he continued with the disastrous news. It concerned the series of events that had taken place down by the sea front, which lead to

Russell, Ceri and Milky coming down mysteriously with first-degree food poisoning.

An unnatural addiction to the strange large beans meant that the café owner didn't need to go searching for his victims. The Pro-Plus that he normally mixed in with the bean ingredients ensured that he always had hungry customers, which in turn, boosted his sales turnover. So that morning, he knew they would return like flesh-eating zombies in search of their next meal of lovely tasting belly-button skin.

Three oval plates of the best giant beans, which had 'accidentally on purpose' been injected with some homemade salmonella, helped the café owner to keep his promise to the Brigadier.

By the time that Russell, Ceri and Milky started to wander back to the hotel their gentle stroll turned into a mad dash for the nearest toilet. Ceri and Milky were the lucky ones. They reached the safety of the toilet with a few seconds to spare. Unfortunately, Russell, who insisted on finishing off the last remaining beans and licked the plates clean, had fallen way short.

Stomach cramps, followed by an almighty explosion of the lower regions not only destroyed Russell's favourite shorts, but had also been responsible for pebble-dashing a passing school bus.

The poor kids that had been on that bus during the unexpected shit attack sadly experienced temporary PWDS (post-war diarrhoea syndrome). This left most of them with snow-blindness but only through chocolate-coated lenses and an acute bout of constipation that lasted six months.

During the next four hours, the three poisoned victims had not got off the pan and had lost half a stone in weight. The local doctor, who had been kitted out with special breathing equipment to examine the three, prescribed strong Diocalm tablets normally given to horses, a butt-plug and extra strong air fresheners.

'They have been told to stay near a toilet for the next forty-eight hours,' Brian informed the waiting crowd.

'Fuck it!' said Big Ken. 'Who else is missing?'

This was the part of the missing jigsaw that they had all been dreading telling the big man. Keith made sure that he was out of harms way before he slowly announced that Alex, Kinsey, Jac and Lusty were no where to be seen. All the Adams' apples in the lounge area, including the waiters, took a large gulp and took shelter underneath their chest bones.

'Lusty? Lusty?' Big Ken screamed out and his knees buckled. 'Where the fuck is Lusty? We need to find him.'

He actually shouted out his name like someone looking for a pet dog. 'Quick all spread out,' he shouted to everyone.

He took a massive draw on the oxygen.

'Perhaps they have gone straight to the ground. You know what that lot are like,' Keith mentioned from behind the sofa.

Big Ken ran out of oxygen so he breathed deeply into a brown paper bag. He was ensured that although they had many of their stars missing, they were still good enough to beat that Evesham crew. They headed off to the ground.

The large crowd already started to assemble at one end of the ground. Of course, the Old Boy's High School, were already there, warming up out on the field in matching track suits and confident grins.

The Dowlais boys sat in mourning in their changing room. There was no sign of Lusty and the gang, which didn't bode well for the eighty minutes to come. Keith instructed Matthew to go in search of them. He was starting to enjoy the power of delegation and the responsibility. The rest of the team prepared in various ways for the game. It involved lying around, or smoking or both. Two of the boys were actually being sick in the showers.

This was not part of Big Ken's master plan. This should have been his big wedding day. But there was no White dress, or cake, just a gaggle of misfits who turned up after the bride and groom had left. His frustration finally poured out of him like lava from a volcano. 'Fuck it, it's over!' He kicked a kit bag right across the room. It smashed into Rob, the first aider, sending him sprawling into the showers. This made all of the boy's sit up in terror.

'Look at the lot of you. I'm ashamed of you. Bloody animals, half pissed, drug taking junkies. You cannot be trusted. This is the first time we have ever reached a final and you fuck it up for us all. I'm sick to death of all this, fucking half-bred animals. Bobby Stokoe never had to put up with this shit.'

He turned and stormed out of the door.

'Was Big Ken getting soft in his old age or had he finally been pushed over the edge,' they all collectively thought, 'and who the fuckin' hell was Bobby Stokoe when he was at home?'

They were glad that at least he hadn't paid his normal visit to Eardrum City.

After the dust settled, Keith followed him outside. Big Ken was sitting on the steps, large head in large hands.

'Ken?' Keith said. 'Ken, why don't you ask the Major if we can postpone the kick off for about an hour? That will give us time to find Lusty and the boys and get ready.'

At first, these words didn't register with Big Ken because he was not at home. In his private world the curtains were drawn and the gas cooker had been turned up to maximum level. He was about to try to squeeze his head into the imaginative oven when all of a sudden he sprang back into life.

'Great idea,' he said and actually shook Keith's hand.

Keith nearly had an orgasm. 'Beryl would be so proud,' he thought.

Big Ken headed off towards the table where the Brigadier and the Mayoress, who was in a neck-brace with a plaster covering her ice burns, were sitting, admiring the trophy. Big Ken was not only re-energised but on a mission to recapture his dream. Nothing or nobody would stand in his way.

Lawrence saw the figure of Big Ken bounding towards the top table through his binoculars. He was amazed just how big that man's head actually was. He put his brown briefcase down and decided that he would try to find out about Big Ken's teams tactic's for the game.

'Everything all right, old chap,' Lawrence said to his opposite number.

'Fuck off, you little ponse!' Big Ken continued with his journey, mouthing what he was going to say.

'Hello Brigadier, hello Mayoress,' he said on his arrival.

The Mayoress slowly started to hide underneath the table, her left eye twitched uncontrollably. She was not only scared stiff of the physical presence of this man, but she also couldn't understand a word this big beast said.

"I was wondering if I could ask you a big favour." He stared into the Brigadier's eyes.

The Brigadier had already been informed about the boys' in the cell and the unfortunate messy episode with the school bus, so he was well prepared for this conversation. 'You would like to take a photo of the trophy to take home with you,' he sarcastically motioned to the peasant that had the nerve to stand before him.

Big Ken was a bit too slow to notice the sarcasm in his comments and innocently asked 'It's just that some of the boys are not feeling to good at the moment…and I was hoping that you could delay the kick-off for about an hour.'

The Brigadier loved confrontations like this; especially when he was up against a half-wit that could not put two words together without the aid of a thesaurus plus operating instructions. He purposely switched on the PA system, so that all present could hear how he would destroy this man with the sharpness of his tongue.

He smiled as he said, 'You would like me to delay the game for about an hour, just because your boys have been drinking all night and God knows what else and now they don't feel so well.' He took a deep breath and turned to face the listening crowd. 'What do you think this is…a charity shop? Oxfam? The answer my good man is a definite NO!'

As far as competing in the speech arena, Big Ken would not have been allowed to sell hot-dogs, never mind going face to face with such a force. He was completely out of his depth. If it had been a scrap to the death, the Roman Emperor would have shown him the thumbs down sign long ago.

He tried desperately. 'But Brigadier, it's only an hour. I don't think that anyone would mind, and it's such a lovely day.'

This was like food and drink to a word fighter of the Brigadier's standing. The Oxford Debating Society had been his second home. He had been bred for such occasions.

He raised his voice for maximum effect as he went in for the kill. 'You don't think anyone would mind, do you?' The words were delivered with Shakespearean poise. Even Olivier would have taken refuge in the wings during this masterful performance.

The dialogue came flooding to the surface. 'How would you know what normal people would or wouldn't mind? If we were talking about animals in a zoo, I could understand, because you are the Chairman of the biggest and most sorry looking bunch of half bred animals that I have ever had the displeasure of coming into contact with.'

He was enjoying this. He wished he had continued with his amateur dramatic studies in his Thespian period during '66. He could actually feel an erection growing with every lash he inflicted on his obviously inferior opponent, 'And for your information, and just to make it clear to you, this is the last time that Dallas Rugby Football Club will ever play in my tournament again. So if you don't mind, I would like to present this wonderful trophy to this year's winner – Evesham High School Old Boys.'

He passed the cup to an elated Lawrence, who in turn held it above his head like he was on the steps at Wembley. The rest of his team began to cheer and hug each other.

But the Brigadier was still not finished. He could taste blood and wanted to show these valley types what the real world was like. 'And now I am going for a spot of lunch and I hope that you and your tribe of weirdoes are not around when I get back.'

He turned his back and took his well-earned curtain call.

A mentally bruised Big Ken was looking down at the floor in utter silence. Keith and Brian had seen this behaviour before and they quickly moved away from their leader's side.

After doing a little jig, Lawrence held out his arm to Big Ken. 'No hard feelings old chap. I am really sorry that we didn't have the chance to beat you fair and square in the first place.' He thought that he would join in with some of his own mental punishment after witnessing how the Brigadier had turned the big man into a speechless jelly.

Fortunately Big Ken was not finished yet. In his mind this was only half time. He remembered the nursery rhyme concerning how sticks and stones could break his bones but words would never hurt him. This gave him the strength and the courage to speak up.

His reply may not have made the top ten sarcastic responses of all time, but it made its point. 'Firstly, it is not DALLAS Rugby Football Club; it is DOWLAIS Rugby Football Club. Wrong fucking country and wrong fucking sport.'

Even the people around the field could sense that this was one speech not to interrupt.

'Secondly, no one calls my boys half witted animals, unless it's me. Now I would like an apology, Sir. Then I would like you to postpone the game for an hour. Do you understand?'

The Christian hot-dog seller was not only back on his feet but he had somehow obtained the right equipment to defeat the lions and bring down the whole Roman Empire.

The Brigadier looked bored with this entire irrelevant comeback and cried in a more personal tone, 'Look, you in-bred, overweight rhinoceros, let me spell it out for you. It's over, it's finished, and the game will not go ahead. And you will definitely not be getting an apology from me.' Game, set and match, he thought.

'Oh…Fuck,' said Keith, who hid behind Brian.

'Oh…Fuck,' said Brian, who put his hands over his eyes.

'Oh…Fuck,' said the rest of the team joyfully.

The betting started in earnest, but the odds on a Big Ken victory were slashed from ten to one, to even betting.

The big man walked towards the table. Now there have been many examples of major mistakes undertaken by mankind down the years. Some of these have been well documented; such as the safety officer of the Titanic who decided to sell all of the lifeboats to the owner of the Thames Boating Club. When asked on a price for the brand new swag, he apparently said that they would talk greenbacks when he got back from the maiden voyage. Or the man who turned down an up-and-coming pop group called The Beatles, and insisted that the drummer looked good, but the rest of them couldn't hold down a good tune even if it fell into their laps.

But Lawrence Reid's action on that day probably topped the lot. Years later, some said that it was the actions of a real hero. Others were less complimentary and terms such as clown or idiot were used to describe his foolish actions.

As Big Ken approached the man who had viciously mocked him in public, Lawrence stepped across his path. The do-gooder saw the anger in the big man's eyes but completely missed the backhander which sent him sprawling back into the gathering crowd. The trophy sailed into the air, along with Mr Reid's two front teeth.

Now the rules had changed. They were no longer treading the boards in some make believe Broadway theatre, this was down at street level, where big complicated posh words were not the currency of survival. This was Big Ken's ring and God help anyone who stepped in it without a gum shield, head protection and a fuckin' elephant gun.

Without any effort Big Ken picked up the table and threw it over his head into the crowd. The Mayoress fell off her chair and rolled head over heels down the embankment. A truck carrying a cargo of oranges and immigrants destined for Liverpool just missed her head.

'Come on then, Brigadier; let's see who the half breed is now,' his words spat hatred onto his fire.

The Brigadier looked around for physical and moral support. His normally obedient servants had also heard about the 'Queeny Tight Pants' wrestling massacre and made excuses, and then left hurriedly. The Brigadier considered trying to talk his way out of the situation but thought that talking had been the root cause of the situation to begin with. Without too much deliberation he decided to leg it across the rugby field with his challenger in hot pursuit. The watching crowd, who had been silent up to this point, came alive, cheering and hollering wildly.

Lusty and Alex turned up with their kit bags over their shoulders to witness an even stranger scene than the madness that they had just been involved with.

The Brigadier now realised how frightened those fifteen-year-old virgins must have felt as he chased them around his mansion. There was no escape and only one outcome for the poor girls and boys being pursued by the hairy human with the rampant tickling stick.

He scrambled to the goalposts with the maniacal man not far behind. A fence blocked his way and although his mind was racing, his legs could carry him no further. He wished that he had his hunting rifle and horse with him. Then the advantage would swing back to him. He would not be so soft with the big over-sized monster if he could change the circumstances. One bullet, or maybe three would stop him in his tracks, then he would have his large head stuffed and mounted in his smoking room. He would feed the rest of him to the pigs. But sadly he didn't have his gun or favourite black cob with him and as the thud of footsteps grew louder, he started to climb and claw his way to the safety of the top of the goalposts.

Big Ken arrived in a cloud of red mist. He followed the Brigadiers up the goalpost, managed to grab his left leg and started to pull him back down. The other leg began to kick out and it caught Big Ken in the jaw. There was a loud communal 'OOOOH' from the crowd. Big Ken retaliated by biting a lump out of the Brigadier's calf. Both men let go of the goalpost and hit the ground with a thump. Big Ken got hold of the Brigadier and piled in to him with both fists. Everyone dived in to stop the Chairman killing his prey.

The police arrived and took Big Ken away.

Alex and Lusty walked back to the pub.

Chapter 16

'The last train out of Talybont'

The next twenty-four hours saw complete bedlam in the holiday town of Albufeira. Firstly, the armed guard were immediately called in. Tanks rolled down the street and helicopters littered the skies. Next, all of the Dowlais party were rounded up and held under 'Hotel arrest'.

Snipers were positioned on the rooftop and dogs patrolled the perimeter fence. All communication links were cut to the outside world. Lisa Bari, who had wind of a sensational story, was stopped at the Portuguese airport. She was threatened with deportation to the Gurnos shops if she continued with her journey.

Big Ken was locked up in a maximum-security prison. He was not allowed any visitors and his request for a change of clothing, (he was thinking of a nice pair of cream slacks and bright red Fred Perry with matching cardigan), were denied. The British Embassy were notified and told that a political situation was unavoidable. Envoys were parachuted in and all the town's women and children were locked in a church for their own safety.

The hotel's electricity was cut off at nine pm and not switched back on until eight am the following morning. Even Lusty (the original Milk Tray man) decided it was too dangerous to venture outside. But that didn't stop a lovely dark haired beauty abseiling into his room at about two in the morning dressed to thrill.

The only one that managed to escape that night was Wigsy, who had cracked after the waiter had refused him a pint on the strict orders of the management and police. After drinking all the duty free Wigsy had started to shake violently and foam at the mouth. The armed guards decided they could either let this deranged animal through the barricade or simple shoot it. They let the beast go, but attached a bleeping system to his shirt and had two marksmen sat opposite him in the bar.

Even at the hospital Justin, who was oblivious to the whole episode, had a rifle trained on him all night. He was prescribed elephant tranquillisers mixed with his cocoa.

Sniffer dogs were sent in to try to retrieve the Brigadier's precious trophy, which had mysteriously gone 'walkies' during the commotion at the playing fields. No such trophy was ever found, however the dogs did uncover a small amount of drugs, a room full of X-rated porn books, two blow-up dolls, one blow-up sheep and a month's supply of pork pies.

The Mayoress immediately quit her post and decided to go back to the circus. She assured her husband and children that the high trapeze was definitely safer than her present role. She would even consider working with 'One-eyed Dirk the dagger thrower,' who had been banned from owning a set of steak knives, never mind throwing sharp objects of death at a spinning wheel with a pretty girl attached. She made her mind up that dagger wounds could always be repaired.

Even though the last twenty-four hours had not been the most enjoyable for the team, especially the cold showers followed by intense interrogation, the boys still felt unhappy about leaving the place. This was always the worst part of the trip. Lips quivered with sadness at the depressing thought of returning to the asylum known as 'Home'.

Their bags were packed with slow abandon and long faces squeezed through the bus door. The bus driver had been replaced with a suicide bomber, who had 25lbs of gelignite strapped to his back with a sign above the window which read, 'Any funny stuff and the bus will be blown to smithereens.' The entire population of the town signed it.

They were treated like rabid animals at the airport. No one spoke to them and all eye contact was lost. One old woman spat in their direction and shouted for them to 'Stop hunting Whales and killing all the newly born children in the country.'

She was arrested, certified insane and the police hid her in the Dowlais kit bag. She was not actually found until two weeks later when Brian took the kit bag into the launderette. After a quick interrogation by the local blue rinse brigade and a cup of tea with two sugars, she was offered a job at Castle Bingo.

She soon became an important member of the community and was held in high esteem, until she started the bizarrely named 'Eyeball for Jesus' religious cult. The followers of this weird group would pluck out their left eye with a spoon and eat it with salad cream. No one knew why, but within a month, she had recruited thirty-eight followers, who would all wander around the precinct, eyeless, frightening small kids. This madness was finally stopped, when the council paid a man with a big club to kidnap her and then roll her up in a carpet and deport her back to Portugal or to wherever the first plane was going.

As the team walked through the airport's metal detector in single file, it went off with an almighty sound. It was one of those all whistle and bell type of devices. The noise was deafening. All the staff dived for cover. On further inspection the security guard pointed to Keith's pocket. Keith slowly took out a shining Sheriff's badge with his name engraved on it. The guard confiscated the badge to use for his next fancy dress party.

Like ants marching in line up a damp wall, the boys slowly walked across the runway to the waiting plane. The pilot already started the engine and had his impatient foot on the accelerator pedal. Matthew, who stapled the arms of his PJ's back together, climbed the steps. Kinsey shuffled along close behind with the hospital's gown wrapped around his body, his stiff member leading the way.

A big black limo jetted across the runway. The squiggly warm heat lines on the horizon also exposed the Indian scout on all fours bounding behind the car. The two men dressed in black jumped out clutching weapons that were positioned on the inside of their thick woollen Crombie coats. A handcuffed Father John was bundled from the back of the limo and roughly manhandled up the aircraft steps. All heads inside the plane jockeyed for position at the tiny windows to see what was going on.

One of the men produced a badge with the words 'Church Police' in big gold letters and flashed it to one of the airhostesses. She wished she phoned in for a 'sicky' that morning. She knew the plane was already full up to the brim with a right motley crew and there were still more to come.

The religious pack headed for the tail of the plane with the scout at the front chewing on a large dog bone. A black and bruised Father John acknowledged some of the boys as he passed. Two colourful Bishops made up the convoy; they made numerous signs of the cross and sprinkled all the passengers in Holy water.

Next on the runway of fools appeared an ambulance, which carried Justin. He was mechanically transported up the stairs and into a special handicap seat. He had his leg in plaster, a neck brace and two black eyes. He was still asleep from the sedatives he had received the previous night.

Then a police car screamed to a halt with all its lights flashing. Four policemen got out in full riot regalia. They in turn wheeled Big Ken out of the back of the van in full Hannibal Lector Gear. It included a straightjacket and muzzle. The four occupied the vacant seats right at the front of the plane with Big Ken sandwiched between the lines of serious looking policemen.

Two albino twins, who intended to hijack the plane and fly it to Arkansas, asked the stewardess could they get off before it took off. They phoned their leader and mastermind of the operation, (who happened to be their mother), and informed her that after observing the passengers on board the 747, it was impossible to imagine any government coughing up the ransom money they would ask for. They pictured themselves flying around the world getting refused entry from all the civilised countries, including Holland, like some kind of unwanted tanker with a highly radioactive chemical cargo in its hold.

It was not long after take-off that the rigours and pressures of the trip finally caught up with them all. Their empty shells of bodies fell into a much needed sleep. Wigsy was of course still drinking. He was determined to fight the demons that tugged at his eyelids and sat necking can upon can. The table in front of him was soon full, so he started to balance the empties on Kinsey's erect penis. The leaning tower of Stella cans reached eight high before collapsing to the ground with an almighty crash. No one stirred. Russell was cwtching up to the tournament trophy, which had already been engraved (using a Stanley knife) with the name of Dowlais as the winner of the competition.

Jac was still full of life. His batteries never seemed to wear out. He was a living dynamo of mischief, which completely recharged itself on less than thirty seconds of shuteye. He threw peanuts at the back of Big Ken's head. The target was easy; a worm with a club-foot would have hit his enormous cranium, nine times out of ten. The impact of the nut bomb's made Big Ken move violently in his seat, his muzzle preventing him from shouting out. This instinctive movement caused the police officers to pull out their guns and edge back from the mad man. They were taking no chances. Rumours spread like wild fire since the attack on the Brigadier at the rugby field. No one wanted to have the responsibility of escorting this beast out of the country, but a promise of triple pay with time off in lieu and free lifetime membership of the new video store in the town clinched the deal.

The peanut attack lasted all of the flight.

The plane finally touched down on the runway at Heathrow. The groggy, odd-looking set of passengers strolled across the tarmac to the terminal. Suddenly, what appeared to be an airport mechanic jumped onto Matthew's back and started to beat him up?

'Hello Sarah, how's the kids?' Alex said to Matthew's wife who was kitted out in overalls and was biting the poor boy's ear.

Everyone ignored the grappling couple on the floor and walked on. The Portuguese police placed Big Ken onto the suitcase-conveyor belt on the ground floor. He was transported with the rest of the luggage up into the arrivals hall. A kicking and struggling Hannibal the Cannibal appeared up the ramp and was being paraded along the conveyor belt along with all the other baggage. To the great amusement of all those watching, the committee-men tried unsuccessfully to pull him off. By the time he was released, the build up of anger was too much and he lashed out and sent Keith flying through the 'Nothing to Declare' area. He then proceeded to chase the departing plane with the coppers on back down the runway. The officers thought he was amusing and started to stick two fingers up at him. They also mooned at the insane man, still in his muzzle. But their joy turned to fear when Big Ken stuck his head through a side panel of the plane. The pilot quickly took off with all the terrified occupants in the crash position. Big Ken rolled around in anger and frustration on the wet concrete surface.

Within a blink of an eye, the bus pulled back up outside the rugby club. The four friends piled into Kinsey's car. No one said a word. They drove passed the church, which had a 'For Sale' sign outside and a wanted poster displaying Father John's picture and a reward of £2000 for any information. They thought that the Indian could buy lots of firewater with his blood money.

They dropped off Jac with waves of goodbye. He headed straight for the kebab shop.

Next stop on the journey was Lusty's pad. As they drove into the estate the car swerved to avoid the Pozzoni boys who were on horseback and dressed in cowboy masks, dragging a fruit machine along the pavement.

Lusty opened the door to the cold flat, put the kettle on and checked the milk blob in the fridge.

The remaining passengers escaped unharmed from the estate of death; they past the old garage and witnessed some builders erecting a big sign with a flashing pair of silver tits on top with a poster saying "Like you, Lusty's Big Titty experience will be coming soon. Opening night next Thursday, Come on feel the Tits".

They both looked at each other and laughed in disbelief. Kinsey dropped Alex off at the end of his street.

Alex surveyed the familiar cul-de-sac with affection. It had been a great tour but he was glad to be back. He decided on the long journey home that this tour would be his last. He was getting too old for all of this nonsense and he needed to grow up and act his age. It wasn't fair on his wife. He knocked on the front door and waited in anticipation of it being answered by the girl of his dreams whom he'd been longing to see.

Claire smiled on hearing the banging of the door knob. She was also waiting for her man to arrive. She banished Ethel to the laundry room for the day with a basket full of shirts to iron.

The doorstep lovers looked at each other with animal lust and fell into each other's arms. Alex kicked the door closed, dropped his bag, unzipped his fly, with one tug of his manful hands ripped her cotton panties off and entered her right there on the stairs.

Sixty seconds later, he rolled off and thought to himself, 'I may as well go to Canada next year with the boys, just one last time….she won't mind!!!!!!!'

Chapter 17

'Twist or Stick!'

After a short while, the sensation concerning the fateful tour eventually died down and everyone involved slowly got back to leading abnormal lives. They were extremely lucky that their daily spot on the front page of the local newspaper had been replaced by the discovery of the supposedly dead guitarist of a world famous rock group, who had been found alive and well in St. David's on the Pembrokeshire coast.

The rock star had gone missing six years earlier while out walking with his pet budgie in the mountains. He was discovered working as a child carer at a local primary school.

The headmistress told Lisa Bari she thought there was something wrong when he wouldn't take off his platform winkle-pickers and leopard skin jacket during gym lessons. Her suspicions were confirmed when the under five's always used to sing 'Milk-float Emptiness' in assembly before break time.

Although the Dowlais crew were out of the glare of the public spotlight, things never really got back to the way they had been.

Big Ken suffered a mild stroke in the summer. It was not life threatening, but due to the effects of several facial veins that burst during the experience, it left him with a section of his head bright red. It made him look like an Arsenal football strip on Charlie George's lean frame. He finally retired from his beloved club and burnt his entire wardrobe in an old oil drum in his back garden along with several hand delivered unopened invitations to a Werewolf ball and buffet in Portugal.

He and his wife bought their dream caravan in Trecco Bay and spent most of their time relaxing in their new found paradise called 'The Love Booth.' One day he accidentally came across the Trecco Bay Caravan Park Committee which met every Monday afternoon in the 'Dirty Duck' pub.

That night he stayed up until dawn, designing potential new uniforms for them to achieve the status of best caravan committee-men of Great Britain and he prepared his grand introduction speech.

Big Ken was back!

Keith finally had his dream come true and became chairman of Dowlais rugby club. His first act was to send the remainder of the committee-men on a two day team-building weekend in the Brecon Beacons. He made an excuse and dropped out at the last minute. While they were all away, learning how to sharpen their teeth on tree stumps or getting a good night's kip in the carcass of a dead sheep, Keith called an extraordinary general committee meeting. He attended alone and unanimously voted to change the name of the club to Dowlais Cowboys with immediate effect, and he made it compulsory for all members and players to wear check shirts and waistcoats to all matches.

All future tours were going to Texas.

Justin never really recovered from the traumatic experience of the scooter incident. A phobia for anything mechanical that looked like it was going to move in his general direction turned him into a bedroom hermit. Because of his obsession he threw away his mother's vacuum cleaner and garden mower, and then tried to set fire to his Father's car.

After six months of non-improvement, his parents, on the advice of the town's witch doctor, decided to pack him off to his Aunt Mable's farm in Cornwall. It sounded perfect; it was like going back to the 18th century with not a combustion engine in sight. Gradually, Justin began to overcome his fear and actually ventured outside to enjoy the countryside's delights.

Tragically, he got killed while walking down a small lane. He was run over by a squadron of randy bulls, who were apparently off to a barn dance, which had just employed a troupe of cow lap-dancers.

Charlie Walters the farmer collected the £60 reward money from the Rugby Club.

Father John spent two long years imprisoned in the church jail under the crypt. All his previous priest privileges were denied and his favourite guitar was smashed to bits in front of the members of the parish committee and the Society of Roman Catholic Single Mothers on Benefit. He was made to breed goldfish and then made to eat them on Friday after the owner of the café in Cardiff had exposed him as the mystery customer, who held the record for finishing off the mega mixed seafood grill and double breakfast Friday feast with fish fingers in the fastest time.

When he was finally released, he immediately gave up the priesthood and sold his story to the Sunday red top newspapers. There was outrage at 1A Vatican Way and the Indian scout was again summoned by his holiness to track down the blasphemer in order to redeem him.

Father John fled the shores and disappeared again. Although it was never confirmed, rumours of a defrocked priest living with two Thai girls in Phuket, playing guitar in a post-pop/punk group called 'The Rosary Beads of Sweat', were just the break that Muffy the Scout was searching for. He headed to Bangkok on the next plane.

Sadly for Muffy, he was killed when the aircraft which he had been on was hijacked and plunged into the sea, after the demands of the Albino hijacker's from Arkansas were ignored.

No one survived the crash except an old Portuguese woman who was found, alive and completely mad, rolled up in a carpet bound for Dublin.

The Pozzoni brothers grew older but none the wiser. They still ruled the Gurnos Estate with an iron grip. Due to an addiction to sweet sugary snacks, Wayne not only lost his teeth but also became more unpredictable. He would insist on everyone calling him by his new adopted name of 'Mohammed' Pozzoni and made his mother wear a rapist mask like a veil. Dorian took a strong liking of nailing people's fingers to a lamppost before beating them with a baseball bat. The police were adamant they would catch them soon.

Steve 'Lusty' James became the sole owner of a very successful chain of Titty Mart Clubs and drive-ins. He had franchises in over twenty-five countries. The funny thing was he did actually employ Kinsey's mother in the Rocky Horror 'Mammaries' Show, which, surprisingly, became his biggest cash cow.

He never stopped working and would travel the world in search of the perfectly formed gland. He would spend hours weighing and feeling tits of all shapes and sizes. He never got married but courted some of the world's most beautiful women.

His latest venture concerned opening up a series of 'Cock Boot Sales' later on in the year. Many believed that this would ensure that the town got its first MBE for innovation and export.

Alex awoke on a sunny morning at five am and made the most important and spontaneous decision of his 33-year-old life. He decided overnight that he would leave Claire and the kids and head north of the border to start a new life. He packed his bag and kissed his sleeping children for the last time.

While waiting at the train station he remembered that he had not completed two items off this months 'to-do' list, which was to paint the outside fence and to make pasta linguini. He panicked because he never failed to finish his objectives and made his second spontaneous decision within forty-five minutes.

By the time Claire and the sprogs came downstairs that morning, the table was laid out to welcome the risers with four family sized cooked breakfasts surrounding a fresh bunch of flowers. Even Ethel was impressed when she saw a mini plate with cut up sausages and buttered bread fingers next to Claire's plate.

Later that day, he rubbed being spontaneous off his 'A' list and turned his attention onto achieving that directorship within a realistic timescale.

Billy '2 amp' Kinsey emerged from the other side of his near death experience as a new man. He told people that he had not just seen the light but had danced on its naked flame. He concluded that life was way too short to be angry all of the time, so he moved his family to a commune near Snowdonia.

There he became addicted to the powers of Viagra, and had five kids and smiled all day whilst never wearing trousers. Every year, he sent money to Hugo Puldka's mother and a bunch of flowers to Rory, the one-armed organ player, for saving his life.

He went back to Amsterdam and brought Sabrina back to the freedom of the mountains, where he would sometimes ask her to work her magic with her little digit.

Wigsy became a teetotaller, but only for an afternoon in March. He starred in and directed the best selling video about unhealthy living entitled;

'Drink if you are glad to be a fat fuck.'

Harry and Fred the Taxis, both became victims of their own competitiveness. After losing a game, Harry climbed up the flagpole outside the town hall to tie his underpants to the mast. Unfortunately he slipped and fell onto Fred the Taxi and they were both killed instantly.

Their joint funeral was massive. Jac painted big round domino spots on their coffins for old time's sake. The mystery of who was responsible for the butter factory explosion was finally revealed when the last line of Fred the Taxi's will stated that Harry had done it!!!

This was not the last time the world saw Old Harry and Fred. Two weeks after they were lowered into the ground, some local kids playing trick or treat dug them up. As the morning mist broke in Cefn Cemetery, the silhouette of two dead old men, sitting at a table playing their beloved game, could be seen clearly across the cemetery.

As usual Lisa Bari was first on the scene.

Sadly around that time, Maxy the Tramp was discovered frozen to death in MacDonald's doorway. He had no shoes on his feet and an empty bottle of cider down his underpants. No one could be arsed with giving him a proper burial so instead a council worker threw him in the skip and covered him with rubbish and burnt him.

Peter was locked away in a padded cell where he would try to catch the images of shagging monkeys that were projected onto the wall by a psychotic warden, who had the pleasure of Peter's wife's lips warming his laughing gear.

Jac missed his mates badly. He was all alone. As expected, he carried on playing fuck all on the keyboard of life. He stopped being a carpenter and became a full time prankster. This got him in deep trouble when the Pozzoni brother thought he had become a full-time gangster. It took him four and a half painful hours nailed to a lamppost getting beaten with a big bat until Dorian finally realised what the difference was.

Things started to look up for him until the dreadful night in the Matchstick pub up on the estate. Jac was bladdered after a drunken afternoon's bingeing session with members of the circus, who happened to be passing through.

Showing off a little, Jac threw what he thought was a stuffed cat onto the pubs roaring coal fire. What he didn't know was that the supposedly stuffed cat was actually 'Snowy', the much alive but slightly inebriated pussy that always slept on the bar after being fed a bowl of cider by the regulars.

The shrieks from the half-barbecued cat could be heard for miles. It even cracked the glass of the old town clock. Some of the older customers in the pub were given hospital treatment and old Reggie Green had to have counselling. A special ex-Falklands psychologist, who had provided expert counselling to the islanders concerning their fear of waking up to find a battalion of lost Argentinean soldiers hiding under a lamp shade, was flown in at great expense.

Jac of course thought he was hilarious until he was told the cat belonged to Doris, the Pozzoni's deranged mother, who had reared the cat from a kitten and even breastfed it from her own titties. Jac knew the he would be getting more than nailed to a lamppost this time. He made a few phone calls to his mates.

The mini-bus found itself at the wrong end of town at precisely the wrong time of night. The driver hastily pulled it around the sharp bend and into the relative safety of the well-lit high street. Its windscreen wipers, like some punch-drunk street fighter, sparred with the more nimble, faster drops of rain. The persistent onslaught of drizzle was making it a very one-sided contest, until a sand-brick from the adjacent block of flats ended the bout by shattering the windscreen and frightening the fucking life out of the bus driver.

The sound of smashing glass also startled Jac, who stood alone in the doorway to the kebab shop, waiting for his lift to arrive.

The end

I would like to thank all of the people who have knowingly or unknowingly helped to shape this novel.

Gary Morgan – for the conversation about Gorillas and Monkeys while sitting in a bar in Portugal.

Special thanks to

Nigel Roberts– who gave me the confidence in the first place to write it.

Stay Free

Printed in Great Britain
by Amazon